C0-DAL-075

Beyond The Edge Of Nowhere.

By Ivin Munson.

Marie;
    When I was little & told whoppers my mom would wash my mouth out with soap. Now I'm old & put it down in writing, someone publishes it & I get paid for it. It don't figure. Enjoy the book, if you have enough spare time to read it. Love ya.

Ivin

Copyright © 2001 by Ivin Munson
National and international copyright laws protect this book.
No portion of this book may be reproduced in any manner
without expressed written consent of the author.

Printed by
Writers Press, Inc.
Boise, ID 83706

Printed in the United States of America

I.S.B.N. 1-931041-48-2

This book is dedicated to my wife, Irene,
my children, their spouses, and grandchildren.
The twenty stars which make up my heaven.

Prologue

During the early portion of the sixteenth century, rumors reached Spain of great wealth to be found in Mexico. In 1535 Francisco Vazquez de Coronado sailed from Spain to the New World. The ships were undermanned so those in prison for certain crimes were pressed into service aboard those ships. This is the story of such a man.

Put in debtors prison, Ian Connor was bought as an indentured servant and sent to Wales. Having been sold to a wealthy mine owner, he was put to work digging coal in the underground coalmines. Running away from his servatude, he escapes to Spain where he is immediately arrested as a spy for the English. Pressed into service aboard ship, he sails to Mexico with Coronado. The lust for gold leads the Conquistadors on a quest that takes them to what is now the state of Kansas. Disillusioned with the treatment of the native people, he steals horses and heads in to the uncharted west. Ignorant of the dangers and pitfalls that await him, Ian travels to the land west of the Rocky Mountains. His quest eventually takes him to the Snake River area of Idaho, where he lives with a village of the Shoshoni tribe. Having never seen either a white man or a horse, the Indian people revere Ian as a spirit being.

CHAPTER ONE.

If the situation weren't so serious, Ian Connor would have laughed at the comical trio that sat on the raised dais before him. The fat one on his left was sweating so profusely, that a wet ring formed around his collar and spread down the front of the black robe. The one in the center resembled the scarecrow in his cornfield back home. The long, straight nose seemed to poke from the center of a narrow face, placed between two exceedingly large ears. The one on his right was, perhaps, the most judicious looking one of the three. A man of average height and weight, he appeared to be about fifty years of age. An occasional shock of black hair, streaked with gray, peeked through where the white powdered wig sat askew atop the round head.

"Mister Connor." The high-pitched voice brought Ian back to the proceedings. "Having been found guilty of not paying your debts, it is the judgement of this court that you be taken at once to the prison for debtors. There you will serve the next five years, or until a responsible person purchases you as an indentured servant. You will then serve said person until your servitude has been completed to his satisfaction." The narrow face, belonging to the voice, no longer looked comical. This person had just taken five years from Ian's life. They might as well sentence him to hang; as there was no way he could stand to be locked away for five days, much less five years. "Is there anything you wish to say before you are removed from this court?" The question seemed to be one that needed to be asked, as a matter of law and formality, not as a matter of really caring.

"I do, sir." Ian's voice seemed shaky and a pitch too high to recognize as belonging to him. "I had no intent to defraud anyone, nor did I intend to steal money from anyone, as I have been accused of doing. My only crime was losing my employment when I became too ill to work. My wife died from the fever and I contacted it soon after. The bill for medicine and the doctor's visits continued to mount, as did the cost of food to keep us alive. Soon all of my savings were gone and I had sold everything of value that I had to my name. If you will trust me to work off the money owed, as a free man, I promise that I will repay every penny."

Trying to stifle a yawn the one in the center spoke, as he peered over the top of his spectacles. "It is indeed strange how nearly every one of you people that appears before us can blame everyone, and everything except your own ineptness, for the predicament you find yourselves in. According to English law you have been found guilty of having no visible means of support and owe debts that you are unable to pay. You are here by sentenced to debtors prison."

Ian opened his mouth to protest but rough hands were pulling him out of the enclosure, nearly dragging him toward the door. The leg shackles made it impossible to keep up with the guard on either side of him. Falling, face first to the floor, he attempted to catch himself but his hands were shackled to his waist. While one guard pulled him to his feet by his hair, the other struck him across the back with a short club. The numbing pain shot through his shoulders and down to his knees. He attempted to regain his balance as he was dragged outside. The bright sun was a sharp contrast to the dark interior of the courtroom that he had just so unceremoniously left. It was unusual to have this much sunlight in London this time of the year. Most days were filled with fog, rain or a combination of each.

Raising his head toward the warmth he said to himself. "You had best enjoy this sunlight, for it may be the last that you will see for five long years." A wooden cart pulled buy two worn out looking oxen stood in front of them. A sharp shove to his back, by one of the guards, slammed Ian's shins against the back of the cart, causing him to sprawl headlong into it. The rough-hewn boards sent slivers into his cheek as he slid along them. He bore the humiliation and pain silently, as he knew that any protest was fruitless and would only cause more of the same to be heaped upon him. He had barely pulled his legs inside the cart when the heavy wooden gate was dropped into place, missing his feet by mere inches. Rolling onto his back, he watched the two guards as the oxen were guided down the narrow streets, toward that place of Hell where he would spend the next five years.

Passing through the heavy wooden gates, Ian saw the stone walls close in on him. A state of panic came over him. If it weren't for the leg shackles he would bolt from the wagon and attempt to run from this place, even though he knew that such actions would mean instant death. These guards would like nothing more than to put a musket ball into his back as he tried to escape. He really could not blame the guards however. For if a prisoner escaped, then the guard would be forced to serve the prisoner's sentence in his stead. The oxen halted before the door inset into the grimy, gray stone building. Ian was pulled from the cart onto the cobblestone ramp and a shove propelled him towards the entryway. Once inside the shackles were removed. He was then forced to undress, while he was covered with a foul smelling powder to delouse him, while his head was shaved to find any hidden vermin.

Never in his short twenty-four years on this earth had he been so humiliated. The sheep on his father's farm in Ireland had received better and more humane treatment, however he knew better than to protest, for the treatment would only get worse if he did. His clothing was thrown at him and he was led down a narrow passageway, lined with cells on either side. A large number was placed over each of the barred openings that served as windows in the door. Ian was halted before door with the number 66 above it.

"This is your new home, Laddy," the larger of the two guards said. "If you should need anything, all you have to do is ring the bell. We are here to look after your every whim." The voice dripped with sarcasm.

The other guard laughed as he opened the door and prodded Ian inside. "I'll tell you now, If you make a sound I personally will crack your head. You get one meal a day and you empty your own waste bucket. There are no special privileges, unless you can pay for them that is. Seeing as how you are in here because you can't pay your legal debts, I'm sure that you won't have any money to buy extra favors from us."

The heavy door closed behind him and the key was turned in the lock. Ian heard the two men shuffle away, then total silence, except for the sounds coming from the others in this forsaken hole. Surveying his cell made Ian sick to his stomach. Pacing it off, it measured eight feet wide and ten feet long. The floor, Ian supposed, was stone under the inches of dirt and debris that covered it. Along one wall lay a filthy straw mattress and in the corner was a much-used metal waste pail. High up, on the outside wall was a heavily barred window. Ian estimated it to be about eight inches wide and three feet high. It was much too narrow for anything but an exceptionally

8

small person to slip through, even if they were able to somehow cut through the heavy bars. This opening was the only source of light and ventilation, hence the place smelled dank and terribly dirty from the multitude of unwashed bodies that had preceded him here. A sense of total despair and abandonment swept over him. This is where he must spend what should have been some of the best years of his life, in isolation and abject squalor.

Hesitant to sit on the mattress, but knowing that sooner or later he must do so, Ian placed his cloak on the cover before sitting down. Placing his head in his hands he began to weep. When there was not a tear left to squeeze out, he wiped his eyes with the tail of the shirt that was still waded into a ball in his lap.

"Now that you have that out of your system, let's see what can be done to make sure you survive this hole. You mustn't let them break you, no matter how they try. You have been through tougher times than what you now face. Think of anything but where you are. Keep your mind occupied with more pleasant thoughts." Talking to himself in a low voice, Ian made plans for doing just that. First thing every morning and the final thing at night, would be spent remembering the life that he had shared with Colleen. Though their marriage lasted only four short years, there were ample memories to keep him going. "Keep your mind sharp and dote on what you already know. Think of happier times such as farming, home, family, anything except discouraging thoughts." Looking at his surroundings, it was easier to talk about doing it than to convince him that it could be done. "First things first. Let's see what can be done to make this pig sty livable."

Wearing only his under garments Ian set about the gigantic task at hand. It did not take long in the stifling heat for rivulets of perspiration to soak through his thin garment. It was only the spring of the year. What kind of unbearable Hell would this be in the heat of summer? "Come on old chum. You're having those kind of thoughts that we decided not to have." Rolling the mattress aside he brushed the accumulation of unknown substances from beneath it. Satisfied that there was little else that he could do, he lay the cleanest straw that he could find beneath it and replaced his bed. Ian found that by grasping a handful of straw close to the center it would fan out in a circle and made a crude broom. The pile of debris grew larger as he continued throughout the afternoon, pausing occasionally to survey his progress.

"Well ain't that a pretty sight?" The suddenness of the silence being broken startled Ian. Dropping the straw he spun toward the voice. A guard leered at him through the barred window in the door. "Save your energy Mate. I seen your kind lots of times before. You prissy ones start out the same way. Cleaning the place 'n acting like this place don't bother you. Then you find out that there ain't no hope for you so you up and hang yourself with your own trousers. Seen it many times, I have." Sliding a tray under the door the man continued in a nearly taunting manner. "Guess I can't blame you though. I'd hate to be locked away where I couldn't visit my wife at nights, or take a walk through the square and smell the lilacs in bloom. Yes sir, I can't say that I'd blame you a bit when you decide to hang yourself." With a snicker the guard disappeared from the opening in the cell door. Ian could hear him whistling some jaunty tune as he walked down the passageway, undoubtedly to taunt some other poor, unfortunate soul.

"I wish that you would hold your head underwater waiting for me to hang myself." Ian said softly, not wanting to be heard showing any signs of defiance. He reminded himself of a dog that he had once seen. A much larger dog rushed the smaller cur and Ian knew that the little one would surely be killed. Instead he lay on his back in a sign of submission, while the larger one walked stiff legged around him, his hackle raised daring the smaller one to show any sign of aggression. Finally satisfied that the little one had shown proper respect, the larger dog walked off, leaving a shaken but still alive and healthy pup behind.

"I'll tuck tail now, but someday I shall have my chance to be the top dog and it shall be you cowering before me. That only serves to give me one more thing to keep me going."

Taking the food tray to his mattress, Ian sat down and studied the mess before him. That was a definite mistake. He learned then to eat the stuff, but never study what it was. The cornmeal mush was dotted with weevils and try as he may Ian could not force the foul mess down. That was another mistake. It would be twenty-four hours before he would have anything else to put into his stomach. He was still on his bed, trying to get up enough nerve to eat the solidified lump, when the guard returned to collect the trays.

"Sorry that you did not care for our dinner this evening, your highness. Perhaps tomorrow evening we could serve you pheasant stuffed with mushrooms, or perhaps venison loin smothered in cherry sauce." The voice fairly dripped with venom. "If you don't hurry and bring me that tray I'll come in there and crack your head for you. Get over here and be quick about it."

Jumping to his feet Ian fairly ran to the door and carefully avoided eye contact as he shoved the tray back under the door. "It isn't that I am not content with what you are serving me, sir. The food is more than nourishing, I'm sure." Ian did his best to keep a straight face as he lied. "It's only that my stomach is a bit upset tonight. More than likely because of the shock of finding myself sentenced to five years in debtor's prison. I had believed that I would be given an opportunity to make some sort of restitution, or perhaps be sent here for a year or two at the most." While playing the coward galled him, he was aware that by doing so he may save himself some severe, or even crippling beatings. It was beyond his comprehension as to how one human being could be capable of administrating the beatings, and worse, upon another human being and actually seem to enjoy it. Hatred flared inside of him as he watched the guard walk away, a snide remark casually tossed in Ian's direction as he left.

Traces of stars could be seen through the narrow slit in the wall as Ian prepared himself for bed. Deciding that his undershirt was the most expendable article of clothing, he tore it in half to use as a washing cloth. Pouring a bit from his bucket of drinking water onto the scrap of cloth, he rung it dry and repeated the process until he was satisfied that most of the sweat and dirt was washed out of it. "Because they have made me live like a pig doesn't mean that I must smell like one too." The water soaked rag felt good against his feverish body and he had to force himself to conserve the water in the bucket. Again ringing out the cloth he hung it on a rusty spike sticking from the wall near the door. Feeling a bit refreshed Ian lay on his bed, arms folded behind his head and, peering through the bars, watched the stars play peek-a-boo as he rolled his head slightly from side to side. He then found that by holding his head in one position and closing one eye, then the other, the stars shifted back and forth behind the window bars. Amazing what small things a man will find to entertain himself when he's forced into a difficult situation. In the darkness Ian felt completely abandoned and, hard as he tried, his mind would not shift away from these thoughts of hopelessness. Staring at the night sky he watched as a star fell and disappeared behind the edge of the window. His memory was shifted back to a warm evening, similar to this one, when he had first met his Colleen.

"If you'll be excusing me, Sir." These were the first words that she had spoken to Ian, as she walked through the crowded marketplace. The days had been exceedingly warm, for this time of the year, and most people waited until after sundown to do their necessary shopping. "I hate to be a bother, but may I get through?" Ian had been talking to a friend and was unknowingly blocking the way to the vegetable cart. A very fortunate set of circumstances, he would reflect on later, for he would have never met his Colleen if not for bumping into his friend at just that time.

Moving aside and at the same time turning to apologize, Ian was staring into the most beautiful face that he could ever remember seeing. Tipping his hat he replied. " I am dreadfully sorry, my Lady." His mind raced trying to think of something,.. anything.. that would enable him to keep talking to this beautiful creature, but nothing came to mind and he simply watched as she walked past and disappeared in the crowd. Reflecting back he felt like a fool. He had left his friend in the midst of a conversation and, without so much as a, "Bye your leave," went in search of the woman that he had just seen. Pushing through the sea of humanity Ian would catch an occasional glimpse of the auburn hair and white ruffled collar, only to see them disappear again. Just as it seemed hopeless that he would ever see the magnificent woman again, fate smiled upon him.

"Stop that man. Somebody stop that man, he has stolen my purse." A shrill call for help could be heard above the din of the shoppers. Suddenly a young fellow, of about Ian's age, running full tilt appeared before him. Clasped in his right hand was a woman's purse. Instinct made Ian throw his right arm out to push the man away from colliding head on with him. It was not so much an act of bravery as one of reflex, in either case, the thief was thrown backwards into a table full of merchandise. The owner of the goods was so inflamed at his merchandise being despoiled that he began pummeling the man with his fists, causing him to release his grip on the purse, push himself free and run off as fast as possible. Ian had just picked it up from the ground when the owner arrived at his elbow. "Thank you so much, Sir," a sweet voice said as a hand relieved Ian of the purse. "Every penny I have to my name is in here."

"Think nothing of it. My name's Ian Connor. Would I be too forward if I was to ask yours?" He could not get over the striking beauty of this lady and at the first opportunity he checked the ring fingers for an indication of a ring. Gratefully he saw none.

"I suppose the least I can do for the gentleman that saved my purse is to tell him my name." Extending her hand to Ian she said softly. "My name is Colleen O'Brien. Connor? Did you say your last name is Connor?" Ian simply nodded his head in response to the question. "That's a good Irish name, almost as Irish as O'Brien. Again I thank you Mister Connor for saving my purse, but I really must be on my way. I still have a great deal of shopping to do and it is getting rather late."

Still holding the offered hand Ian knew that if he let her get away now, he may never see her again. "I am indeed happy to meet you Miss O'Brien. It is Miss, isn't it?" Ian held his breath waiting for an answer.

"Yes, it is still Miss. My father's rather old fashion and believes that I'm still a bit too young to be thinking of marriage. Of course I think that he will believe that when I'm forty also." The grin made dimples appear at the corners of the pert mouth and a shallow one indented the chin.

"You can never fault a father for looking after the welfare of his daughter. Especially when she is as attractive as you." Ian's face turned red with embarrassment. "I'm afraid that I have put my foot in my mouth. I have been a bit too forward and I apologize for that remark."

The grin spread wider and a twinkle appeared in the green eyes. "You apologize for thinking that I am attractive. I see nothing to be apologetic for. I am rather flattered by your complement, Mister Connor."

"Perhaps you would allow me to show my sincerity by sharing a spot of tea with me. There is a quaint little place close by and I would deem it an honor if you would join me there." It was then that he realized that he still held her right hand in his. Hesitantly he released his grasp and let his hand fall to his side.

It seemed like forever before she answered. "I really should be going home, but how can I say no to such a chivalrous gentleman as yourself? Perhaps a quick cup and then I really must be going home. First though, I must retrieve my groceries. I dropped them back there when that dreadful creature grabbed my purse."

Ian could not believe his good fortune. The crowd had thinned as he led Colleen back to where she had dropped her grocery sack. Retrieving what hadn't been taken or tromped on, they went around the corner to the tearoom. Finding a table towards the back they sat facing each other and engaged in useless conversation. When the waitress finally brought their tea Ian found that he was a few cents short of having enough to pay for it. Now it was Colleen's turn to come to his rescue.

Two hours slipped away before they realized what time it was. "I really must be going home. I'm afraid that my father is already pacing the floor wondering where I am. I thank you for the tea and wonderful conversation, Mister Connor." As she stood to leave, Ian knew that there was no way he could allow this angel to get away.

"Perhaps I should walk you home. You never can tell what will await you on the streets these days. I would never forgive myself should anything happen to you." Hopefully the guise would work and he could learn where she lived and at the same time appear gallant.

"I would be ever so grateful if you would, however I don't want to put you out," Colleen smiled.

Taking her by the arm, Ian was elated at the invitation. "Don't you worry about putting me out. It would be my pleasure to see you safely home."

That was the beginning of a short courtship, for only seven months later, and just two weeks after her eighteenth birthday, Ian and Colleen were married. That same year, using up all of his savings, he bought in as a full partner in Tyler and Sons Apothecary. There were really no sons associated with the business. In fact Tyler Jensen was a confirmed bachelor, but he thought that the name gave the company more family appeal. An ardent student, Ian soon became proficient in the various stages of pharmacy and associated doctoring. The business flourished and Ian gave Colleen anything that he thought would make her happy. Money was no object. The one thing that money could not buy however was a family. For some unknown reason no children blessed the marriage. Though they were both disappointed they accepted the situation, as a decision made by a Higher Being, therefore there must be a reason for it.

In the darkness of the cell Ian relived many happy moments he had spent with Colleen. As sleep overtook him the visions changed form and became dreams. He could control the thoughts, when he was awake and shut out the ones that he wished to forget. Asleep the thoughts became jumbled, disjointed and at times extremely bothersome. One moment he would be sitting on the porch holding Colleen close and the next she had disappeared and he was standing over the open grave while she seemed to beckon to him. His sleep became fitful as the dreams became more and more macabre. Shovels of dirt were thrown into the grave but instead of covering the corpse in the bottom, each shovel full raised the body closer to the surface.

Awakening with a start, Ian sat upright on the straw mattress. Sweat ran down his face and chest in streams, while his breath came in quick gasps. The once stifling interior of the cell was now cool and clammy with the night air. Drawing his cloak over his shoulders he drew his knees up, until he could rest his chin on them, and stared into the depths of darkness surrounding him. "One day down and only one thousand eight hundred twenty four more to go, before I am out of here." Why in the world he would think of such a thing was beyond him. At least there was something to look forward to, even if it was four years, eleven months and three hundred sixty four days away.

Daylight found him sitting in that same position and before long he heard stirring in the adjoining cells. Walking to the far end of his cubicle he could look outside, through the slit of a window. This morning the London sky was the usual dreary gray. Occasional splatters of raindrops could be seen as they hit the sill and sent a fine mist inside. He was backed against the door, engrossed in the rain, when he heard the voice somewhere behind him.

"I say, number sixty-six. Welcome to the Filthy Room Hotel. Sorry we didn't have the brass band out to greet you. They were busy playing at a special ceremony for old King Henry the eighth and whichever harlot he's married to now."

Pausing only long enough to see that the voice came from directly across the narrow walkway, Ian hurriedly moved away from the opening in the door and went where he couldn't be seen by the others. That fool was talking treason and Ian wanted nothing to do with any conversation that had the possibilities of getting his body stretched on the rack, or worse. The voice continued to taunt him, while all the time hurling insults at the King of England.

"Shut your mouth you idiot," came a voice from close by. "Do you want to get all of us punished just because you have something against King Henry? Believe me, my friend, whatever complaint you have now is nothing compared to what you will have if you keep talking that way. Men have disappeared for saying less, so just hush now."

"This isn't a prison, it's an asylum for the insane," Ian said to himself. The walls seemed to suddenly close in on him and he bit his lip until he drew blood, just to keep from screaming. "Find something to do before you lose your mind also," he thought. Returning to his bed he surveyed the walls surrounding him. They were made of stone blocks, which were freely decorated with various pictures, symbols and gouges left behind by previous room guests. Above his head were a series of parallel lines in a series of four and then a slash through them. Taking them to be a measurement of time, each line representing one day, Ian counted them. One thousand eight hundred ninety one. If he was correct, and each mark equaled one day, that came to five years two months and six days. Each mark must have taken hours to gouge into the hard wall. Running his fingers over the marks he felt a kinship to the faceless man who wore the grooves into the gray stone. In his minds eye he envisioned a figure using a shard of discarded rock, and rubbing it back and fourth until the indent was satisfactory.

"I may as well finish what you have started, my friend. I shall fill in a mark for every day that I am here." Using the abundant dirt from the floor, Ian mixed it with drops of water until a paste was formed. This he pressed into one of the furrows in the stone. Satisfied that it would stay, he did one for this day. "Now let's see. What is a good time of day to work this into my busy schedule? Perhaps I could squeeze it in between my morning swim and stroll." Strutting around the small cell he imitated a pompous gentleman. Grinning at his antics, he wondered if perhaps he was really losing his mind after all. "Don't worry old boy. As long as you know that you're making a fool of yourself you are completely sane. It's only when you don't realize that fact that your sanity is in jeopardy. Besides, who is going to notice in this place, except for a rat or two that were frequently seen scurrying from one corner to another?"

There was a persistent gnawing in the pit of Ian's stomach and he was beginning to wish that he had eaten the mush last night. Taking a drink of the tepid, stale water did little to satisfy his hunger. In fact it seemed to whet his appetite and the pangs grew sharper, while his belly began to growl in protest. Walking to the door he bent until he could look out of the opening into the passageway. Peering down the hall he knew that it was a lesson in futility, for there would be no food for at least six or seven hours yet.

This was the first time that he had taken time to really examine his surroundings. The identical doors were evenly spaced and set in the center of each cell and recessed, about eight inches, into the stonewall. The indent, and small openings, made it nearly impossible to see into any of the other cells except for the one directly across from him. Shifting his gaze to that door, he was surprised to see that it was wide open. There was no sign of activity inside the room and Ian had heard no noise from that direction since the occupant had made the remarks about the King. After studying what could be seen of the cell from his vantage point, Ian was about to turn away from the window when he heard footsteps scurrying toward his door. Around the curve in the passageway appeared an elderly man carrying a bucket and broom. From his bent body and sparse white hair Ian estimated him to be in his twilight years. The period in life when a man should be sitting beside a fireplace with his pipe and paper, enjoying the time he had left on this earth, not confined to this place. Ian watched as the elderly man stopped before the vacant cell across from his and, shaking his head, threw the water from the bucket onto the floor of the passageway. Sweeping motions of the broom sent water in all directions as he scrubbed the flooring stones with the bristles. The tip of the straw broom began to take on a pink tinge. It was then that Ian knew why the floor was being scrubbed. It was to remove all traces of blood that had been spilled onto the floor when the noisy protestor was removed from his cell. The guards had been very efficient in carrying out their duty, as there had been no sounds of a struggle or shouts that one would have expected to hear. Ian shuddered at the thought of the damage the heavy clubs, that each guard carried, could inflict on the human body. When the floor was cleaned to his satisfaction, the old gentleman turned to Ian.

"You're new here. I know most everyone on this floor. Knew that gent 'fore he went and got himself killed," he said indicating with his thumb the open door behind him. " Heard that he was tryin' to escape when they opened his cell to give him some clean straw. Least ways that's what the guards are sayin'. Everyone here calls me, 'Old Crazy.' I might be a bit strange, but I'm the one out walkin' around while the rest are locked up tight."' A high-pitched cackle escaped the narrow lips. "What might your name be?"

"Connor, sir. Ian Connor, at your service." Ian nodded in a gesture of acknowledgement.

"Not much service you can be to me, or anyone else, locked in that cage the way you are, but nice to meet you, Mister Connor." The pale blue eyes studied Ian's features through the bars. "The guards will be through before long 'n let you out for a spell. That's your chance to empty your slop bucket 'n stretch your legs in the courtyard. There's a water barrel in the corner of the yard that catches rainwater. Has a bit of peculiar taste, but at least it's wet 'n quenches a body's thirst. They only let a couple dozen at a time out in the yard, 'n then only for about half hour twice a week."

Ian was happy to see the first friendly face since his trial had started. "Thank you for the advice, Sir. I'll greatly appreciate any help and advice that you can give me."

"Best advice I can give you is to make yourself invisible. Don't make no waves 'n don't do nothin' that'll draw attention to you, like that fella 'cross the hall from you did. As far as help goes, there ain't no help I give nobody. I learned a long time ago to look after myself 'n let the other guy do the same. That way if he goes under he can't take me with him."

The conversation was interrupted when the shuffle of feet was heard approaching from the jog in the passageway. The old man quickly gathered his bucket and broom and walked in the direction opposite from where the approaching footsteps were heard. Ian smiled to himself as he turned away from the opening. "Make yourself invisible," he murmured. A key was put into the lock and the door to his cell swung open.

"Come on Connor. We don't have all day to wait for you." The guard was the same one that had threatened to break Ian's head before and it was plain that he was not to be kept waiting. Grabbing the slop bucket in one hand and the water bucket in the other, he hurried to join the others in line and was marched outside into the fresh air.

"Follow me," a voice behind him said. "There's a place over there where we dump the buckets, but you best hurry. If the guards think you're doddling they'll give you a few smacks with the club to move you along."

The man speaking was now slightly ahead of Ian and heading for the far end of the compound. Following his lead, Ian too hurried in that direction.

"My name's Ian Connor," he introduced himself to the fellow beside him. Sizing up the stranger, Ian estimated him to be about the same age as himself, but that was where the similarity ended. The other man was a good head and shoulders taller than Ian and out weighed him by at least a hundred pounds. The broad shoulders, thick neck and heavily muscled arms were evidence of years of physical labor. The neck length black hair was tied with a piece of dirty ribbon that Ian estimated had been red at one time.

"Names don't mean much around this place. Most of us just go by the number of our cell. I'm sixty-two, but my name's Kale. Kale Brewster." Ian's hand was lost in the ham-like hand as they exchanged handshakes. "I heard them when they brought you in yesterday. From what I could hear you played it smart with the guards. Some of the trustees you have to watch out for. Old Crazy's okay, but some of the others try to better themselves by climbing over the backs of the rest of us."

By the time the exercise period was over Ian had learned that Kale Brewster had worked the docks in Liverpool since he was twelve years old, which explained the massive muscular build. He had been in debtor's prison for the past seven months and was sentenced to a period of three years for a twelve-pound debt that he was unable to pay.

"Has anyone ever been sold into indentured servitude that you are aware of?" Ian asked as they were being rounded up to return to their cells. "I doubt that servitude could be any worse than spending five years in this place."

"About the only time anyone shows up to get indentured servants is when they need some special kind of person, or they need some kind of legal slaves for work nobody else'll do. They have to pay to get us out, so when they do you're owned body and soul 'til your debt's paid off."

Picking up their water and slop buckets they were herded back inside and down the winding passageway, stopping before the various cells to drop off the occupants. Ian and his new found acquaintance exchanged nods as Brewster left the line and entered his cell. Once the door was locked the procession continued to the next, then it was Ian's turn to hear the key turn behind him.

In his ignorance he had filled the water bucket too full and much of the water had spilled over the top and soaked his trousers from the knee down and his shoe made a squishing sound with every step that he took. Setting the buckets down he proceeded to remove the wet garments and hung them to dry. The time in the exercise yard had given him something to think about besides his empty stomach, but now the pangs returned with a vengeance. Dipping his cup into the water bucket, he drank the contents, hoping to control, or at least diminish the growling in his belly. This time it did help and the pangs eased a bit.

The inside of the cell was beginning to become stifling hot as the sun replaced the usual fog and rain. Removing everything, except for his under bottoms, Ian lay on the mattress. He longed for the cool breeze from the ocean. His mind went back to the home that he had shared with Colleen, a cottage on the beach that he had surprised her with. The business was blossoming and the profits grew, as both Tyler Jensen and he were making a very comfortable living. They expanded the apothecary, while the number of people coming to be treated for various symptoms increased also. The treatments were similar in almost all of the illnesses. First remove the bad and infected blood, either by leaches or cutting. If that failed the patient was usually given large doses of laxatives, diuretics and expectorants to clean out the system. If these steps failed the patient was usually deemed incurable. Closing his eyes Ian pictured the cottage and Colleen scurrying around the small kitchen preparing him their first meal in their new home. Things were good and times were happy.

CHAPTER TWO.

Days slipped slowly into weeks and weeks into months, with not much to change the monotony or drudgery that was life in prison. When Ian had filled the gouge in the wall this morning he counted them, as he had every morning since starting the project. Two hundred eighty seven were filled. Nine months, two weeks and three days since he first entered this place. His routine had varied little since that memorable first day. He added a few more things to keep him occupied but all in all he was well satisfied with the way he was faring. Much better than those who were content to mope about and find nothing to do but dwell on the hand that fate had dealt them. These were the ones that the guards would find hanging in their cells.

His hair had long since grown back and his clothes had literally fallen from his body before he was given a change of clothing. The quality of the food had not improved appreciably, but Ian had learned to hide away what he was unable to eat. There were times when they would be punished for some infraction, either real or imagined, and food would be withheld for that day. The rats were a constant problem when he first tried to store food, as they would seek it out and devour it to the last crumb. He tried numerous ways to protect what he was saving before finally hitting upon one that worked. He had been able to get Old Crazy, who had since died, to find him a discarded boot. This he put the scraps of food in, folded it double, and then hung it by the strap from the hook in the wall. Ian smiled when he thought of how he first used this food storage method. Before coming here he would never eat anything that had dropped from his plate, to say nothing of eating food that had been stored in someone's old boot. It was strange how circumstances dictated the way that one would live his life. Things that he would never have thought of doing had become an accepted part of his routine.

It was now the heart of winter and the exercise yard was more of a chore than one of enjoyment. The mounds of snow and frigid temperatures

21

were not something that any of the prisoners looked forward to, but it was mandatory that they spend the full half hour outside. Upon returning to his cell Ian was trying to warm himself when the door to his cell swung open again. Two guards and a man dressed in rather plain but neat clothing entered.

"I am told that you are a physician. My youngest daughter is stricken and you are the closest. I am the warden of this prison and this is your chance to gain great favor in my eyes. Save my daughter and you name your fee. If it is in my realm to grant it, you shall be given whatever you ask. On the other hand if you fail to save her, your life here will be more miserable than you could ever imagine. Do we have a bargain?"

"I am not a trained physician Sir. I have been schooled in the use of leeches and bloodletting and have had some success in bringing down a fever or two, but I was unable to even save my own wife when she became ill. I'm afraid that putting your daughter in my care would be a foolish mistake on both our parts." Ian sat as if the matter was closed and was taken by surprise when he was roughly jerked to his feet, a guard holding each of his arms.

The warden stood nose to nose with Ian. "Perhaps you didn't understand me. You will be tending to my daughter. The outcome will determine whether I allow you to walk around a whole man. Now come with me and no more dawdling."

Having no more say in the matter, Ian was led down mazes of passageways and through doors until finally they entered a foyer, that led into a comfortably furnished sitting room. Red velvet drapes covered the windows and thick pile carpet covered the floor, while bottles of brandy sat on a cart by the matching velvet settee. Ian had no time to completely assess the room as he was rushed through and into the bedroom in the back.

By the light of a single candle Ian could barely make out the form lying on the bed in the corner of the room. "I will need more light, if I am expected to miraculously save this child." Taking the candle as he passed it, he stood over the inert figure. In the dim light he beheld the cherubic face of a young girl of about four years old. Her blond hair, soaked with sweat, was plastered tightly against her face and head. Laying the back of his hand on her cheek he was not surprised to find her burning with fever. "How long has she been this way?" Turning to face the girl's father Ian was sounding a bit hostile. "I need some idea of her symptoms and if there has been anything given to her." Just then a candelabra holding six large candles preceded a rather plump, unattractive woman into the room.

"I heard you order more light," a high-pitched nasal voice was directed towards Ian. "I will set fire to the whole city if you need that much light. Whatever you shall need, you shall have, Doctor." Hovering close to him Ian was revolted by the odor of an unwashed body that emanated from the woman.

Backing away, Ian turned his attention back to the girl. "How long has she been unconscious, and what brought on her illness?" Finding an excuse to rid the room of the unpleasant odor, Ian instructed the woman to bring a tub of cold water, some cloths, and finally to put on a pot of water to boil. According to the warden the girl had complained of a stomachache, but as most children are afflicted with upset bellies they thought nothing of it. Shortly after they had eaten supper last evening she became more feverish and the belly became tender to the touch. The girl slept little during the night and by morning was as she appeared now. At first they thought that she was simply sleeping but, upon trying to awaken her, late in the afternoon for some nourishment, they found her to be comatose. Lifting the hem of the nightgown Ian looked for any tell tail signs on the stomach area, but there were none visible. Pressing and probing around the small belly he got a slight reaction from the girl when he pushed on the lower right quadrant. Shaking his head Ian moved from the bed and sat in one of the stuffed chairs.

"What is it," the warden asked. "What do you need to cure my baby? Tell me and you shall have it immediately." The voice went from one of demanding to that of panic.

"I have told you that I am not a surgeon but only trained in the use of leeches and certain drugs. It is my opinion that your daughter has a ruptured appendix. If that is the case then I am not qualified to remove them. I have only watched the operation done, but never did one myself." Ian hoped that the expression on his face reflected the helplessness that he felt inside. He was not about to tell the father of this little child that both of the patients that he had watched had died shortly after the surgery. "I would suggest that you send for the nearest physician, and do it as fast as humanly possible. In my opinion this child has but a few hours to live unless the surgery in done very soon." The woman returned carrying a pot of water and some cloth strips.

"What are you doing just sitting there? Why aren't you attending to my daughter?" The voice was both demanding and caustic. This woman was obviously one that was used to having things done her way and woe be the poor soul she vented her wrath on. "Here is the cold water you wanted, now get busy and help her."

Ian stared into the pasty face. "As I have explained to your husband, I am not capable of doing the surgery that is required to save her life. Every minute that we sit and chat, is one more minute that decreases her chance to live. There isn't time to go over all of this again. Will you please send someone for the nearest surgeon before it is too late?"

The ear splitting screech as she yelled for the guards pierced the air. Her husband simply sat and held the small hand in his. "Take this useless piece of tripe back to his cell." Placing her hands on her abundant hips she glared at her husband. "Are you going to just sit there, or are you going for the doctor? It's evident that this one you brought from the cells can do nothing."

The last thing Ian saw before he was hustled out of the room, between two guards, was the expression of total hopeless surrender on the face of the warden. "I suppose that we all are in a prison cell of one type or another. The only difference being that some don't have visible bars on the windows and slab doors," he thought to himself. It was more than evident that in his way the poor warden was as much of a prisoner as Ian, or any of the other inhabitants of the cells that he was being hurried past. The entire way from the bedroom to his cell was accomplished in complete silence. The usually overbearing guards were strangely gentle in the handling of their prisoner, also the banter and abuse was not there. When the door was locked behind him Ian felt his way to his mattress. In the darkness, as he undressed, he uttered a silent but sincere prayer on behalf of the small child that he had just left. Sleep came hard the rest of the night, most of it filled with disjointed dreams of a feverish little girl.

Daylight was streaming through the barred window when Ian was awakened by the sound of the door to his cell slamming. Before he was fully awakened a booted foot was planted sharply against his behind. "Just wanted to let you know that you weren't much help last night. The little girl died about an hour ago. I don't envy you a bit, there number sixty-six. You'd better give your soul to God, 'cause the rest of you's going to belong to the warden. No sir, I don't envy you at all."

Trying to focus on the guards face and at the same time absorb what he was saying, Ian pulled himself to a sitting position. "I told them that I was not qualified to heal her. She needed a physician not merely one with my limited talents. Surely he can't blame me for being inept, when I am not trained in the art of surgery." His voice began to tremble, as he comprehended the seriousness of the situation. "Perhaps if I could speak to him, I could make him understand that there was nothing that I could have done to save her. I doubt that any trained physician could have done much for her."

The guard's face showed a slight sign of sympathy. "The warden's given orders that you are to get just enough food to keep you alive, and at the first chance your carcass is to be sold into indentureship. If it helps any I feel for you, but there's nothing I can do to help you. Anyone caught giving you aid will join you in this cell and it's better you than me. There is to be no more exercise out of this cell and after I leave, no one is allowed to talk to you for as long as you are here." With that he turned and without a backward glance, closed and locked the cell door. The key turning in the lock seemed a thousand times louder than it ever had before.

For an interminable amount of time Ian simply starred blankly at the wooden door, trying to assemble his thoughts. This couldn't be real. How could he be punished so severely for something that was beyond his control? Perhaps if he had treated the child and then she had died there would have been some reason for it. As it was, he was completely innocent of doing anything wrong. A chill passed through him, even though there had been no change in the room temperature. Gathering the remnants of his cloak about him he tried to get his mind off this unpleasantness and on to something lighter, but to no avail. Was this to be how his life would end? Closed away from the rest of the world and slowly starved to death? No matter how hard he tried to change it, his mind was occupied by the circumstances that he now found himself in.

"Buck up, old boy. You haven't come this far just to give in now. Remember how Colleen looked the time that you asked her to marry you?" Try as he might the picture escaped him and the face of the sick child haunted his memory.

When the daily meal cart came around Ian's door was bypassed. Looking through the barred opening he could see the bowls being shoved beneath the other doors, then the trustee vanished from his sight. "I wonder how long a body will live on only water to sustain life? Perhaps I shall learn soon," he thought silently to himself. Returning to his mattress he resumed his seat and once more stared at the door, as if by doing so his meal would magically appear beneath it. Dejectedly, he finally lay down and looked at the ceiling. The patterns were indelibly etched in his mind, for he had studied them so many times before. Closing his eyes he could visualize each indent and protrusion on the rock surface above him.

Just as he began to doze off there was a scraping sound at the door to his cell. With barely enough light to see by he hurried to the doorway. Picking up the bowl, that had been shoved beneath the entryway, he returned to his bed. By the dim light from outside he saw that he was receiving the uneaten scraps from the other prisoner's meal. Bits and crusts of dried bread, and an unknown substance that resembled what had been fed to the hogs on his father's farm. There was no spoon so he was forced to eat the concoction with his fingers. Learning long ago not to question what he was eating, Ian devoured the meal in a short time and pushed the bowl back under the door whence it came. The void in his belly temporarily satisfied he again lay on his bed and was soon fast asleep.

The days dragged into weeks of constant boredom. His water bucket was only filled once a week; also this was his only chance to empty the slop bucket. He dared not even allow himself the luxury of an occasional body washing. His hair had become long and matted, as had his beard. His meals were anywhere from meager to nonexistent, depending upon how hungry the rest were. Some nights he had to be satisfied with nothing more than one crust of bread and a sip of water. His clothes, ill fitting to begin with, now hung on his lank frame without any form to them. It became a constant battle to keep his trousers from falling about his ankles, as they were not allowed to have belts. His cloak had finally become so rotten that it was a useless scrap that he wadded up under his head for a makeshift pillow.

The marks on the wall indicated that he had been in this tiny cubicle for one year, four months and thirteen days, when he was to receive his first visitor, of sorts. It was on a stifling hot and humid afternoon when the cell door was opened and a portly man, holding a handkerchief to his bulbous nose, entered. Ian was in the midst of an afternoon nap when the guards roused him.

"On your feet Connor. This gentleman wants to have a look at you." The rounded end of the club prodded Ian in the ribs. Turning to the stranger the guard said sarcastically, "This is as close to a physician as we have in this place. The warden has already told you of his ineptness, but if you want him he's for sale." A smirk twisted his lips. "Right cheap too, I'll wager. The warden would more than likely pay you to take him out of here after what he's done, or hasn't done would be more like it." Jerking Ian to his feet the guard turned him in circles for inspection.

"Not much flesh on those bones," the man commented. "are you sure that he'll live for me to get him back to Wales? Wouldn't give more than twenty pounds for the likes of this one. I don't suppose that it matters much though. A year or so in the coal mines and if the work don't kill him the black lung will. Bring him along with the rest, but only twenty pounds for him mind you. If I wasn't in such bad need of a medical man I'd leave this one for the rats to feed on. Do you know how to set broken bones and treat bad cuts and such?"

Seeing an opportunity to finally be rid of this prison Ian would have lied to God himself. "Yes Sir. I am very capable of doing those things. I have set many broken bones and treated more illnesses than I could count. I promise to serve you well, Sir."

"Bring him along and be fast about it. The stench in this place is making me nauseous." The portly man hurried out of the cell followed by Ian and the guards. Ian was elated when they stopped at the door of Kale Brewster's cell. In a matter of moments Kale had joined the procession. By the time they had arrived at the end of the corridor seven more had joined their ranks. "Chain them together and I'll settle up with the warden. Have them outside and ready to leave when I get there."

Unaccustomed to the bright sunlight, Ian squinted against the brilliance as they walked outside. The group was herded to a small building at the back of the grounds. A place that he had no idea existed. Smoke rose from a small forge and, as they entered, they were taken one by one to the anvil. A shackle was put around the right ankle of each man and a chain was fastened to a ring on the outside of the manacle. Ian watched in horror as

27

each one ahead of him was forced to place his leg next to the anvil. A red-hot bolt was taken from the forge and driven into the shackle and hammered closed. The proximity of the heated metal to exposed flesh caused an excruciating burn on the ankles of the unfortunate prisoners, until they could submerge them in a tub of water at the end of the anvil. Kale was next and then it was Ian's turn.

"It can only hurt for a short time and then you shall be free of this madhouse. What's a little pain compared to what you have already endured here?" Trying to think of anything except what was about to happen, Ian lifted his right leg to the anvil. He was not ready for the sudden jolt that sent shock waves of pain all the way to his hip. The burning of the bolt was bad enough but the twisting of the shackle as it was secured made him think that if it lasted any longer, his anklebone would surely break. A few deft blows of the hammer and he was allowed to hobble to the tub of water. The tepid water sizzled as he submerged his leg into it. Although it did little to relieve the throbbing pain, it at least stopped the burning from going deeper into his flesh.

When the final three were secured to the rest, they were prodded toward the gates. The same ones he had entered so long ago, or at least it seemed long ago to Ian. It took a while for the prisoners to become accustomed to the chain binding them together. Many times they would have to stop and pick up one of their members who had fallen, which caused the rest to stumble. Finally they learned to walk in unison. A two-wheel buggy and a rickety wooden cart stood awaiting their occupants. "I don't need to guess which one we get to ride in," Ian heard Kale mutter, but it mattered little to Ian. He was finally going to be free of those great stonewalls forever. Whatever awaited him beyond today couldn't be as bad as the year, plus, that he had endured inside here.

Standing in the oppressive heat for much of the day did little to relieve the discomfort of the shackles around his ankle. The guards were also becoming disgruntled with having to stay in the heat. When Ian asked for some water for the men, he was given a slap across the face for his efforts. The sun was disappearing behind the prison walls before their new owner appeared with the warden in tow.

"Men," the warden announced, "this is your new owner, Master Dole. He has paid good English silver for you. If any man fails to fulfill his obligation to him, at his discretion, that man will be punished as he sees fit.

You are no longer wards of King Henry but chattel of Master Dole. Long live the King." With that he shook hands with the portly man and withdrew through the gates.

"Get them into the wagon. We still have a ways to go before night fall," Dole ordered the guards. "Treat them gentle. I don't want any broken bones, least ways not before they get a few days work under their belts." Prodded and shoved the nine men were loaded onto the wooden cart. Holding the reins of the mules, that pulled the cart, a huge black man sat on the driver's seat. This was only the second person of that race that Ian had ever seen and he was fascinated by the superb specimen. "Gentlemen," Dole stood before them, "I'd like to introduce you to Ham. He settles all my disputes for me and hasn't lost one yet, so I'd suggest that you not do anything to incur my wrath. That club of his is never more than an arms length away. Show them, Ham."

The one called "Ham" picked up a large club from the seat beside him. "I have seen smaller trees than that," Ian thought to himself. "If a man was ever hit with that, it would drive him into the ground up to his knees."

The Black grinned, showing rows of even yellow teeth. "Yes 'ir Master Dole. I ain't never lost an argument yet and I don't see nobody that'll change that either." Surveying the contents of the wagon his gaze stopped at Kale Brewster. "That 'un looks like he's the only one big 'nuf to be of any mind." Shoving the butt of the club against Kale's chest he pushed harder. "You ain't gon'na cause ol' Ham no trouble, now are ya mister?" The only response from Kale was a slight shaking of his head.

Climbing into the buggy Dole motioned for the cart to follow and they started down the same street that Ian had entered over a year ago. Excitement and anticipation replaced the hopelessness that was his for this past time. The prospect of being able to see the sunrise and feel the fresh dew on the grass, instead of the dirty floor and walls of his cell, lifted his spirits. Whatever lay ahead for him couldn't possibly be worse than what he had endured lately. He had heard little of the Welch coalmines, except for they were a place as close to Hell as could be found on earth. The fact that Dole had purchased him to do the doctoring gave Ian hope. Perhaps he would be spared the arduous task of working beneath the ground. Ian shuddered at the thought of being shut away in a narrow tunnel, with the only light being that from a lantern and no fresh air.

"You worry over nothing," he thought silently. "At least wait and see what fate awaits you before you turn yourself into a wretched wreck of a man. Just make certain to stay on the good side of Ham. That giant could make mincemeat of a bull." Glancing at the somber faces of his traveling companions, he wondered if they all shared his feelings. For no apparent reason a Bible passage came to mind and he found himself mentally repeating it. "The Lord is my shepherd, I shall not want." The words flowed one after another until he came to, "Thy rod and Thy staff they comfort me." Looking at the huge club by the side of Ham, he felt little comfort.

Closing his eyes Ian attempted to think of happier times. He pictured the green pastures of home and the happy times of his childhood there. His father sat in his chair while mother scurried around the kitchen preparing dinner. Despite the jostling and bumpy ride of the wagon Ian fell asleep. The characters changed from his parents into him and Colleen. He could smell the fresh bread that she had taken from the oven only moments before. Sitting close to him, she laid her head on his shoulder and he could feel her warm breath on his neck as she nuzzled closer to him.

A sharp jolt as the cartwheel hit a rut in the road brought Ian back to reality. Opening his eyes he found the head on his shoulder and breath on his neck belonged to the man chained next to him. The fellow had also fallen asleep and had found a pillow on Ian's shoulder. Hesitant to move he thought to himself, "Oh how I miss you my darling Colleen. I love you more than life its self. Whatever awaits me at the end of this journey will never diminish that love. If not for the memories of the moments we had together, I would have gone mad long ago." With that he closed his eyes again, hoping to revive the same dream but it escaped him. "Colleen," he murmured although he was fast asleep.

CHAPTER THREE.

Throughout the long and tedious journey the only relief, from the jolting of the cart, occurred when Dole needed a break from the monotony or to stretch his legs. The prisoners were allowed out of the cart and able to walk in a circle, under the watchful eye of Ham. There was to be no conversation between any of the men during the trek, for as Dole explained it, "I want no escape plans being made, so there will be absolute silence. The only time I want to hear from you is if one of you dies."

When they finally arrived at their destination, Ian was surprised to see a bustling community in the center of a green valley. A dozen or so buildings surrounded the town square, while houses numbering in the teens were on the outskirts. Dropping down from the low-lying hills the cart made it's way to the edge of town where Dole called for a halt. Walking to the cart he held a brief conversation with Ham then walked back to his buggy. Clicking to the mules, Ham drove toward the far outskirts of town and over another hill beyond. Nestled in the center were about seven long, dilapidated shanties. Smoke rose from the crooked chimneys, forming a haze in the narrow valley.

"Take a good look at your new home you deadbeats, 'cause here's where some of you are gon'na die. You belong ta Master Dole and I'm here ta see that he ain't cheated when he bought you. Get any notion 'bout runnin' out 'a your head right now. What we do ta runners ain't a pretty sight. Work hard and don't make no fuss and we'll get along just fine. Slack off 'n make trouble and you'll rue the day you was ever born. This ain't no threat, just fact." The yellow teeth, showing between the black lips, reminded Ian of a rabid dog that he had seen as a young boy. The sight was indelibly etched in his mind, as though it happened only yesterday. The large black mongrel bared it's teeth and snapped at anything in his path, while everything and everyone cowered from the onslaught. Like with any bully there was someone stronger and braver than the mad dog. It's rampage ended with a well-placed rifle ball.

Urging the mules into a semi trot Ham soon pulled them to a halt on the banks of a narrow creek. Dropping the tailboard he ordered the occupants out. Like Ian, most of the men had trouble standing for their legs had long since gone to sleep. The needles began to dance in his feet and legs as the blood began to circulate again. The lone building, close to where they had stopped, was a clapboard one-room shack with no door.

"Get your worthless hide out here 'n earn your keep." Ham hollered in a thunderous voice toward the cabin. "Master Dole got another batch for you to fix up. Bring your scissors 'n razor 'n meet me at the creek." Turning to the chained men he grinned. "When you get all prettied up I want ya ta get in that water and scrub that lily-white skin 'til it's pink as a baby's butt. There's lots of sand on the bottom of the creek, and I want you spankin' clean when you get out." Lifting his pant leg he took a large knife from his boot. Walking to the first man in line he proceeded to cut away all the man's clothing. When they were all standing completely stripped of any clothes, he ordered them to sit on the ground. An aged man with one cloudy blue eye and one brown eye cut and shaved their hair and beards. When it came Ian's turn he was more than a bit apprehensive, over having a man with only one good eye and a shaky hand use a straight razor on him. The piles of hair fell in his lap as the scissors did their job. A strong smelling soap was lathered on his scalp and face then the shaving started. Closing his eyes against the scraping on his tender skin, Ian was more than grateful when the torment ended with only a few nicks to show for it. When the old man finished the last in line Ham ordered them into the creek.

"I want ta see all 'a you scrubbing yourselves clean. There's lots 'a sand on the bottom of that creek, so don't be stingy using it. I want every inch 'a that lily-white skin pink as a baby's bottom. Any man what comes out and don't look that way'll have old Ham give him a scrubbin' that he'll never forget. When ya get out, there'll be clothes waitin' for ya on the bank. Don't bother puttin' on the trousers 'cause we're gon'na take them shackles off 'n don't want no tears in the trouser legs. Now, get in that water." No one hesitated at the order and soon all were scrubbing the coarse sand into their skin under the critical eye of Ham.

"One more time back and forth with this sand and I'll hit muscle," Ian heard one of the men say in a barely audible whisper. Ian simply nodded in agreement, afraid to say anything that might be heard by their overseer.

Finally the order to get out of the water was given and one by one Ham inspected each man from head to toe. Satisfied that they were all clean enough he allowed them to pick up their clothing. A baggy pair of well-worn trousers, with a brass ring at either side with a foot long length of rope tied to one ring. The rope was to be fed through the other ring and tied in a knot to act as a belt. The top consisted of a loose fitting, tunic type shirt with no sleeves. All of them had seen too many washings and the holes were crudely sewn into a gathered lump of material. A pair of one size fits all sandals completed their outfits.

"Hardly a fashion statement," Ian thought, "but at least they're clean." Slipping the thong of the sandals between his big toe and the next, he tightened the lace to hold the thing to his feet. He imagined the pathetic picture they painted, standing there wearing only the oversized shirts and sandals.

"If ya will all be so kind as to folla me, gents, we'll relieve ya 'a them ankle bracelets. I know how you've got a likin' ta 'em, but they ain't no more use to ya. There ain't nowheres ya can run that we can't find you. One thing I forgot to tell ya, Master Dole has a rule here. If anyone does escape the camp, the men sleeping on either side of him also gets hanged. It's ta your best interest ta see that your bedmates stay put. Now we all understand how things will be, ya follow me." There was no doubt in anyone's mind that Ham was thoroughly enjoying his roll. Silently they followed him to the blacksmith shop, the anticipation of more pain hung heavily on all of them. It had not been that long ago that the hot rivet had been searing the flesh of their legs and ankles.

Entering the lean-to, which served the Smithy, the first thing that Ian noticed was the man himself. He was, if anything, larger than Ham and just as black. Shirtless, his pectoral muscles rippled while the stomach muscles resembled a washboard. Broad at the shoulder, he tapered to an almost feminine waist and the massive thighs sought to burst the tight trouser legs. The round head was shaved smooth and not a hint of chest hair. His biceps seemed to be as large as Ian was around his middle and the well-developed forearms completed the most perfect specimen of man that Ian had ever seen. Without a word he motioned for the first in line to put his leg up. Placing the ankle next to the anvil he put a punch to the rivet and with a single blow drove it from the shackle. One by one he repeated the process until the final one was freed. Only then did he utter a sound, saying something to Ham in a foreign tongue. The two conversed for a time, then the Smithy turned back to his forge and Ham ordered them all to put on their trousers.

The sun was disappearing behind the far hill when they were led to the line of shacks that were to be their new home. Stopping before the first shack Ham ordered them to stay still, then he disappeared inside. A moment later he reappeared and the procession went to the next, where he selected two of the new arrivals to follow him inside. On to the next, and the next, until there were three left, Ian, Kale Brewster and a weasel-faced Cockney. Stopping again he pointed the butt of his club at Ian. "You, step out." Ian did as he was told and stood before the Black. Surveying the remaining two he pointed at Kale. "You'll make a good bed partner for this runt. You step out too." Kale followed Ian's lead and the two were marched into the shack. As they entered the narrow doorway Ham gave Kale a hard shove from behind, as if trying to goad Kale into a fight, but he met no resistance. The walls and the center of the one large room were lined with tears of bunks, three high. Leading them to a pair of empty bunks Ham pointed to the top one. "This one's yours runt. Your friend gets the bottom below you."

Ian looked at the crude boards covered with a thin straw mattress. A length of rope went from the top through the middle bunk to the bottom one. Picking up the rope Ham grinned. "Every night you get tucked in 'n this rope tied ta your ankle 'n those of the other two in this row. Ya ain't ta untie this rope for no reason 'til ya are told ta. If you're found untied ya'll get ten lashes for it." Looking at the two his gaze stopped on Ian. "Ya look like ya got a problem, runt. Don't ya like your sleeping arrangements?"

"It's not that, sir. What do we do if we have to go to the bathroom during the night?" Ian's serious question brought a guffaw from Ham.

"Ya best control yourself," he answered. "If ya don't the fella below ya might get awful wet 'n more 'n a mite mad. Once you're in bed, nobody'd better be caught out 'a his rack. Them's the orders from Master Dole himself. Got any more questions?" Ham asked swinging the club menacingly.

"No sir," Ian said looking at the floor. When he glanced up again he was looking at the back of the giant of a man exiting the doorway, leaving Ian and Kale standing there and wondering what they were to do next. The question was answered for them in a short time when a sandy haired man of middle age approached them.

"Welcome aboard gents," the man said as he stood next to Kale and extended his hand. "Me name's Donavan. I'm the overseer a' this bit o' heaven. Tis my job ta keep the peace 'n make sure ol' Dole's rules aren't broken in here 'n help new arrivals fit in. Outside ye take orders from everyone else but in here ye take orders from me." The thick Irish brogue was music to Ian's ears, reminding of the hills where he had lived as a child.

"Me name's Connor, Ian Connor," he smiled, attempting to match the brogue that was now foreign to him. Taking the offered hand he pumped it mightily. "Tis nice ta shake the hand of a Gaelic gentleman again. This is my friend Kale Brewster."

"Connor, tis it? Well Mister Connor, the pleasure's all mine." Turning to Kale he shook hands, then sat on the bottom of the three bunks. "Like I said, I'm here ta help ye get adjusted ta being here. The rules 'r simple, ye just do everything yer told ta do. The food's good but the work's hard. Inside the mine's 'bout fifty degrees hotter than the hubs of Hell 'n little fresh air ever gets there. Some shafts have water up ta yer knees 'n others the dust's so thick ye could cut it. We eat twice a day. Once at sunup and once just 'fore sundown, in between there's a bowl 'a soup 'round midday. The scudder comes 'round with all the water ye want ta drink while yer down the shaft. Everyplace ye go will have an overseer like me. It ain't by chance that we got to where we are, it's 'cause we scrapped 'n kicked our way up. Any 'a us that don't cut it gets thrown right back where we come from, 'n I ain't 'bout ta let it happen ta me. Just so we understand each other. Your job's ta do what yer told 'n mine's ta make sure ye do. Is there any questions ye have?"

For the first time since leaving the prison Kale spoke. "Are all of the men here indentured servants, like us?"

"Indentured servants, is it? Well Mister Brewster, that's just another fancy word for a slave 'n that's what we are. We were bought with hard silver 'n we ain't no better than some African bought on the slave block. Ye're owned lock stock 'n barrel by Dole 'n ye ain't free 'til he says so. By the time a man's freed from this place there's only a shell 'a him left."

"But I was sentenced to five years in prison and have already served nearly a year and a half there. That means that I should only have three and a half years here before I'm a free man." Ian sputtered.

"That might be how it looks ta ye, laddie, but until Master Dole figures you have paid back every schilling he gave for your hide, ye belong ta him, even if it takes a thousand years." Donavan shook his head. "We're all sail on the same ship here. 'bout everyone 'a us came from one prison or t'other 'n mostly we try ta look out for one another, but to survive look out for yourselves first."

Ian felt his spirits drop to a lower level than they had been since his so called trial. There he had been sentenced to five years, now he was hearing of a possible lifetime of bondage. The look on Kale's face told that he shared similar feelings.

"Buck up lads. It's not as bad as it sounds," Donavan said trying to sound convincing, "I been here fer nearly four years 'n look at me. Don't go down the mines no more, 'n all I got ta do tis keep this place clean 'n look after newies like ye. I'll get yer blanket 'n be right back." With that he left Ian and Kale alone.

"Do you really believe that we are in this place forever?" Ian asked, his voice shaking as much from anger as fright at the prospect. "My sentence was five years and no matter what, that's all I'm going to serve anyplace." The anger grew as he spoke.

A somber look came over Kale's face. "You heard what Ham said about hanging the two men on either side of anyone trying to escape. If you run I my neck gets longer by a foot, and that really isn't a very appealing thought. I think we ought to make the best of our situation and see what it brings. I do believe that we should be careful who we say what to. Anyone here could run to Dole and tell him there's trouble brewing and we'd be over our heads in hot water, or worse." Their conversation was interrupted when Donavan returned carrying two threadbare blankets.

"Here ye are, mates. These 're the best we got right now. You'll get better when someone moves out, or dies." Staring at the razor nicks on Ian's face he clicked his tongue. "Ol' Evil-eye's getting' shakier every day. Hate ta have him shave me again. Most of the men here keep their hair 'n beards cut clean 'cause it's so bloody hot in the mines. They trade the dessert, we get once in a while, ta Ham 'n he lets 'em borrow the scissors 'n razor ta clean each other up with. That Ham sure got some kind 'a sweet tooth."

"Speaking of Ham," Ian said. "I have never seen a larger man until the one in the blacksmith shop. I'm curious about them. Are they indentured also?"

"In a way I guess they are, they're brothers. Their parents was in the Dole family for a long time. Master Dole's father bought 'em off a slave block. All I know is that they're Nubian 'n when they were small their pa got riled and killed their mother. Master Dole had him took out ta the creek 'n drowned him for it. They was raised by some woman the elder Dole bought, 'til she died too. By then they were old enough to put ta work, 'n when they got big Master Dole figured they would keep the rest 'a us in line. They do a mighty good job of it too. Nobody wants ta tangle with Ham 'n Cain. Together they could whip the whole lot of us at one time." He ceased talking when some men entered the shanty. Each was naked and dripping water, forming puddles as they crossed the room. Ian didn't know whether to stare in disbelief or look away in embarrassment. "They have to bathe in the creek 'n wash their clothes while they're at it," Donavan explained, seeing the look of astonishment on Ian's face. "The clothes 're hung outside to drip 'n then they put 'em back on ta finish dryin'. Can't have 'em naked as a jaybird while we're tryin' ta eat. Speakin' 'bout eatin', it's getting' close ta time."

Just as Ian opened his mouth to ask Donavan another question, a swarthy man with bushy eyebrows stepped between them and sprawled on the empty middle bunk. Standing shorter than Ian, the man reminded him of the stove in the kitchen at home. His stout body and short legs gave him a nearly box-like appearance. The deep-set eyes were almost black in color and peering from those craggy eyebrows gave him a sinister and foreboding look.

"This is Poulos. He's a deaf mute. Only noise ya'll hear out 'a him is a grunt when he wants something. Keeps ta himself 'n don't cause me no trouble. Workin'st fool I ever did see. Well gents, got ta tend ta my flock. If ya need me just yell, but not too loud. Most of these guys'll be sleeping 'til they ring the bell for mealtime, then don't be in their way or you'll get trampled." Turning away he joined a conversation with a group on the other side of the room. Occasionally they would look in the direction of Ian and Kale and the two knew that they were the topic of conversation.

Surveying the shack, that was to be his new home, Ian counted two rows of bunks against the two opposite walls and two rows down the middle. "Eighteen men in a room," he thought. The solitude of the prison cell suddenly didn't look quite so bad. At least there he had some privacy away from peering eyes, here there was absolutely none. "Cozy arrangements, aren't they Kale?" Before he could receive an answer the sound of a bell was heard not far off and Donavan appeared at their side again.

"That's supper, mates. Best hustle or you'll get the leftovers." Reaching down he shook the shoulder of the man introduced as Poulos, making a motion like he was putting food to his mouth. The stout fellow jumped to his feet and hurried to the door. "Follow me 'n I'll take ya ta the line. Next time it'll be up ta you ta fend for yourselves. When ya hear that bell ya best start hustling over there." Leading them to the doorway Donavan explained some other ins and outs of the camp. Once outside they turned sharply around the corner of the building and toward a long lean-to type structure, where there was a long line of men waiting. An obnoxious stench assailed Ian's nostrils as they approached a slow running ditch not twenty feet from the back of their shack. "This is where you go ta relieve yerselves. Slop buckets smell up the place inside 'n Ma Nature takes care 'a dumpin' it fer us out here. Nothin' fancy, but it gets the job done."

Arriving at the very end of the line gave Ian a chance to study a bit more of the camp. At the very edge of the flats, where they now stood, a series of hills extended as far as he could see. Black holes were dug into the sides of most of them and, as Donavan explained, these were the mines. Some were still active while others had played out. Huge piles of coal dotted the countryside. "It would take forever to burn all that coal," Ian commented.

"Not when ya figure that Wales furnishes most of the coal fer all of Great Britain," was Donavan's response. "What ya see here's only a small part 'a what's mined in these parts. The big mines are farther ta the south. Wagonloads 'a coal goes out 'a here every day 'n we still have a hard time keepin' up. Them fancy ninnies in England's big cities think this stuff comes out 'a coal wagons. They ain't got no idea that some man breaks his back fer every lump they burn. Tomorrow you'll have yer chance ta add ta them piles there."

Ian hesitated at asking the next question, for fear that Donavan might think that he was seeking special treatment, but went ahead anyway. "I was brought here to treat sicknesses and broken bones. Am I still going into the mines?"

"That's where most 'a the sickness 'n broken bones are. We got nearly a hundred men here, 'n 'less the bone's stickin' through the skin we just wrap it up 'n he goes back ta work. Can't have men off fer every little ailment or we'd never get no coal dug. You'll dig like the rest 'til yer needed." Donavan's emphatic answer was not exactly the one Ian had hoped to hear and the conversation ended as they were next to be served.

Taking the metal tray, that Donavan offered, Ian held it toward the man ladling out of a big cauldron. Chunks of boiled mutton and potatoes were slopped into the tray and a piece of bread was added. A pottery cup of water completed the meal. Picking up a large spoon from the pile, Ian waited for Kale and Donavan to join him.

"I was hopin' fer some dessert tonight. Been a long time since we had somethin' sweet," Donavan grumbled. Looking for a spot to sit, he finally led them to a clear place on the outer fringes of the sea of humanity. "Hope ye like mutton 'cause that's what we get most of. Once in a great while an old milk cow of the Doles 'll die 'n we get a change fer a time, but it's mostly boiled mutton 'n these beautiful Irish potatoes." That ended Donavan's contribution to the conversation, as his mouth was busy chewing the fatty meat, while sopping the up juice with his bread. When he was finished he laid back and a loud burp escaped his lips. "That, gentlemen, is in appreciation of such a fine meal." Waiting until there was nothing on either Ian's or Kale's trays, except for a few puddles of solidifying mutton grease, he motioned for them to follow him. Arriving at the lower end of the creek, in which they were earlier bathed, he proceeded to wash his spoon, tray and cup with sand and rinsed them in the water. Satisfied they would pass the most stringent inspection for cleanliness, he looked at the other two men's also. Nodding in approval he led them back to the lean-to and placed the tray in the pile to be used for the next meal. Putting the cup and spoon in their respective places, he waited for Ian and Kale to follow suit.

It was dusk when they entered the shanty and found most of the others already in their bunks sleeping. Loud snores reverberated from wall to wall, leaving Ian wondering if there was to be any sleep for him this, or any other, night. Leaving them to their own devices, Donavan moved to the bunk closest to him and proceeded to tie the length of rope to the ankles of the occupants. Moving around the room he was soon at the tier occupied by the two new arrivals. Poulos was already asleep. "Ye best get some shut-eye, mates. The sun comes up early this time 'a year 'n so will ye." Waiting for them to climb into their respective racks, he loosely tied them, then walked away without another word.

The first solid and filling meal that Ian had in his stomach, since he couldn't remember when, was now beginning to revolt. His system was not used to having so much at one time in his empty belly and he had to fight to keep it down. He wondered if Kale was going through the same torment. Not daring to move he simply lay there, listening to the ever-increasing crescendo of snores around him. Sometime around midnight exhaustion caught up with him and he drifted off to sleep. Too tired to dream, or at least to remember what his dreams were, his heavy breathing joined the rest.

It seemed his eyes had only closed when he was awakened by loud shouts. A single lantern sat on the wooden table, casting weird shadows on the walls. "Wake up gents. It's gon'na be another beautiful day here in Purgatory. Get yer bones out 'a here, soon as I let ye loose."

More than a few profane comments were directed toward Mister Donavan, mostly casting aspersions on his parents, for having been awakened. Ian lay there almost in a state of suspended animation. The straw mattress did little to cushion the hard slab and his body ached from sleeping on the board beneath him. Waiting to be untied he held his throbbing head. When Donavan arrived at their tier he first shook Poulos awake then undid the rope.

"Ye know the ropes by now mates, so grab yerself some food 'n I'll get ye after yer finished. I'll introduce ye ta the section boss 'n he'll take ye ta yer place in the mines." With that he moved to the next tier of bunks.

"Just a few moments more," thought Ian, closing his eyes again. He had barely shut them when he felt a hand gently shake his shoulder. Turning his head he was looking into the dark eyes of Poulos. All that was visible was the top of his head to the bridge of his nose; the rest was hidden below the edge of Ian's mattress. Rising up on one elbow he could see a broad smile on the Greek's face. Poulos beckoned for him to come down and follow him, motioning to Kale in the same way. The simple clothing made it easy to dress and, after slipping their feet into the sandals, the trio made it's way to the line of men waiting to be fed.

A low hanging ground fog covered the moors, leaving the grass covered in dew. The rolling clouds of mist played over the hills, giving the entire scene an ominous but at the same time beautiful appearance. The rising sun, on the water vapor, reflected rainbows of color into the morning air. The cool air and the conversation with Kale made Ian nearly forget about his nagging headache and sore body.

"If it's not too personal Kale, how did you end up in debtors prison? If I'm being too forward, just tell me to mind my own business." Ian hoped that he hadn't overstepped the bounds of their friendship with such a question.

"It's not too personal at all. I don't mind talking about it." Kale answered. "It all started when I was about thirteen years old. You see, I never knew my father and my mother worked as a cleaning woman for some rich snob in Liverpool. One day he got fresh with her and I figured that rather than get mad, I'd get even so I started stealing things from his home. Little things at first, then they got bigger and more expensive. I'd find some sucker off the street to buy them. There's always someone looking for a good deal, cheap. I'd stash the money away and never spent a penny until I had enough for my mother to quit. I told her that I'd found it buried while I was looking for something. I doubt that she really believed me, but we were so poor that money was money no matter where it came from. Stealing came easy to me, so I found other places to take from. When mother died I had a sizeable amount of money stashed away. It was easy to get and just as easy to spend. I would dress in nothing but the finest clothes and drove the shiniest buggy. Everyone was aware of my wealth, although no one knew how I came by it. Soon different places were fighting for my business. Offers to extend me credit, if I would do business with them, poured in. I could go into the fanciest tailor in London, have a suit made and walk out the door without leaving a shilling behind. The debts mounted and so did my appetite for the finer things, things that I had been denied as a child. By this time I was nearly nineteen years old. You can't imagine what it does to a nineteen-year-old ego, to have people trip over themselves to wait on him. The women were something else. Any pub in England would set up drinks for me, just because of my prosperous appearance."

The conversation halted as they were served the morning meal. Ian was surprised to find that it was the same boiled meat and potatoes that they received the previous night. When the trays were filled Poulos beckoned for them to follow him. Leading them to a pile of wood the three sat and Kale resumed his story.

"Now let's see. Where did I leave off?" He scratched his head as if that would help his memory. "Oh yes, the pubs. Well, I had no idea of how much I owed and I really didn't care. I could always get more, where I got it before, and I kept spending. Things started to get tough in England and soon everyone was calling in my credit slips. I had not nearly enough money socked away to pay my debts, so I started stealing again. Thankfully, I got caught on the first thing I tried to take. I broke into a house in the middle of the night. In the past I had only picked well-to-do homes in the richer parts of town, but this one was on the outskirts of London and not prosperous at all. An elderly woman came into the room just as I was taking the only thing of value in the house, one silver candleholder. Her hair was stringy and the patched robe she wore reminded me of the many times that I had seen my mother that way. She started screaming and I dropped the candlestick and ran. Right then I developed something that I hadn't had in nearly six years, a conscience. I took what money I had, which was still considerable, and disappeared from sight. The last thing that I ever stole was a pair of worn trousers and a shirt from a clothesline. I put them on and threw all the fancy stuff in a garbage can. Traveling at night I worked my way back to Liverpool, where I got a job working on the docks. I had decided to repay everyone I owed money to, no matter how long it took. I started with the people I could remember stealing from. I would put money in an envelope and tuck it under their doors. The only one I wouldn't repay was the man who had taken advantage of my mother. I figured he owed that to her anyway."

Ian had been so engrossed in Kale's tale that he was surprised when Donavan clapped him on the shoulder. "Come with me mates. Ye best get yer trays cleaned, it's nearly time ta go ta work."

Kale grinned, "I guess the rest'll have to wait. It appears that Mister Donavan is calling us for a command performance. Perhaps when I finish my story you will tell em yours, Ian. That is if I haven't killed you with boredom." With that they followed Donavan to the creek, where again the trays were washed. Their first day working for Master Dole was about to begin.

CHAPTER FOUR.

Ian was soon to find that Donavan's description of the mine, as the "Hubs of Hell" was a just and fitting name. The temperature at the back of the digs was well over one hundred degrees and, once the digging began, plumes of coal-dust filled the cavity with a choking cloud. The rag that was given each man, to cover his mouth and nose, did little to keep the dust from entering the lungs with every gasp for air. He had not expected a walk in Picadilly, but neither did he expect these harsh conditions. "No wonder no one escapes from this place," he thought to himself, "they die inside this bloody mine first."

When he and Kale were taken to the mine overseer, they were given a very brief description of what they would be doing. Ordered to take off their shirts, they then joined Poulos and six others as they were led into the narrow entrance. Coal oil lanterns hung precariously from pegs driven into the rock walls. At times the openings were so small they had to crawl before it opened up into the next chamber. Arriving at the end of this particular digging the overseer gave Ian and Kale each a long pry bar, pointed in one end and flattened on the other. Four of the others went to work punching holes into the face of the coal-vein that covered nearly the entire back section of the wall. One man held a four-foot star bit while the other pounded the end with a large hammer. The bit turned after each hit of the hammer and a gradual hole was made in the coal face. The other team was doing the same thing on the other side of the seam. After a series of holes, about a foot deep, were punched it was Ian and Kale's turn to work. Placing the points of the bars into the holes they would peel off hunks of coal, which would fall to the ground causing another cloud of dust into the stagnant air. Ian could feel it settle on his head and for the first time he was happy that his head was shaved.

"Are we having fun yet?" Ian heard Kale say. Looking at his friend he saw streaks of sweat mixing with the coal dust causing rivulets of black to run down his muscular chest and soak into the baggy trousers. He began to laugh at the picture before him, but then realized that he must look just as bad.

"Not yet, but I'm working on it," came Ian's reply. "Another ten or fifteen years and I'll be having tremendous time. It's just a matter of pacing ones self so you don't have all the enjoyment at once." The friendly banter drew laughs from the other men, all except for Poulos who was oblivious to anything but the job to which he had been assigned.

"I think we'll get along just fine," one of the men said. "My name's Kerr 'n my partner here's Patrick. Them two over there's Wheeler 'n Wheeler, they're brothers. Makes it real easy when ya need 'em. All ya got 'ta do is holler fer one of 'em 'n they both answer. You already know Poulos. Don't see none of that coal fallin' out by its self so we best get to it." With that Ian and Kale resumed pulling slabs of the black mineral from the wall.

A constant stream of men carried, or dragged, the full baskets back to the entrance, where other men separated the coal from the stone. They reminded Ian of a bunch of ants, scurrying around in a headlong attempt to get everything finished in a minimum amount of time. Hardly had Poulos filled one basket when it was snatched away and an empty one replaced it. Ian was thankful that he hadn't been assigned the job of moving the baskets. He was to learn later that the ones with that job had fallen into disfavor with the overseers, Ham or Master Dole and this was their punishment. One fellow had the nerve to ask for a second helping of food and this was his answer.

By the time the overseer told them it was time to quit for the day, Ian was near collapse from exhaustion. His arms felt as though they would be torn from their sockets, while his back had muscles that were not even discovered yet. Laying their tools down they made their way to the fresh air outside. Tearing the cloth from his face Ian took a deep breath. Letting it out slowly he savored every last bit, as if that would be his final one. He was nearly run over by the stampede of men behind him as they hurried past. It was all Ian could do to put one foot in front of the other and these fools were nearly running. Reaching the creek he soon found why. Everyone wanted to bath at the head of the water. The ones below got the run off of dust from those above.

"Looks like we learned another lesson today." Kale was standing beside Ian with his hands on his hips surveying the stream full of humanity, while others waited on the banks for a spot. As soon as one had washed himself and his clothing, he got out and a shoving contest erupted to take his place.

"I'm in no hurry," moaned Ian. "If I got in that water right now I swear I'd simply drown. There isn't enough strength in my arms to hold me up." Falling to the ground he laid back and closed his eyes. Kale sat beside him waiting his turn. Just as Ian began to doze he was brought back to reality when Kale nudged him with his foot. Opening his eyes he looked into the grinning face above him. "Just let me die in peace Kale. When you see the angels hovering over me, don't get in their way," he groaned, closing his eyes again.

"Move it Ian," Kale commanded. "You'll feel better after you get twenty pounds of coal dust off you." Picking Ian up by the arm he dragged him into the water. "Best hurry or we won't get any dinner tonight."

"How in the name of anything Holy can you think of food? I don't have enough strength to chew much less swallow. All I want to do is go to bed and sleep far a week, then get up, get a drink of cold water and then sleep for another week. Maybe by then I'll consider eating." He hated to admit that the cold water was offering some relief to his sore muscles. Even the coarse sand felt good as he rubbed it into his skin and watched patterns of coal dust float away. With himself and his clothes washed, he was about to climb out of the water when Kale took his arm.

Pointing behind Ian's left ear, he asked. "Are you saving that for something? You missed a spot." Ian rubbed his finger against the indicated area and looked at the results. A black smudge covered the tip of his finger.

"Thanks Kale. I doubt if there is enough sand in all of Wales to get all this off. What I can see on the outside is bad enough, but it's what's in the inside that worries me. I've seen what Black Lung does to a body. A person slowly suffocates because his lungs fill with coal dust and there isn't room for the air." A look of real concern wrinkled Ian's brow. "We have to get out of that mine somehow, you 'n me." Despite the heat of the air goose bumps formed on his body, as much as thoughts of the dreaded Black Lung as from the cold creek water.

"We have to take the hand dealt to us," Kale said somberly. "I found that the best thing, is to keep your eyes open and your mouth shut. That way we'll learn what goes on and how everything's run here. Now get out of that creek 'n we'll have a bit of time to rest before the supper bell rings." Pulling himself from the water Ian threw his clothes over his shoulder and followed Kale to the shack. Without another word each fell into their respective bunks. Hardly had their heads hit the mattresses before they were sound asleep, only to be shortly awakened by the loud ringing of the bell.

"Come on, Ian. Let's get some food before the good parts are taken," Kale said as he poked Ian. "Maybe we'll be lucky and have some boiled mutton and Irish potatoes tonight."

"You go without me," Ian begged. "I'm really too tired to even eat. Nestling as far down as the hard board allowed he attempted to go back to sleep, but Kale continued to harangue him.

"You're going to eat even if I have to chew it for you and shove it down your throat. Now get your lazy carcass out of that bed before I throw you out." Ian opened one eye and looked to see if the expression on Kale's face was as threatening as the sound of his voice. There was no smile on the normally placid face and Ian was not certain if the threat was real or not. Finally deciding that he really did not want to find out, he pulled himself from the bed and followed Kale outside. Taking their clothes from the line, they dressed as they went.

"Thanks for looking out for me, Kale. I would have simply remained in that soft, comfortable bed and wasted my time sleeping." A note of sarcasm sounded in Ian's voice.

"Don't thank me. My motives were strictly selfish. You don't eat, you get weak, you get weak and I have to do the work of both of us. I have no thanks coming, I'm just looking after my welfare." Ian looked at Kale to see if his face indicated whether he meant what he was saying. The face was somber, however a slight curl at the corners of Kale's mouth indicated otherwise. Again the two were near the end of the line when they arrived.

"Seems like this is the only place we really get to talk," Ian said looking at the long line of hungry men before them. "Tell me the rest of your story, 'cause it looks like you'll have plenty of time."

"If you really want to hear it, I'll be glad to share my misspent life with you. I don't even remember where I left off," Kale said looking at Ian, as if trying to determine if he really wanted to hear it or was only being polite.

"It was where you nearly got caught stealing from that old lady," Ian quickly replied. "You'd gone back to Liverpool 'n got a job on the docks."

"I changed my name from Kale to Kyle and Brewster to Banister. Kyle Banister. Has quite a ring to it, what say?" Not pausing for an answer, Kale continued. "Every penny I earned, I sent to people I owed. I built a shack, from broken shipping crates, at the back of a dock so I didn't have to spend money on a flat in town. I ate just enough to keep my strength and never spent one shilling on an unnecessary thing. The day came when I could say I had paid everyone off, except for one Taylor in London. As luck would have it, a ship came in loaded with dry goods. I was carrying a bale of broadcloth from the ship when the only man I owed stood at the bottom of the gangplank. I attempted to hide my face but he followed me and, when he was certain it was me, he yelled for a bobby. I was arrested. Because they couldn't prove my past burglaries and because I couldn't pay him on the spot, I was sent to debtor's prison. That's about the size of it. Here I am paying for being a fool and choosing the easy life instead of working like an honest man should."

Pausing to pickup his tray Ian waited to be served next. "Surprise," he exclaimed to Kale in a low voice, "no boiled mutton tonight." A strong odor of fish permeated the lean-to. A ladle full of thick, boiled barley was heaped on his tray. Ian thanked the server and moved on to the next one. A thin sliver of pound cake, sprinkled with a minute bit of sugar, was given him. "Donavan got his dessert," he smiled to Kale.

Finding a spot away from the crowd they sat down to eat. Ian had nearly forgotten how tired he was. There were flakes of fish mixed in the barley and, as disgusting as the mess appeared it was quite tasty. Both were quiet during most of the meal, then Kale broke the silence.

"I'd appreciate it if you didn't say anything about what I just told you. I'm not a bit proud of my past and since I let God into my life I am a changed man."

Ian stopped eating and looked at Kale in astonishment. "Let God into your life," he exclaimed. "What big favor has He done for you? You're a slave, digging coal for the rest of your life, for a man who bought you from a prison that was just one step above this place. I used to be a regular Church goer but now I really question the usefulness of all that nonsense."

Kale stopped eating and a hurt look crossed his face. "It wasn't God who stole those things from innocent people, it was Kale Brewster. God didn't even make me do it. My own greed and laziness were the cause. My mother raised me that stealing was wrong and I knew the consequences if I got caught, but I took that chance. Now I'm paying for my sins. Haven't you ever been in a desperate situation and prayed for deliverance, without realizing you were praying? Everyone needs to believe in a higher being." Kale's voice had a nearly pleading sound. He then said something that Ian would remember for the rest of his life.

"Haven't you ever wondered what's out there beyond the edge of nowhere? Out there in the vast sea of stars there must be someone that created all of them. I can't believe they all just happened. If He could master such a task, as to create all those stars and this very ground we dig in, why do you question His existence?" Looking down at his tray, Kale apologized. "I really didn't mean to preach. Every man is entitled to his own beliefs and no one has the right to infringe on them. I didn't mean to push my theories off onto you. Please forgive me, it's just something that I feel very strong about." Saying nothing in return, Ian simply stared at the food in his tray. "I'm sorry if I made you angry, Ian."

"You haven't made me angry. It's something you said that I've never stopped to consider before. 'Beyond the edge of nowhere.' I was taught about the creation and such but never considered where the stars came from. I just took for granted that when the sun disappears they would appear in its place. I guess you have a valid point. One, that if it keeps me awake thinking about it, may raise more questions than answers.'" Ian patted Kale on the shoulder. "I guess I'm just feeling sorry for myself for being here. You see I didn't steal anything, or wrongfully take what wasn't mine. I was sentenced here because my wife and I became ill. The bills piled up, my business failed because I wasn't there to run it after my partner died and the whole world fell in on me. When my Colleen died I didn't much care if I died also. The creditors started to hound me for money before she was even in the ground and I gave up trying. I couldn't figure why, if there is a God, He didn't step in and help me rather than let me fail so miserably."

"I would hate to believe that out there somewhere, someone sits and reads from a book exactly what our lives are to do next. To have every minute of every day planed for us would make mankind nothing more than puppets. There would be no free agency and while life may appear simpler there would be no reason for our existence." Kale spooned the last bite into his mouth and stood up. "We'd best get these trays washed up and head for bed. I may have to pry you away from that mattress, come daybreak, as it is." The trays washed, placed in the stack with the rest, the two friends had climbed into their bunks before the conversation ended.

Lying in the darkness, Ian's mind flashed back to a period not so long ago. "The Lord is my shepherd. Yea though I walk through the valley of the shadow of death. I guess I have prayed for deliverance, however this isn't exactly where I had in mind," he thought to himself as fatigue finally closed his eyes in slumber.

As the days in the mine progressed, Ian became more used to the heavy labor. His back became stronger and his shoulders filled out, as did the muscles in his arms. He had been there for nearly four months and had yet to be called on to use his doctoring skills. He was beginning to wonder how anyone could go this long without some kind of serious illness or injury? The food continued to be very basic, lacking salt, or any spices, it was extremely bland, but still nourishing and plentiful. Dole realized that he had an investment in each man and one that was starved couldn't dig as much coal as a healthy one. Occasionally Ian's mind would flash back to the prison and the scraps he was given, after the incident with the warden's daughter. The work was hard and the hours long, but at least he had something to look forward to at the end of the day.

Dole was a devoutly religious man; consequently there was no work on the Sabbath. Sundays they were allowed to sleep until the bell sounded for the morning meal, which was sounded an hour later than normal. After the trays were cleaned, everyone was to attend the religious services conducted by the Master himself. He would spout scripture to his captive audience, while making wild gestures with his hands. His favorite chapters of the Bible always seemed to have something to do with giving your all for your master. There was no doubt that in his case he was referring to himself, not God. After an hour of ranting Dole would close with a long-winded prayer and the congregation would be excused for religious meditation for another hour.

"You bloody hypocrite," Ian thought to himself. "I wonder if you have ever heard the passage about loving your neighbor as thyself?" This particular Sunday Ian was sleeping when he was aroused by a shout from the doorway.

"Connor, Ian Connor. Come quick, Donavan's bad off 'n I can't get him to move." Peering toward the voice, Ian saw Kerr motioning for him to hurry. Jumping to his feet Ian followed Kerr towards the moor. "We was standing there talking 'n he suddenly grabbed his chest 'n keeled over. He never said a word 'n his face's a terrible color." Pushing through a cluster of men before him, Ian saw Donavan lying in a heap on the ground. Ankle-deep grass partly hid the lower part of his body and head, while his eyes stared vacantly skyward, the pupils fixed and dilated. Bending over the man that he had come to call, "Friend," Ian knew there was nothing that he could do for Donavan, but perhaps something he could do for himself.

"You men back off and give me some room to work," his voice was a bit more commanding than he had intended for it to sound. "Get me two or three blankets and let's move him out of the sun." Two men ran off to fetch the blankets, while more than enough eager hands lifted Donavan's limp body. Following Ian to the shade furnished by the woodpile, where he, Kale and Donavan had shared so many meals, he was gently lowered to the ground. No sooner was he straightened out than the blankets arrived and were placed over the inert form. Going through a mock examination, Ian felt the throat for a pulse and placed his ear to the open mouth.

"Is there something I can do to help, Ian?" he recognized the voice of Kale standing behind him.

Without lifting his head Ian responded. "You can clear everyone out of here except for you and five others. We don't need an audience but I may need some help with Donavan. Someone bring me a basin with about an inch of water in the bottom and someone else find me a small feather." Looking up he saw nothing but puzzled looks on the faces surrounding him and no one moved. "Do I have to leave this man and do it myself?" he snapped. "I need the stuff now, not tomorrow." Ian realized that his requests were strange and he wanted them to sound just that way. Most of these men were common laborers and had never even been attended by a doctor. The charade continued as Ian uncovered Donavan to the waist and, opening the shirt, put his ear to the man's chest. In an instant a basin of water was shoved toward Ian. Taking the offering he placed the container on

Donavan's naked chest. Leaning over the liquid he stared at it for a time before removing it and placing it on the ground beside him.

"I didn't know where to find no small feather so I caught one of Master Dole's geese. Will one of these do?" Kerr held out a handful of freshly plucked goose feathers. "I'll probably get whomped for this, but Donavan's worth the whippin'. Is there anythin' else I can get for ya, Ian?" The voice was almost pleading. Meanwhile Kale had selected four men to stay with him and Kerr and sent the rest away.

Still playing to his now meager audience, Ian selected one of the smallest of the feathers. "I need you to take these blankets and form a circle around me and Donavan. There can't be any breeze when I do this next test." Kneeling beside Donavan's head he waited until the blankets were satisfactorily placed then gently put the feather between Donavan's mouth and nose. Carefully balancing it in the philtrum Ian slowly leaned back and examined the bit of down. Shaking his head he removed the feather and, using his thumb and index finger, closed Donavan's eyes forever. "There is nothing more anyone can do for Mister Donavan." Ian said dramatically as he rose to his feet. "He will no longer be tormented in this earthly life. May he rest in peace." Dropping the blankets most of the five men crossed themselves, all except for Kale, who simply bowed his head. "Someone needs to go to the great house and let Master Dole know what's happened." Without a word Kerr took off at a dead run for the Dole house. Ian covered the corpse with one of the blankets and awaited instructions from Ham, who he knew would appear to take charge. After all, Master Dole couldn't be bothered with such a small matter as the death of one of his beasts of burden.

Kale perched himself on the woodpile and was soon joined by the remaining men. "What's all that mumbo-jumbo with the basin of water and the feather, Ian?" Taking a sliver of wood from one of the logs he picked his teeth with the pointed end.

"That was no mumbo-jumbo, my friend. That was the latest in the tests for death. The water would pick up any vibrations, from the chest, if there was a sign of a heartbeat, and the feather would have moved if there had been an expulsion of breath. Unfortunately there was neither." Ian was pleased at the looks of admiration from his companions.

"How the devil did a man as smart as you end up in this place?"

One of the men asked. "Seems to me that if you know what yer talkin' about, you'd be makin' lots of money in London or someplace. You sure ya ain't puttin' us on, now are ya Ian?"

"Believe me, this is the latest technique used by every knowledgeable doctor anywhere. You have seen water ripple by the slightest disturbance. Even walking close to the basin will send shock waves into the liquid and cause slight ripples to appear on the surface. These ripples may not be discernable to an untrained eye, but to someone that knows what to look for, they are as plain as the nose on your face." Wondering if he was spreading it on a bit thick, Ian was thankful when they were interrupted by the appearance of Kerr and Ham.

"Pull that cover off that man 'n let Ham have a look at him," he ordered Kerr. Doing as he was told a shaky hand pulled the blanket from Donavan's face. Satisfied that he was really dead Ham nodded for Kerr to replace the blanket. "The Master 'll want ta talk ta all 'a you. Follow me back ta the great house." Without another word Ham set off across the moor with the rest following behind.

Dole sat in an easy chair on the veranda sipping a drink when the group arrived. "You all stand down here," indicating a spot at the bottom of the steps. "Don't allow the likes of you on the porch."

"'The likes of you,' indeed,'" thought Ian. "You over grown pompous slob. We are all better men on our worst day than you are on your best. That is if you have ever had a best day." Seething inside, Ian stared at the ground, as did the others. Looking the Master in the eye was considered an act of aggression or defiance and neither was tolerated.

Setting the silver goblet on the arm of the chair Dole leaned forward. "From what I understand, I have lost Mister Donavan. I had a large investment in that man and now it is lost and I want to know how." The tone of his voice was more than unkind, it was threatening to the point of sending chills down Ian's spine. "Mister Donavan was one of the few that I could trust. If I find that there was foul play involved with his death the perpetrator will wish he was dead a thousand times before he actually is. Was anyone there when Donavan died? If so I want to know who and what he saw."

A very meek and visibly shaken Kerr stepped forward. "I was standing next to him. We was talkin' 'n Donavan was in the middle of a word when he grabbed his chest 'n fell over. Honest Master, I never touched him. He just fell over. I ran 'n got Doc here 'n he did all he could, but Donavan died anyhow. Ian worked on him for a long time but it didn't do no good." Ian was both pleased and a little apprehensive about the praise being heaped upon him by Kerr. Pleased, because it may make him look the hero in Doles eyes, apprehensive, because Dole might find Ian to blame for not saving his patient.

"Who's this Doc person?" Dole demanded. "Ham, go fetch that man 'n bring him to me. I want to know more about that one"

Ian stepped forward, his eyes still downcast. "It is I, sir. My name is Connor. You purchased me nearly five months ago as an indentured servant."

"Raise your face so I can get a look at it." The steely gray eyes seemed to burn a hole to Ian's very soul. "Bring that man up here Ham, I can't see anything from here." Ham was none too gentle as he shoved Ian toward the waiting master, reminding Ian of the same treatment just before being sentenced to prison. In place of the three judges, there was but one that held the power of life and death over him. Standing before Dole Ian began to tremble with fright. "Now I remember you. You're the one that killed the Wardens daughter and now you have done the same to one of my most valuable servants. Get him out of here Ham before he kills the rest of my men. You know what to do with him." Ian felt the huge arms engulf him and squeeze as he was being dragged down the steps. The vise-like grip tightened around his chest and he fought for every breath. He remembered what Kale had said. "We have to play the cards that are dealt us." He had tried to bluff a man that was playing a pat hand, and lost.

"If I may sir?" It was Kale's voice. "You have already lost one investment today and before you lose another, may I point out something to you? There were a number of us that witnessed everything that Connor did and he did nothing wrong." Dole motioned for Ham to halt, then looked at Kale.

"You are a nervy one. Don't you know I can have you flogged for speaking to me without being told to?" Dole's voice betrayed his curiosity. "If you have something to say do it fast, or you'll join your friend there." A disappointed Ham released his hold on Ian.

"We were in the shack when Mister Kerr ran in and yelled for Ian to come quick. I followed him to where Donavan was laying on the ground. There were already at least two-dozen men there when we arrived. I have never seen a doctor at work before, but nothing that Ian did could have possibly harmed Mister Donavan. I believe that every man that was there at the time will testify to that fact." Every one of the assembled group nodded in agreement. Kale went on to relate the entire happenings all the way up to being summoned to the house by Ham. "It is my strong belief that no one could have prevented that man's death. I was also at the same prison that Ian was in and it was common knowledge, that there was nothing anyone could have done to save the warden's daughter. Ian begged them to get a trained physician for her, but they demanded that he heal her. It was the stubbornness of the warden and his wife that killed that little girl, not Ian." Dole sat silently, as if digesting what he had heard.

"You and you stay here," Dole ordered, pointing to Ian and Kale, "the rest of you get back to where you belong." Quickly obeying the order Ian, Kale, Ham and Dole were soon left alone and for over an hour the two friends were questioned about every facet of Donavan's demise. Finally satisfied that he was getting the full truth, Dole stroked his chin. "As you both know, Mister Donavan was the overseer of the shack. He was that, because I could trust him to do as he was told and also keep the men in line." Pointing at Kale he asked, almost politely. "What's your name?"

"Brewster, sir, Kale Brewster." Now it was Kale's turn to sound concerned. Shuffling his feet nervously he stared at the steps before him.

"Brewster, is it? Well Mister Brewster, you look big enough to handle yourself. You will take Mister Donavan's place as overseer. You may already be aware that if a man escapes the two sleeping on either side of him also hangs. You may not know that if it's through your negligence you join them. Do you understand what I am telling you?" Kale nodded in disbelief at his good fortune. No more working inside that stinking coal mine.

"I understand completely, sir and I am truly flattered that you would consider me for such a high calling. If you would allow me though, it was Ian who was the hero today, not me. If anyone deserves to be raised to a higher rank, it is him not me."

"That man isn't big enough to put the fear of God in the men that needs to be there. I have chosen you and there will be no arguments." A stern look crossed Doles face, for he was not used to being corrected on any matters. "I have plans for Mister Connor." The steely eyes shifted to Ian. "I may need another houseboy and it would be nice to have a medical person close. Tomorrow Ham will give you some real soap, which you will use vigorously. After you are given some decent clothes you will come to the house. You will clean during the day and return to the shack at night." Pausing to take a sip from the goblet, Dole eyed the two men before him. "Do me a good job 'n you'll be rewarded. Mess up 'n you'll be so far back in the mine that you'll never see daylight again. Ham, take them back to the shack and show Brewster here what to do for tonight, then in the morning you will fill him in on the rest of his duties." With a wave of his hand they were dismissed.

The walk back to their sleeping quarters was completed in silence. Neither Ian nor Kale dared to rejoice in their good fortune with Ham there and they followed behind him quietly. An occasional pat on the back and exchange of smiles were all the excitement they allowed themselves. Once inside the shanty Ham announced in a loud voice.

"Master Dole's said that this man Brewster is the new overseer in this room. Ya all best do as he says, same as ya done for Donavan. Everybody get in yer bunks now, so's I can show Brewster how ta tie ya in fer the night." Always eager to display his power Ham set about snuggly tying each man's ankle. Kale followed him about the entire room and observed. With the last one tied Ham turned, his stare was full of venom and the obvious dislike for Kale showed on the black face. "You'll mess up some day 'n when ya do it'll be me that gets ta put the rope around yer neck. I thought ya were trouble when Master Dole picked ya up at that prison. Don't know exactly why, but I never did trust some Dandy that talks as slick as you. You're big enough ta give ol' Ham some trouble 'n then talk yer way out with that sugar tongue 'a yers. I'm warnin' ya now, give me one lick of problems 'n I'll break yer back like a twig." Without waiting for a reply Ham turned and stalked outside, disappearing into the evening. Picking the coal-oil lamp from the table Kale made his way to where Ian was laying. In the flickering light the broad grin on his face revealed his elation.

Bending, he whispered in Ian's ear. "You got us saved there Ian. Thanks to you there's no more digging coal for us. All we got'ta do now is watch our step 'n it's easy living, compared to where we have been. Thanks for helping me."

"I owe you for saving me," Ian whispered back. "If you hadn't stepped in Ham would have crushed my ribs in another second. Let's just say, ' We owe each other,' and let it go at that.'" Reaching out he grasped Kale's hand in his. The bond between them became stronger than ever as they exchanged grips. With a final nod Kale left Ian and walked to his new bunk by the door. Ian watched him until the lamp was extinguished and the room plunged into total darkness. Ian fell asleep with a feeling that for the first time, since being sent to prison, everything was going to be all right.

The morning sun was streaming through the windowpane and the smell of biscuits baking awakened Ian. Colleen bent over him and kissed him lightly on the forehead, as she stroked the wild shock of hair from his face. Her tender touch sent waves of passion through his body as he embraced her slender form. Holding her close, her he attempted to pull her onto the bed but she pulled back and protested.

"Behave yourself, Mister Ian Connor. I have Biscuits in the oven and still have to make the gravy for them and I don't have time for your shenanigans. You still have a full day's work ahead of you and you need to save your strength." She laughed lightly as she pulled away and returned to the stove. Watching her from the bed, Ian couldn't remember when he had ever been happier. Business was good, he had a beautiful wife who was totally devoted to him and it seemed that nothing could be better for him. Pulling himself to a sitting position he reached out to receive the platter of biscuits and gravy from Colleen, when his dream was shattered by the incessant clanging of the meal bell and someone shouting.

Opening his eyes Ian was surprised to see that it was still dark outside. Kale had lit the lamp and as he turned the wick up the light slowly found it's way to the edges of the shack. The shouting grew louder as the noisy one came closer then Ham burst into the shanty.

"Come quick. The house is burnin' somethin' fierce." By the light of the lamp Ian could see the normally stoic face had turned to one of sheer panic and helplessness. The hair on one side of the black head was singed away and blisters were already forming on his face. The men were untying themselves and rushing for the doorway to see what the excitement was all about. Ham ran from shanty to shanty waking up the occupants to fight the fire.

Ian's heart sank as he made his way outside. The horizon glowed with an orange hue in the direction of the great house. In the confusion many of the men used this opportunity to make a run for it, while others simply stood and stared, not believing their eyes. Ham ran back and forth in desperation, pleading for help.

"Every man to the house," Kale ordered. "Let's save what we can." Running up the hill and across the moor in the darkness was not an easy task. Upon reaching the house the group stopped. The entire structure was engulfed and they watched helplessly as the roof fell in, sending waves of sparks into the darkness. Silently, the assembled mass stood and watched until there was nothing but a few spots of flame and dying embers of the once magnificent home. Ham stood with tears streaming down his cheeks and for the first time since he had seen the man, Ian felt nothing but pity for the giant. The once feared servant was reduced to a blubbering mass of nothing. His brother, Cain stood at his side staring at the rubble as if attempting to comprehend what was going on.

"The Master, he got drunk tonight 'n I carried him up ta bed," Ham began to explain. " I got him undressed 'n tucked in next ta the Mistress when he started wavin' his arms around 'n knocked the lamp over. It landed on the bedcovers 'n before I could do anythin' the whole bed was on fire. The Mistress was screamin' fer me ta do somethin' 'n she was on fire. The Master was so drunk that he slept right through it. I tried ta put the fire out but there was too much coal oil 'n the whole place went up. They's gon'na blame ol' Ham fer this, I just know they will."

"There is no blame," Kale stepped forward. "It was an unavoidable accident. You did all you could under the circumstances."

"If we ain't got no master no more, that means we're free men," came a voice from the outer fringes of the crowd. Others joined in, in agreement and soon the vast majority was yelling. A very confused Ham stepped forward. The responsibility of keeping the men in line had always fallen on his shoulders, and even though the master was dead he still felt that responsibility.

"There ain't no such thing as a free man, long as Ham's here. Ya still belong ta the Dole family 'n me 'n Cain are here ta see that ya stay." The two brothers stood facing the ever-threatening crowd, which had now turned into an uncontrollable mob. "Now everybody get yerselves back ta yer beds 'til sunrise. By then I'll know what ta do with ya all." Seeing their chance at freedom slowly slip away violence was inevitable. Some of the men behind Ham and Cain grabbed the largest rocks from the fallen fireplace and, with a downward sweep, sent them crashing into the heads of the two Nubians. The brothers neither felt nor saw the blows that ended their rein of terror. Lying in identical heaps on the ground they were no longer a threat to anyone. Ian began to kneel beside Ham, but was halted by a threatening voice.

"If ya try ta save them two, yer gon'na be next. We're free men 'n anybody in our way's gon'na join them two in Hell." Looking into the faces that surrounded him left Ian no doubt that this wasn't a threat it was a fact.

"You fools," Kale's voice boomed over the others, "you have turned this from a chance for freedom, to one of murder. If you had simply ran, all you could be charged with was being an escaped bond servant, now it's murder charges that you face."

"Either way you can hang just as dead," came the reply. "I seen a man hang once 'n I really ain't hankerin' to be the main attraction at one. Everybody that's wants out 'a here follow me. Let them two stay 'n try ta explain ta a bunch 'a Dole's friends what happened here."

The mob broke into splinter groups, all with but one thought, that being to put as many miles between them and the mines as possible. Left alone, Ian and Kale discussed the dilemma facing them. If they stayed, and the rest ran, they would be alone to face the other mine owners when word of the fire got around. There was a better than fair chance that they would be accused of being responsible for the deaths, simply because they were the only ones left around to blame. Weighing all the options they finally decided that they too should run, and run they did. Approaching the shanties they saw groups run from one to another. Soon the night sky was aglow with the flames shooting from every building and even from the mouth of the hated coalmines. Ian and Kale used the madness to make their escape before others wanted to join them.

"Because I worked on the docks in Liverpool, I have some friends that might help us get out of England where we'll be safe," Kale told Ian as they ran. "As long as we stay in this country we'll be hunted fugitives. Our best bet is to find a ship going anyplace but another port in Great Britain." Working their way to the outer fringes of the compound they broke into a faster run.

Staying away from the traveled routes and moving around mostly at night, the two companions found themselves in Liverpool, seventeen days after leaving Wales. Hooking rides on the backs of an occasional passing wagon they worked their way to the waterfront. Finding help out of the country was more difficult than Kale had imagined. It seemed that nearly everyone that he approached wanted money to smuggle them aboard a departing ship. Neither Ian nor Kale had even seen any money to call their own in so long, that they couldn't remember when they had two shillings to rub together. Knowing that the word of the fire and killing of Ham and Cain had gotten out by now, they were desperate to leave as soon as possible. The moors would be covered with posses looking for all the runaways. Then Kale came up with an idea.

"We'll take the cargo out of one of the large crates and hide inside. Once we're in the hold we can get out and stowaway." Selecting a crate large enough to hold them both, they emptied the goods inside and threw them into the bay, to be carried out to sea with the tide. Climbing into the vacant crate they pulled the lid shut and secured it from the inside. Making themselves as comfortable as possible, in the cramped quarters, they waited. For what seemed an eternity they sat quietly, afraid that any movement would give them away. Finally the crate was pushed from side to side and they were hoisted into the ship's hold. Waiting to hear the hatch over them slam closed before they dared to move, they endured another long period of cramping muscles. At last the long awaited noise announced that the hatch was closed. Prying the inside latch open, Kale peered into the dark hold. "I can't see my hand in front of my eyes," he whispered. Feeling his way to a bulkhead he felt along until his hand touched a lamp. Using only his sense of touch, the oil lamp was soon casting an ominous light into their surroundings.

"You are a nice guy Kale, but you're sure not a fun date. Imagine bringing a gentleman such as myself to a place like this." Ian's attempt at humor was not wasted. "What time do you serve dinner on this ship anyway? My stomach is beginning to think that I have forgotten how to eat."

"The way our luck is running I'd be more concerned with my ability to tread water, than filling my gut," Kale retorted. "For some reason we seem to be destined to fail in everything we touch. I wouldn't be surprised if this ship should sink."

"I thought you didn't believe in predestination," Ian reminded him of their conversation on religion. Though it was said in jest, Ian became concerned at the look on Kale's face. Lines of worry creased the forehead and between his eyes. "Are we really that bad off, Kale?"

"The one thing I neglected to mention to you, is that the only way out of this cargo hold is through that hatch up there. I have seen the temperature raise to well over a hundred degrees in a ship's hold. I was hoping that perhaps we may have been in a crate that was stored on deck. That way we could have slipped out during the night and hidden forward and below decks. If we try to push open the hatch it will make too much noise and someone will surely hear it. I'm afraid that in my desperation I may have put us in a worse predicament, I'm sorry Ian."

"You didn't drag me onto this ship, I came of my own will. There are no apologies necessary, my friend." The ship was clear of the harbor and well out to sea by this time, and the gentle rocking was doing strange things to Ian's stomach. "This is the first time that I have ever set foot on a ship and you can forget what I said about needing something to eat." With that he rushed to the far corner of the hold where Kale could hear Ian retching. When he reappeared Kale met him with a slight smile.

"While you were off enjoying yourself, I took the liberty of looking on that crate we hid in, to see where it was bound for. We are going to Spain, Ian. That's far enough away that Dole's goons will never find us. We could never have asked for better. Depending on the winds, we should be in Spain in a matter of a few days."

"Sure," Ian groaned. "All we have to do now is live through the next few days, and then what?" His stomach was churning uncontrollably and the urge to retch returned, even stronger than before. "I take back what I said about you not being a fun date, Kale. You're a terrible date." Off to the corner he ran again.

It seemed that just as Ian was getting used to the rocking and pitching of the ship, Kale informed him that there seemed to be preparations being made on deck to enter port. He had heard the shout, "Land Ho," from the crow's nest, followed by an abnormal amount of scurrying overhead. Deciding that the best way to get off was the same way they got aboard, they latched themselves back in the crate again. Fortunately, they had been one of the last loaded so they were one of the first to be taken ashore. The thump as they hit the dock sent Kale flying on top of Ian, who covered his mouth to keep from groaning. The hot sun beat down on the crate, making the heat inside nearly unbearable. Just as they were about to burst out of the enclosure and make a dash for it, the noise around them ceased.

Undoing the inside latch, Kale opened the upper corner of the crate just a sliver. Holding his eye against the crack he peered out. Leaning to Ian he whispered, "I see stars out there. All the dock-hands will be gone soon and then we get out of here as fast as possible." Sweat soaked their clothes as they waited for the opportunity to leave, but at last Kale whispered, "Now's as good a time as any, let's get out of here." Following Kale's lead Ian exited the crate and they ran to safety under the dock.

"The first thing we must do is find some suitable clothes," Kale said softly. "We're dead giveaways in these garbs from the mines. We may be in Spain, but I'm sure they know what prisoners look like here too." Motioning for Ian to follow, and moving silently, he worked his way along the shadows to the edge of the waterfront. Traversing through back alleys and peering over fences, they finally found clothes hanging on a line to dry. Finding something to fit Ian was no great challenge; Kale was a different story however. His broad shoulders would not fit any of the clothes there; so the search continued until they at last found some that at least passed. Having nothing of value to leave in exchange for the stolen garments, Kale vowed to somehow find a way to repay the owners. Using a pointed rock he scratched an X on the wooden fences of the houses that they took clothes from. Noticing Ian's curious looks Kale smiled.

"That way I know where to look when I can pay them for these," he explained.

"I thought that you had finally lost your mind," Ian replied. "Do you think you can find a fence to carve into indicating that we stole something to eat too? I seem to have left everything I had back on the ship."

"What we find to eat may not be what you're used to, but I'll do my best." The narrow alley was heaped with garbage on both sides, leaving Ian wondering how he could possibly think of food. Following Kale he made his way through the darkness and farther away from the waterfront. Winding through this alley and that alley, Ian was about to call a halt to the travels when Kale stopped abruptly. A doorway, opening onto the alley, stood ajar and Kale slowly pushed it open. The moonlight through the front windows showed they had entered the kitchen of a small home. Helping themselves to some food they hurriedly consumed what they could and took a small amount with them.

"One more person we owe," Ian said as they hurried away, eating as he ran. "You may not be a fun date Kale, but you certainly an adventurous one." Daylight found them far from the ship that had smuggled them into Spain only yesterday. Finding a bridge that spanned a creek, the two hid far back beneath it and settled for some well-earned rest. With full stomachs and tired muscles they immediately fell asleep.

Traveling only at night, they worked their way deeper into the countryside, with no inkling where they were going. One week after leaving the ship, they believed they were far away enough to be out of harms way. Seeking some way to earn money to live on was a great problem. Neither spoke one word of Spanish and it seemed that no one here spoke English. Cutting wood here and cleaning out chicken coops there gave them some coins, but they were also unfamiliar with the rate of exchange. They worked for an entire day at one place, chopping down trees. When they were paid they immediately went to the market to buy food. There they learned that they had earned the equivalent of three pennies English, for the day's labor. After that they were quick to learn the monetary system in that area, as not to be cheated again. Finally getting steady work on a hillside farm, the future looked bright for the two friends. Just as it looked as though they were finding some sort of stability, their luck soured again.

They were in the fields hoeing rows, when a dozen-uniformed men on horseback approached. Riding slowly up and down the rows they studied each person before moving to the next. Stopping before Ian and Kale, the one in the lead pointed a riding crop at Ian.

"Nombre?" He said. Ian looked at Kale, who just shrugged his shoulders in response. "Nombre?" The man said louder in a more threatening tone. Moving closer to Ian he raised the crop as if to strike him.

"I sure wish I knew what you want, mister. If I did I'd sure give it to you." Receiving no answer the leader turned to Kale and repeated the same gibberish that he had to Ian. Kale was just as ignorant about what he wanted as Ian was. Receiving no response from Kale either seemed to infuriate the man. Before they realized what was happening both of the Englishmen were on the ground and their wrists tied behind them. Shouting in Spanish to the onlookers the soldier looked around. An older woman stepped forth and after a short conversation with the leader she approached the two lying on the ground. Bending between the two she said in halting English.

"I talk little English. The Capitano wants I tell you, you are arrested for.... How you say...spies for English. He say you run, you die."

"Spies?" Ian said aloud. " What makes them think we're spies?" The absurdity of the idea. What spying could they do hoeing furrows in the middle of a farmer's field. Did they think they were taking secrets of how to hold a hoe? Looking at the woman he pleaded, "Tell him that this is absurd. We are no more spies than you are." The woman simply shook his head.

"No comprende," the woman said as she stood and walked away. Their last vestige of hope had deserted them. Pulled to their feet each was unceremoniously thrown over the hindquarters of different horses. A shout from the Captain and the soldiers left the field with the spies in tow.

"I sure don't like the looks of this," Ian thought to himself. "Here we are in a foreign country, where we can't speak the language, and now we're accused of being English spies. May God have mercy on our souls."

CHAPTER FIVE.

It had been over a week since their arrest and the time spent in the tiny cell was weighing heavily upon Ian. The uncertainty of what the future held for him and Kale played on his mind continually. The walls of the tiny cell seemed to close in on him even more as the days passed. He and Kale were separated upon arriving at the jail, each locked in a barred room with barely enough room to move about. The food seemed to be of the standard as that in debtor's prison, except less of it. They had been taken before, what Ian believed was a high ranking official. Unfortunately, speaking no Spanish and the man spoke no English; they were cast into these cages, still not positive of the reason.

"You awake, Ian?" Kale's voice carried down the narrow passageway, his voice bouncing off the walls.

"I'm awake," Ian answered. "I'm just laying here counting fly specks on the window." Concern crept into his voice as he asked, "What do you think will happen to us, Kale? It seems forever that we've been in this place and we still don't even know why. That old lady didn't speak English very well but the way I understood her, they seem to think we are spies of some sort for England. We'd be pretty dumb spies to enter a country totally broke, not know one lick of the language, get odd jobs hoeing vegetables and stay in a town with a population of less than fifty people. What in the world could we learn here, even if we were spies?"

"You've convinced me," came Kale's response, "now all you have to is convince a judge, if we ever get before one that is. From the looks of things, our chances of getting out of here are slim and none. I don't know what Spain's equivalent of the Bastille is, but that's where England sends spies. From what I've been told once they're in there they never come out again. They just mysteriously disappear. In hindsight, I'd say we'd have been better off staying at Doles." Neither man said more, each contemplating what the future may hold for them. It was near time for their meal when they received their visitor.

"My name's Juan Hernandez," said the man in flawless English, appearing at Ian's cell door. "I am here to represent you and your friend at your trial." Speaking to the guard in Spanish he waited for Kale to be brought to Ian's cell and the two entered. With barely enough room for one person, the cubicle was very crowded with three. Shaking hands all around the man continued. "As I said I am here to be your barrister, as you call us where you came from. I assume that you are English?"

"We are," Kale admitted. "I'm surprised to find someone that speaks any English at all here, much less one that is as fluent as yourself. I am Kale Brewster and this is Ian Connor. Perhaps you would be so kind as to tell us exactly why we are here?"

"I was educated in London. My parents are both Spanish, however my father was an attaché to the royal court of England, hence my English education. It seems that diplomatic connections between your country and Spain are strained to say the least. Each is casting a suspicious eye at the other, over who should rule the seas and trade routes. At the present time Spain has a mighty armada but we are aware that England is building a navy that may rival ours. Any strangers are looked upon as potential problems, especially those from Great Britain. Now, I must ask you to tell me exactly why you are in Spain? I also must caution you to be perfectly truthful with me." With that the two friends told Juan everything, beginning with debtors prison, through the fire at Dole's, sneaking aboard the ship and everything leading up to their arrest.

"That's about all there is to tell," Kale finished speaking. "We know nothing of spying or any diplomatic connections. We only want to live as free men." Leaning casually against the bars of the door he awaited Juan's next question.

"You're telling me that the soul reason you are in Spain is that you are runaway bond servants and are only looking for a place to hide. Is that correct?" Looking from one to the other, he studied their faces as if to find the truth in their demeanor. As he stood up and offered his hand to each of the two men he smiled. "I don't believe that we will have a problem convincing a magistrate of your innocence. I will prepare your defense and then we will go to trial in about six or seven days."

"There is one big problem," Ian said as the man turned to leave. "We have no money to pay a barrister to defend us. There may be a shilling or so from the farmer we were working for, but not near enough to cover your expenses."

"I knew that before I even entered your cell. My motives are strictly selfish ones. You are being tried as spies from a country that Spain will certainly go to war with, sometime in the future. If I am able to get the court to find you innocent of these charges, it will boost my standings in the community. If I am not able to get you freed, I have been involved in a high profile case and my standing hasn't been injured a bit. So you see, I win either way the decision against you goes. Goodbye gentlemen, you shall hear from me shortly." Opening the cell door Juan stepped out and disappeared down the hallway, leaving Kale and Ian staring at each other in consternation.

"It's certainly nice to see that someone wins in this situation," Kale said as the guard led him back to his cell. "I would hate to think that all this is a lesson in futility." There was little humor in Kale's remarks and Ian was left wondering how hard Juan Hernandez would try to defend them?

The promised week passed and stretched into two with no word from Juan. About ready to give up any hope of a resolution to their incarceration, Ian and Kale spent the days in idle conversation. Eighteen days passed before Hernandez appeared at the cell door and was admitted.

"I have had a very difficult time arraigning for a trial date for you two. It seems that most of the judges do not want to touch your case, or have already found you guilty. There is one that will hear us but it must tomorrow morning. Is there anything else that you can tell me that may help our case?" Ian looked at Kale and they both shook their heads. "Then gentlemen, I shall see you bright and early and good luck to us all."

"It's about time that we had some good luck," Kale retorted. "Everything we've seen lately is far from that." With a smile Juan walked away and Kale was taken back to his cell.

There was little sleep for either of the two facing trial. Visions and hopes flashed through their minds throughout the night. Before dawn broke both were sitting on the edges of their beds and Ian could hear Kale offer a prayer in their behalf. "Amen," he echoed as Kale finished the prayer.

Sunlight was just breaking through the windows when the guards came for them. Both were manacled wrist and ankles and a chain was fed through the rings attached to them. Led outside into the morning air, Ian wondered if this would be the last time that he would enjoy it. The walk to where the trial would be held was almost too short for them to bask in the morning light. Taken into a large room they were placed behind a waist-high railing. A long table faced them from across the room and two smaller ones between them and the long one. Juan Hernandez sat at one of the two tables, while three men shared the other. A hawk-faced man sat at the long one looking directly at the accused men.

What went on after that neither Ian nor Kale had any idea, as everything was said in Spanish. Juan stood up and gave, what appeared to be a very passionate speech. When he sat down the other three conversed before one stood, and delivered one that sounded exactly the same, to the two men behind the rail. Juan jumped to his feet and the four men engaged in a shouting match, before the magistrate pounded for silence. The banter went on for the better part of an hour before the four were called to the long table. A lot of head shaking and verbal arguing went back and forth. Finally Juan walked slowly to where his clients were chained.

"Well gentlemen," Ian didn't like the sound of his voice. "This is the best I can do for you. I have explained exactly what you are doing in Spain and that is no way that you are English spies. The prosecution argues that your story is exactly what someone would dream-up to protect themselves if they were caught. The magistrate seemed to lean a bit to the side away from you, but I planted enough doubt in his mind that he has offered you four choices, rather than pronounce sentence upon you himself. Here are the choices and none of them are ideal. You may spend the rest of your lives in a Spanish prison, or be sent back to England in chains and turned over to the authorities as runaway bondsmen."

"There were four choices and to be perfectly honest with you, I really don't care for the first two." The furrows between Kale's eyebrows deepened as he spoke. "I hope that you aren't telling us that those are the best of the four options."

"I warned you that none of them were ideal. The third option is that you must leave Spain and never return."

"We'll take that one," Ian blurted out. "Point us to the quickest way to the border and we'll run for it." Finally it appeared there was hope for them, but it was soon dashed.

"Not so fast my friend," Juan interrupted. "You are given the choice to leave Spain but not where you will go. Word has reached the King, of great cities made of pure gold somewhere in the New World. He is sending Don Francisco Vazquez de Coronado to search for such a legendary place. If it proves true, Spain will become the richest country in the known universe. As we speak there are preparations being made for their departure. There is a shortage of men to accompany them, so this is your chance to escape the gallows in England as runaways, or rotting in a Spanish prison. Granted, you will be no more than the surfs that you once were, but at least you will be breathing fresh air."

Ian was almost afraid to ask the next question. "And the fourth choice?"

"You will be taken out at sunrise tomorrow and shot as spies. Those are your options. We must have an answer immediately, or the choice will be made for you." Juan said as he paced nervously before them. "Those aren't much for a solution, but they're the best I could do and please believe me I did try."

Kale looked at Ian while he stroked his chin, as he always did when perplexed. "As far as I'm concerned the last choice is definitely out and I'm not too crazy about numbers one and two. What do you say Ian? It's your neck too."

"It looks like we are going on another boat ride. Lord I hope it's a short one. The ride from England to Spain about killed me. That's our answer Juan." Ian took Juan's arm in his hand. "Thanks for all your help. Until you can be better paid, I guess that's all we can give you." Juan smiled as he returned to the long table where the others were impatiently waiting. A very brief conversation followed, then Ian and Kale were returned to their cells.

The following day Juan appeared at the door again. "I guess this is goodbye, gentlemen. They are coming to take you to the coast where you'll be put aboard the ship. I realize this is a rather facetious remark, but I do wish you well in your travels." That was to be the last time that they saw the man who saved them from execution, or worse.

The journey that had taken them such a long time, running through alleys, was covered in a matter of a few days. Ironically, they stopped at the exact same dock where they had climbed from the crate. After they were turned over to the ship's first mate Ian and Kale were taken to the cargo hold and put to work loading cargo. Mounds of food supplies, bales of hay, casks of water, gunpowder and countless casks, crates and barrels were crammed into the center below decks. Crude stalls lined the starboard side, while cages and pens stood against the port bulkhead of the ship. These would hold the horses, pigs, sheep and cattle to be taken on the journey. Two identical ships were also being prepared in the same manner for the trip abroad. Other Spaniards had been to this destination before and returned with wondrous tales. King Ferdinand was determined to make this part of the Spanish Empire. Conquistadors were being sent to explore every facet of this uncharted land. The year was fifteen hundred and thirty-five and both Ian and Kale wondered if they would live to see the sunrise on another year.

The ships were finally loaded and, with great fanfare, sailed out of the harbor into the open sea. The dangers ahead, on the westward course, forgotten in the promise of great riches in gold. Even Ian and Kale felt a tinge of anticipation at seeing great cities made of the precious yellow metal. It was no wonder that the soldiers, who would share in these riches, were so excited to leave.

Once underway, those remanded to below deck attempted to make their quarters somewhat livable. Every available open space a hammock was hung. Ian and Kale had a difficult time finding a space for theirs. The choice spots, that were near the open hatch, went first and territorial fights were not an uncommon occurrence. Winding their way through the maze of crates and humanity, the two friends finally found an open space at the ship's stern large enough to accommodate their needs. After many futile attempts the two canvas slings were hung to their mutual satisfaction. Kale had slept in one of the beastly things before, however Ian was a novice. Fortunately he was not alone and the hold was filled with thuds and curses, from the unfortunates that kept falling out of them. After repeated demonstrations from Kale, Ian at last managed to stay inside, rather than falling from the canvas sling.

"Now I know what the Spaniards use to get confessions from their victims. They simply made the poor souls spend an exorbitant amount of time in one of these contraptions," Ian groaned. "I would admit to anything right now, and I've yet to spend the night in here." The rocking of the ship, mixed with the stench from the many animals, soon added to the seasickness that plagued a good portion of the men below decks. Ian wasn't spared this malady either and soon he was joining the crowd at the rail. Fighting to climb back into his hammock he turned to Kale. "I have but one question to ask you. 'Why, on Gods green earth, didn't we choose to be shot when we had the chance?' At least it would have been a quick and merciful death, nothing like this.'"

"Believe it or not, you'll live through all this and in a day or two you'll be as right as ever." In the darkness Kale was glad that Ian could not see the smile on his face. He remembered well the first time that he had been aboard ship and knew exactly what the others were going through. "You could stand to lose some weight anyway. All that soft living we've had lately has put a paunch on you."

"Soft living? I haven't had a moment of soft living since I met you. I'm beginning to wonder if perhaps we are nothing but a pair of Jonahs. Maybe we'll be fortunate and they'll throw us both overboard, like they did with that fellow in the bible, except I hope we drown. I definitely don't want to get swallowed by some big fish, it smells bad enough in this sty." With that statement Ian was running topside again. Sunrise found him still draped over the rail, weak from the nausea that tormented him constantly.

There seemed to be no dawn, as Ian had known it. One minute it was barely a streak in the east and bright sun the next. The entire group of those sentenced to serve was gathered on deck, where they were separated into two groups. Those who spoke Spanish and those who did not, they were then divided again. The ones that had seen duty aboard ships in the past placed in one group, and those who had not in another. When questioned, Kale denied his sea duty so he and Ian were placed into a group of nine others, which had not seen sea duty nor spoke Spanish. This group was turned over to a boson, who spoke very fragmented English and some French. The large belaying pin stuck in his belt signified his authority. This group was sent to clean the cages and stalls below deck, which did not set well with Ian's stomach. Once the stalls were cleaned the horses were each exercised by a brisk walk around the line of crates. This meant that all the hammocks had to be taken down and put back up when they were through.

Once the animals were all fed it was time to feed the men. The food was worse, if possible, than that at the Spanish prison. The thin gruel was like eating paste and not nearly as tasty. Lumps of uncooked porridge stuck to the roof of the mouth, making Ian wonder how anything so thin in appearance, could be so thick in texture? One cup of water was issued to every man, with a stern warning that anyone caught pilfering either food or water would receive fifty lashes. "Why would anyone want to steal this garbage?" Ian thought to himself, still fighting to keep down what he had been able to swallow. By late afternoon he was beginning to become accustom to the rolling of the ship and did feel a bit better. Back below decks the chores began all over again and by nightfall the eleven workers were tired to the bone.

"Perhaps tomorrow will be easier," Kale said as they climbed into their slings. "It could be worse for us. We could be one of those fellows climbing around in the riggings. I'd much rather be cleaning stalls, than walking around on nothing but a rope that far in the air."

"I have a question," Ian said thoughtfully. "Why is it everywhere we end up someone has to carry a club? The guards in prison, Ham and now that fellow that bosses us around here, I'm beginning to think that no one trusts us." Kale shrugged and before long both were snoring loudly.

The next day went as the previous one, as did the weeks that followed. When they had been to sea for nearly five weeks the word spread that they would put ashore for supplies and refill the water casks. Excitement went through the entire ship as the day approached to dock, but there was no dock. The ship was anchored off shore and small boats were sent ashore to fetch the supplies, leaving all the rest longfully gazing at the green palms, so close yet so far away. Standing at the rail Ian and Kale talked of how it would be to set foot on solid ground again. They were still there when the boats returned and they were ordered to help unload and stow the cargo. Much to their pleasant surprise they were each given a fresh fruit for their efforts, which they eagerly consumed. Back on deck they watched the island disappear on the horizon and soon nothing but open ocean was in sight.

Many months, and islands too numerous to count later, the end of their voyage neared. In the far distance the coastline of the New World was barely visible, one or two more days and they would land at their destination. The anticipation grew the closer they drew to land, everyone strained their eyes to be the first to see the famed golden cities, but none appeared. Perhaps they lay just a bit farther inland, away from the destructiveness of the sea air. The landmass grew larger and when the order to drop anchor was given a huge roar went up from the masses. Anxious to be ashore there was little sleep for anyone that night and daylight found the longboats lowered and ready. A skeleton crew was to be left aboard while the rest would accompany the soldiers ashore.

Both Ian and Kale were in the first group selected to go ashore. In separate boats, they put their backs to the oars as they pulled toward shore. Coronado was in the boat which was between Kale's and Ian's. Standing erect in the bow, with one booted foot placed on the seat before him and holding a flag of Spain high, he reminded Ian of a portrait rather than a living person. His breastplate and helmet shone brightly in the sunlight and, as pompous as Ian thought he was, there was still an air of royalty about the man. The oars dug deeper into the water and with every pull the boat shot ahead with a jerk, nearly dumping Coronado into the sea. Deciding that discretion was better than showmanship, he promptly sat down and handed the flag to one of the men behind him.

When the bottom of the boats rubbed against the sandy bottom they were quickly emptied of soldiers. The ones manning the oars were ordered back to the ship for another load. Ian wasn't certain that he could pull another group of heavily armored men back again, for his arms and back already ached from the first trip. When they pulled along side the mother ship they were ordered out of the boats and a new team of rowers was put aboard, along with the next group of soldiers. So it went until all of the men, including Kale and Ian were ashore. When there was a sufficient audience Coronado dramatically claimed this portion for Spain and said a prayer of thanks for their safe arrival. Hardly had he finished when, from the foliage lining the outer portion of the beach, came ten times the men that Coronado had brought on all three ships. Feeling threatened the musketeers raised their rifles nearly in unison, while the pikemen lowered their lances to form a pointed barrier.

"I'm not sure we were the fortunate ones by getting to come off the ship," Ian whispered to Kale. "We may end up in someone's stew pot and be the main menu for tonight's dinner." Standing on the far fringes of the soldiers he felt some safety, but not enough to be thoroughly comfortable. As the sea of dark skins advanced closer, Coronado drew his sword and raised it in the air, preparing to give the order to fire the muskets. The natives stopped their advance a scant fifty yards away and one walked closer, holding his arms toward those on the shore, as if in a gesture of welcome. A smile showed clearly on the brown face, while he continually nodded his head.

Coronado was uncertain as what to do next. The man's demeanor seemed friendly enough; still there were enough of the natives to easily overcome his troops if it came to a fight. Replacing his sword in the scabbard, he walked to meet the oncoming native. Stopping within arm's length of each other the two studied the one before him, attempting to discover if there was any kind of threat. Neither spoke the other's language, so a great deal of gesturing and nodding passed between them before Coronado returned to his men.

"It appears they are friendly enough," he said in Spanish. "We will follow them to their villages, perhaps our golden cities lay just beyond the edge of those trees." The group surged forward in anticipation of what they might find, leaving Ian and Kale standing ankle-deep in water, as they hadn't understood a word of what had been said.

"I suppose we had best follow the crowd," Kale said, "I only hope we aren't the lambs being led to the slaughter. They don't appear to be a threat."

"An open flame doesn't appear to be a threat to the moth either, until it gets it's wings singed," Ian replied as he scanned the landscape for the fastest exit should trouble arise. "Somehow the safety of debtor's prison is starting to look pretty good to me right now. At least there I could be certain that I would be the eater and not the fare." The feeling of uneasiness grew deeper as they entered the outskirts of the town of mud-baked buildings. Carved stone faces stared back from arches as they drew deeper into the interior and the plain houses gave way to grander buildings. In the center of a large plaza stood a magnificent structure, with steps of stone rising taller than any Ian had ever seen. In contrast to most of those they had seen upon entering, this one was made entirely of close fitting blocks of hewn stone. Carved effigies on each corner and lining the entrance, gave Ian the impression that this must be some sort of a religious place.

"That's a beautiful architecture," Kale said, "but it's certainly not made of gold. From the looks of the work I have seen so far, these people certainly not primitive savages, but exceptionally fine craftsmen. This stonework would rival most of the statues in England." Kale continued to marvel at the building as they passed by. The procession finally halted before a stone edifice nearly as grand, but not nearly as large, as the preceding one. Seated on a huge carved throne-like chair was, what must be, the head of the village. Descending the steps he spoke to Coronado, who looked about for help in understanding the gibberish. When none came he spoke back to the man, who was as confused with what he heard as the Captain was. "At least he now knows how we feel," Kale said softly to Ian. "He can't understand a word of what's being said to him either." Ian smiled and nodded in agreement.

The hot sun continued to beat down on the assembled group, and Ian could imagine the torment those wearing the metal breastplates and helmets were going through. It would be like climbing into a heated oven and slowly baking. "Those soldiers will earn every once of gold they get for this journey," he thought to himself. For once he didn't envy them in the least. For a long time the two leaders simply stood facing each other, as if neither knew what the next step should be. At last the chief said something to a native standing beside him and the man disappeared. When he reappeared he carried a robe made of feathers, similar to the one worn by the chieftain. Carefully the chieftain placed it around the shoulders of the Spaniard leader and beckoned for them to follow him.

"Perhaps we will be lead to the gold and we can leave here," Kale said softly to Ian. "I have a bad feeling about this place. They seem almost too polite and friendly to be real. Can you imagine the reception that a group of them would receive if they landed in England like we have here? Perhaps I'm being overly cautious, but I'd suggest we watch ourselves carefully." Ian was deep in his own thoughts and barely heard what was being said to him.

They were led to a courtyard, with a covered center, where Coronado and his officers were then seated. The rest stood in the blazing sun while those inside attempted to communicate with each other. The sun was but a glow in the western sky when they finished and the men returned to the ships. It was decided that there was little danger from those on the mainland. Tomorrow they would take the animals ashore and a permanent camp erected near the town. Again Ian and Kale were chosen to accompany those not being left on the ships. With mixed emotions the two discussed their fate as they lay in their slings, awaiting sleep to overcome them. Tired and sore from the strenuous workout of the day, it was not long before conversation ended and an exhausted sleep took it's' place.

Sunrise found the ship bustling with preparations to return to the land. Water casks were emptied, their spouts sealed with pitch and then tied on either side of the pigs and sheep. It was a crude but efficient floating device and there was little danger of losing an animal to drowning. They would be tethered to the back of the longboats and dragged to the beach, where the kegs would be removed and taken back to the ship for the next batch.

Waiting for high tide the soldiers and crew passed the time in various games and discussions of what they would do with their share of the gold. As the excitement grew, wagers were made with riches they hadn't even obtained yet. At last the tide rose and the anchor was away. Using only the foremasts the ships slowly made their way closer toward the sandy beach. A sailor stood well forward of the ship throwing a weighted line, that was marked every so often, into the water. As the ship passed over his spot he would look at the markings on the line and call out the depth of the water below the ship's bow. Before it had gotten too shallow the anchor was dropped again and the interminable wait for the tide to recede began.

As before, a relay of oarsmen took boatloads of soldiers ashore to receive the incoming animals. It was on the last return trip to the ship, that Ian felt the boat being propelled faster toward the large vessel. The outgoing tide gave a shove to the tiny craft in its hurry to return to the open waters.

The confusion on deck of the ship as terrified animals were shoved overboard was a comedy of errors. Men ran helter-skelter chasing loose critters while others strained to force stubborn pigs from the ship. Eventually all were towed ashore and safely secured in hastily constructed holding pens. The last animals to leave the ship were the dozen or so horses. Above all these were the most valuable possession and great care was given as they swam the short distance to where they could walk ashore.

The tide had completely receded, leaving the ship grounded and helpless, as there was no way to move it in case of any attack. The cannons were manned and armed men lined the rails, waiting for the next tide to float them to safety. A dozen men, among them the two Englishmen, were given the responsibility of tending the stock as they were brought ashore.

The entire village turned out to stare at the strange animals that were invading their land. Of special interest were the huge beasts that the strangers would climb on the backs of and ride. These creatures must be Gods. They must be to have dominance over such animals.

Slipping his foot into the stirrup and mounting his sleek white stallion, Coronado led the parade through the streets of the village and beyond. Selecting a suitable location, he ordered that this would be where their community would be. The surfs were put to work immediately clearing brush and setting up temporary enclosures for the officers, while each soldier worked to fix his own place to live. No one, except themselves, gave a thought to where the servants would stay. It was of no great concern as there was absolutely nowhere they could run to. Even if they did lose one or two that was just a few less to worry about. There was always more where these came from, even if they must be taken from the native village.

CHAPTER SIX.

To the native people, the shiny yellow metal was nothing but one that was easily found, melted at a relatively low temperature and was easily malleable. They could not understand the white skinned ones intense interest in the ornaments they wore, or the effigies that were made from it. As the months passed the whites seemed to become more aggressive toward the naïve natives. The once passive Spaniards became belligerent masters, demanding all the yellow metal be brought to Coronado. The chieftain was tortured to make him disclose the location of the cities of gold, however he constantly held steadfast to his story that he had no idea what they were talking about. Tiring of his stubbornness, the Spanish captain ordered that he be shot while the entire village was forced to watch. Reverence and awe were replaced with terror and hatred in the hearts of the Indians. Soldiers would appear at the homes of the natives and take a handful to lead them on expeditions, searching for the wealth that had consumed them. Beatings became commonplace as the rein of horror continued. Coronado had moved into the Chiefs palace, while he continually demanded more and more tribute.

"I don't like the looks of this Ian," Kale said. "These people will only be pushed so far and then explode. I'm afraid that they won't care who was responsible for these actions and every white will have his throat cut. The brutality is rampant and beneath the terrified looks on their faces, hatred is in their eyes. I almost wish we had been left on the ship instead of witnessing this."

Ian had just returned from treating another of the soldiers. Not used to the tropical diseases, malaria and fever ran rampant among the whites, while the natives seemed immune to the bite of the anopheles mosquito. The mixture of the two cultures was just as deadly for the ones with the brown skin. The European diseases were taking their toll also. Funeral pyres burned constantly, while wails of mourning were the norm rather than the exception. "If the Spaniards keep dying off this way, we won't have to worry about it. Two more bit it today from some fever and there isn't a thing I can do to save them. The natives aren't faring any better I'm afraid."

As time progressed the people became virtual slaves in their own village. Forced to dig gold from the earth, from daybreak to dusk, and treated like abused animals, they finally revolted. The camp was awakened by the sound of musket fire and yelling came from near the palace occupied by Coronado. Rushing to see what the excitement was all about, Ian and Kale hid in the tall grass while watching the fiasco unravel before their eyes. Natives, armed with nothing but clubs and knives, were no match for the musketeers and lancers of the Spanish army. Row after row fell before the onslaught of infantry and horsemen. The silence that followed was almost deafening. Brown bodies littered the ground, while others less fortunate, cowered before Coronado's troops.

A hurried meeting between Coronado and his officers was held on the spot. It was decided that come morning the remaining soldiers would be divided into three groups, two large and one small. The larger groups would divide the bondservants and male Indians, while the smaller group would return to the ship. On the next high tide the ship would return to Spain and load with people and supplies to settle this newfound land. Each group placed under one of his most trusted officers and one group under Coronado himself. Coronado would search for the Cities of Gold while the others would find a suitable place for settlement. Drawing straws was chosen, to see what group would leave for Spain and which stayed. Heading in the direction away from the sea, those looking for a settling place would travel as far as they could in one fortnight, then return to this place and report their findings. If they should find nothing promising they were ordered to stay another week in pursuit, however at the end of the second allotted time they were to return anyway. Anyone not here by that time would be considered either dead or deserters and their share of any found gold forfeited. The officers in charge could select the men they wanted to take with their group, but naturally only after Coronado had selected his men. When the meeting ended the charge officers each ran to grab the most able for themselves. Risking the wrath of their leader, none wanted to get the culls so they took their chances. Hoping to hide away the most valued men for themselves, thus insuring their own success.

"I don't know what that's all about but I have a feeling that we aren't going to like it, whatever it is," Kale said softly into Ian's ear. Pulling back from their hiding place the two made the way back to their hammocks. No sooner had they climbed in and began conversation, than they were rousted out by one of the charge officers. Motioning for them to follow him, he set out for the deeper part of the jungle. The moonlight was insufficient light to travel through the tangled roots and overhanging vines. Finding a fallen log the officer motioned for the other two to sit behind it and be quiet, then silently slipped away.

"What do you think that's all about?" Kale asked, completely dumbfounded by the events. Attempting to look over the log and into the camp he strained to make out what was happening, but to no avail. "It's so bloody dark and these trees are so thick that I can't see a thing."

"Save your energy," Ian replied, "I'm sure well find out soon enough. We'll probably have the job of burying all those bodies back there. Those poor souls never stood a chance in Hell of ever pulling that off. Why do you think they went against such odds?"

"I don't know," Kale answered thoughtfully. "I guess that a body can only take so much abuse then it switches to the survival mode. These people have been deceived, robbed, enslaved and murdered. I think they have a good enough reason to revolt."

Throughout the night they speculated what was going to happen to them. Sunrise brought resolution to their questions when the officer returned and motioned for them to again follow him. Doing as they were bid the two followed into the center of the village, where there were groups of three divided. Coronado was standing in the shade of the veranda and ordered the officer, leading Ian and Kale, to come to him. Doing as he was told he received a sharp slap with the heavy gauntlets of Coronado's, along with sharp words of rebuke.

"I don't understand the words, but you don't need to speak Spanish to understand the wallop he got. I just hope we aren't next," Ian said softly, afraid to be heard by the leader. The words were no sooner out of his mouth than Coronado pointed at them and motioned for them to come forward. Hesitating at first they were prompted by jabs from pikes to move. Approaching the most feared man on this continent the two stood before him with bowed heads.

"Docator?" Coronado asked, pointing at Ian. "You docator?" Ian nodded in the affirmative wondering just what that meant? Pointing to Ian he motioned for him to join the group behind him and another motion sent Kale to one across the way. Panic replaced wonderment.

"They can't be separating us," Kale wailed. "We have been through too much together to be separated now." The tone of his voice was like none that Ian had ever heard before. Refusing to budge, the two friends clung to each other's arms. Rough hands tore them apart and they were dragged to their respective places. Tears welled in the eyes of both men, each wondering if they would see the other again.

Shortly after the noon meal the groups went their separate ways. Ian and Kale kept track of each other until the jungle hid them from sight. "Goodbye, my friend and may God bless and look after you," he said aloud as Kale disappeared from view. The snorting of the horses and the laughing of the soldiers drown out his words. Ian could not remember when he had felt so dejected and alone. He was not allowed any time of mourning however. A large knife was thrust into his hand and he was taken to the front to help chop a path through the heavy foliage. With every swing of the machete he pretended that the head of Francisco Vazquez de Coronado was at the edge of the sharp blade. The face of his friend haunted him and he could hear Kale's laugh ring in his ears, one that he doubted that he would ever hear again. It was April in the year fifteen hundred and forty, a date that would be firmly fixed in Ian's mind for the rest of his life.

The further inland they went, the thicker grew the vegetation. Greater effort was required to hack through the undergrowth, leaving the men soaked with sweat and their heads spinning from the exertion and humid temperatures. When they were finally allowed to rest they fell where they stood. Exhausted and miserable Ian didn't particularly care if he ever got up again. "Just leave me here to die in peace," he thought, but such a merciful end was not his just now, for soon they were back cutting a swath again.

As the day progressed the heat became unbearable and many of the conquistadors shed the heavy metal breastplates and other armor. Even the vain leader had taken his off and carried it behind the saddle. For obvious reasons the Indians were not to be trusted with the sharp machetes so they were reduced to beasts of burden. Carrying heavy loads of food and supplies on their backs, they were herded ahead of the soldiers. Those that faltered were either whipped to their feet or summarily slain. Ian was not accustomed to such cruelty; even in the worst prison he could not imagine this kind of inhumanity happening.

Just as he thought that he could not swing the knife one more time, the vegetation began to thin. On the third day, since leaving the camp behind, they emerged into the high desert country. The rolling hills were dotted with spruce and firs, which gave way to cedars and junipers the farther inland they traveled. Sandy soil and low sagebrush replaced the rich loam and thick trees, but the most noticeable was the heat. The heavy humidity of the jungle was left behind and a dry air took its place. Those, like Ian, with fair skin became severely sunburned; even some of the darker complexioned Spaniards suffered the same fate.

As there was no need for the way to be cleared with the knives anymore, Ian and the rest were relegated to helping the Indians carry the loads. Their portions weren't heavy and Ian found it almost relaxing after the tedious job of chopping through the underbrush. The Indian guides kept motioning the group ahead and jabbering something that only they could understand. To Ian the sign language seemed to indicate that the place they were seeking was just over the next hill, but there was only another sage covered mound, and another, and another after that. The same monotonous scene greeted them for as far as the eye could see. Picturing the rolling hills of home and the moors of Wales, Ian wondered how the same Creator could have made this place also? It was as though He had started something, then tired of the task and left it unfinished. "Perhaps this is where He dumped everything He didn't want," Ian said to himself, wondering if Kale was facing the same boredom as he.

The vista flattened out to low desert and the vegetation became more sparse and stunted the further they went. The guide continued to urge them on, and like so many sheep, they followed. The weeks blended into one another, until Ian had no idea how long they had traveled. Crossing rivers, up mountains and crossing deserts too numerous to count, the caravan trudged on. Just as it seemed that all hope of finding the Seven Golden Cities of Cibola were waning, the guide waved them on as he ran to the top of a plateau. The ones walking in front of the mounted horsemen were nearly trampled by the onslaught, as the animals were urged into a gallop to the top. Pointing to a distant table-top mountain the guide spoke excitedly, as Coronado and his officers arrived. Those on foot ran as fast as possible to see the end of their quest.

"Run on you idiots, the cities aren't going anywhere," Ian said aloud as the soldiers rushed by, him leaving him to breathe great clouds of dust they left in their wake. Actually the excitement was mounting inside Ian also. Not so much as seeing the fabled place but that this meant the search was over and they could return home. He was even looking forward to hacking his way back through the jungle again, but this time he knew what was on the other side. Stumbling the last few steps he joined the rest on the top. Straining his eyes in the indicated direction, he could see no shining city, only dots on the far plateau. The guide continued to yell excitedly and nodded his head continually. Urging them to follow, he took off at a dead run down the hillside. Picking up his load Ian followed the rest, but with less enthusiasm than before. "There are no cities of gold," he thought, " this is only a lesson in futility. How many more will you Spaniards torture and kill before you see what fools you are?" The hatred mounted with each step until it became a consuming fire inside. They had separated him from his best friend, one that he looked upon as a brother, murdered innocent people and forced the rest into slavery, and for what? The promise of gold that no one had ever seen but only heard about through legends. "You are indeed an idiot," he muttered looking at the back of Coronado, "a pompous idiot. May you rot in Hell."

Urged ever onward by the speculation of what lay ahead, the once organized army became a mob. Each man, wanting to be the first to claim his share of the golden treasure pushed and shoved those in front. At last they topped the final barrier between themselves and the purported riches. Ahead stood no city of gold, but only adobe buildings filled the plateau.1 Excitement and greed were replaced with disappointment and hate. The poor guide that had urged them on was thrown from the top of the mountain, to land in a broken heap at the bottom of the cliff.

Refusing to give in to defeat the soldiers pounded holes in the mud buildings, in the hope that a thin veneer covered the precious metal, but to no avail. The terrified Indian residents ran in panic, some throwing themselves over the edge and joining the unfortunate guide at the bottom. The survivors were quickly rounded up and herded back to the center of the village. Having seen neither a horse nor muskets before, the terrified villagers cowered as the soldiers ran rampant through the area. Especially frightened by the strange sticks that the whites held to their shoulders and, amazed by the smoke and noise coming from the end, causing holes in whatever it was pointed at. For a fortnight the village was pillaged, sacked and nearly destroyed before Coronado called a halt to the rampage. All there was to show for it all was a few gold trinkets and a bit of ore, while the natives were forced to sit helplessly and watch the destruction of their homes.

By now they were well past the allotted time set by Coronado himself. The days had shortened considerably, and the nights cooled to the point where morning frost formed on the grasses. With no more time to waste the conquistadors became more savage questioning the innocent Indians. When threats to throw a half dozen women and children over the cliff drew no results from the men, the victims were hurled to their deaths. Not understanding exactly what it was the foreigners wanted, all the men could do was stand helplessly by as their loved ones died. Unable to watch the slaughter Ian hid behind the rocks, but nothing shut out the screams that would haunt him forever.

Three more days of inquisition passed with no results. The Spaniards knew that it was now too late to return to the coastal area. Light snow began to fall and the varying hare was a mottled brown and white, winter would soon be upon them. Crowding the Indians into less comfortable places, the invaders occupied the larger houses themselves. The slaves and bondsmen were relegated to the upstairs rooms over the soldiers. Loneliness weighed heavy on Ian and there was little he could do about it. The days were still filled with taking care of the horses and whatever chores were beneath the conquerors. It was the nights that he dreaded. How could a person be so alone in a room full of humanity? The only one that even acted like Ian existed was an Indian slave, brought with the group from the coast. Ian had taken care of a small puncture wound for the fellow a while back. Since that time, whenever the opportunity arose, the man was at Ian's side. Neither spoke the other's language, so usually nothing more than a smile passed between them. As Ian sat against the wall of their room, the man sat beside him and shook Ian's arm.

"Cunga," he said pointing to his chest, "Cunga." Uncertain whether the man was saying his name, or that he was hungry, or exactly what, Ian hesitated to answer. Pounding on his chest with his fist the native repeated, "Cunga."

"Cunga," Ian mimicked, pointing to the man. A smile spread over the brown face and his head nodded so vigorously that Ian wondered if it was attached to his neck? Pounding his own chest as Cunga had done he said, "Ian." So began a strange friendship. Every waking moment that they were together, Ian would attempt to teach the Indian English. In exchange he attempted to learn the dialect spoken by Cunga. Much to his surprise the Indian was learning English far faster than Ian was learning the simple Indian words. Mispronounced words grew into fragmented sentences, but Cunga never gave up and would smile broadly at any word of praise.

"Is good, okay?" He would ask Ian, after he believed that he had mastered a particular word.

"Is good, okay," Ian would assure him that what he had accomplished was acceptable. It was strange how a thing as simple as a word of praise could mean so much to a person. Cunga would try so hard to please Ian and then bask in the smallest praise given him.

One winter evening the two were engaged in their verbal lessons, when Cunga tapped himself on the chest. "Jaguar," he said cupping his hands near his mouth. The roar that came from the man startled Ian. It sounded exactly like the sound he had heard many times while cutting the way through the jungle. Smiling Cunga made other animal sounds. It finally dawned on Ian why the native was learning English so fast. He was only mimicking the sounds Ian was making. He had no Idea what he was saying. So began the process of teaching Cunga what each sound meant. By the time the snow was starting to melt they were able to have a fairly decent conversation with each other.

Preparations were being made to return to the outpost of Culiacan, from where they began their quest. Ian and Cunga were storing supplies in the various packs when the native, for no apparent reason, said to Ian. "Cunga knows a city of gold. My father said about it to me." Taking a stick he drew an X representing where they now were and one higher and to the right. Between them he drew a wavy line connecting the two. "Much gold," he said too loudly, for he was overheard by one of the soldiers.

"Oro," the guard said. "Que oro?" Greed had reared its ugly head again. Ian knew enough Spanish by now to know that oro was the word for gold and que was the word for what.

"Now we're in really deep stuff, Cunga. Why did I ever teach you to speak English?" Taking Ian by an arm and the Indian by the other they were hurried to the house occupied by Coronado. A quick exchange in Spanish between the two and the guard led his leader to the scratching that Cunga had made in the dirt.

Pointing to the top X the excited guard exclaimed, "Oro, Don Coronado, mucho oro." Pointing to a shivering Cunga, the guard identified him as the one who had drawn the map. The two were returned to the house and questioned well into the night. A handful of soldiers, that spoke very little English, were ushered in to help with the translation. Between them and sign language it seemed that Coronado was satisfied that what Cunga was saying was legitimate.

As Ian and Cunga were leaving the building the Indian tripped and fell down the last three steps. Writhing in pain and holding his leg his cries would be heard in London. Rushing to his side Ian lifted the man's head. Cunga motioned for Ian to come closer and as he placed his head nearer he saw a wink and slight smile. "Cunga okay, don't want us should walk. You docator you fix." Looking at the assembled crowd still standing at the top of the steps, Ian shook his head. Breaking an imaginary stick between his two hands, he tried to look as dejected as the situation would let him. Pointing to the still writhing Indian he made the motion of riding a horse. "Can't walk," he explained, hoping that he wasn't signing the man's death warrant. But gold-fever had struck again.

The word spread like wildfire through the camp and by morning every man was ready to leave. Ian was ordered to stay by Cunga's side to interpret what was said and also to look after the broken leg, which Ian had bound with cloth holding two sticks as a make believe splint. When their mounts arrived he was a bit disappointed to find that they were each to ride a small burro, but anything was better than walking. By midmorning the caravan was underway, leaving many jubilant villagers behind. With the burros in the lead they made their way in a northern direction. Patting the neck of his burro Cunga looked at Ian. "Is good, okay?" he said showing his bright teeth in the largest grin that Ian had ever seen.

"Is good, okay," Ian echoed. "I only hope that you know what you are doing," he said under his breath, "or we'll both be in hot water." Cunga kept talking though out the day but Ian only heard, or at least understood, a small portion of it. The native had a habit of mixing the Indian words with English, leaving Ian wondering just what he was saying, but this time Ian's mind was elsewhere. He was wondering what had become of Kale and if his friend was all right? Just to be able to talk with someone in fluent English again would be at the very top of his list of things he wanted. His mind wandered to the many conversations that the two had shared through out their association. Recalling some of Kale's funny stories brought a smile to his face. He was so engrossed in thought that he hadn't realized that Cunga had stopped his animal until he heard his name called. Turning his burro around he returned to where the Indian was now dismounted and standing on his supposedly bad leg. Hurriedly he got off his own beast and bent over as if to examine the splint.

"I'm afraid that we must take a break. I must examine this leg to make sure the bone is set right," he said loudly to Coronado. "There is always the chance of the bone pushing through the skin in this type of injuries." The look on the Spaniards face left no doubt of his disgust at having to stop already but he motioned for his men to rest. Calling his officers together they held a meeting, while occasionally glancing in the direction of the injured man.

"Does your leg give you pain?" Ian asked, loud enough to be heard by the soldiers.

"Pain?" Cunga repeated. "What is pain mean?"

"Pain. Hurt," Ian explained, "does your leg hurt?"

"No pain here," the Indian replied pointing to his leg. "Much pain here," he said rubbing his backsides. "No ride, Cunga walk," he said as he made gestures with his index and middle fingers, as if a man was walking.

"Like heck you'll walk," Ian said emphatically. "I couldn't explain to the soldiers your miraculous recovery. You think your behind is sore now, just wait until I get through kicking it. Now, get back on that mule and behave yourself." In his anger Ian had talked so fast that Cunga couldn't understand what was being said to him, but the tone of Ian's voice left no doubt that he was displeased.

"Is not good, okay?" the native asked looking into Ian's eyes.

"Is not good," Ian said slowly. "Cunga ride no walk. Leg bad, much pain." He felt like a fool speaking Pidgin English, but he knew no other way to make the man understand. Patting the burro's back he repeated, "You ride now." Dejectedly Cunga climbed back on the burro and the journey continued.

Riding behind Cunga's burro gave Ian a good view of the poor wretch ahead. Constantly leaning to one side then the other, shifting forward then back, trying to relieve the pressure on his tortured behind. It had been years since Ian himself had been astride a horse and he was suffering the same as Cunga was. He had the advantage of being able to get off and lead his animal, while poor Cunga had to submit to the constant beating. Catcalls echoed from the Spaniards every time that Ian dismounted, but it matter little what those heathens thought.

Two months into the trek, during a stop for the night, Coronado and some of the men who spoke a little English approached Ian and Cunga. Thoughts of doubt ran through Ian's head as the soldiers drew closer, the firelight played on the hilts of their swords.

"Don Coronado wants to know where we are going and how much longer will it take to get there?" One said in very broken English. "The Don is getting impatient with this savage," he snarled, pointing to Cunga. Ian was filled with indecision. He had no more idea where Cunga was leading them than Coronado did. How could he explain what he didn't know himself? The soldier stood over them tapping his foot, while waiting for an answer.

"Lord," Ian prayed silently, "let Cunga have the answers these men want to hear." All this time the Indian was searching from one face to another, trying to figure out what was happening. "Cunga," Ian said, speaking very slowly. " Don Coronado wants to know how much more are we going? How long?" he asked drawing his hands apart in a gesture indicating distance.

Cunga watched Ian carefully as he spoke, then looked into the faces surrounding them. Hate and distrust were evident in the Spaniards expressions. Shifting his gaze to the open sky he thought for a moment before answering. Making an X in the dirt with his finger, he drew a line upward to another X, the line less than an inch long, to another mark. Pointing to the first one he said, "Village." Following the line in the dirt he stopped at the second, "We here," then to the third, "Gold here. Maybe part day," he said holding up one finger bent in half at the knuckle. Without another word the Spaniards turned and walked away.

Ian noticed terror in the eyes of the Indian and by the expression on his face he was noticeably upset. "Do not be afraid, Cunga. They only want to find the gold you are leading them to."

"No gold," Cunga muttered. At these words Ian jumped to his feet, looking around to see if anyone was within earshot.

"What do you mean, 'No gold?' These people are not playing games. They have followed you for miles because they thought you were taking them to a rich mine. Why did you make up such a story in the first place?'"

"Cunga see what white men do to people of village. Cunga not want to die so he makes story so they not kill him. If he no good they kill him like rest of people, so he make story to look good." Tears of fright were streaming down both cheeks as he finished his confession.

Patting his friend on the bowed head Ian said softly, attempting to sound reassuring. "Don't worry, I will try to think of something to get us both out of this mess." Although he knew deep down that it was easier said than done.

Looking up at Ian Cunga sobbed, "Cunga have Ian in trouble too?"

"Nothing we can't find a way out of. We fooled the Spaniards into believing that your leg was broken, didn't we?" His attempt to lighten the conversation was wasted.

"No want Ian in trouble. Me tell lie, me pay, not Ian." The sobs grew stronger as he spoke. "Ian tell Cunga what do now."

"The first thing we do is go to bed. Let me think about how we can get out of this and I'll tell you in the morning." Pulling Cunga to his feet Ian guided him to his blanket beside the fire. Sleep was slow coming but eventually exhaustion overtook worry and Ian fell asleep, only to be awakened shortly after sunrise, by a sharp jab from the toe of a boot.

Trying to focus his eyes, he was jerked to his feet and propelled to Coronado's camp spot. Bewildered by the events, he waited for the Captain to address him through an interpreter, such as he was.

Looking at Ian the Spanish leader rattled off something then paused for the translation. "Your friend told all and I know he told you too."

"I have no idea what you are talking about," Ian lied, hoping his voice didn't give him away. "I have been asleep and still would be if this man hadn't awakened me. Cunga told you that the gold was just over the next hill, less than a half days ride. What else is there to tell, Sir?"

"He lied about the gold and you knew it too. Someday I will prove it and you will join your friend in Hell." The veins stood out on Coronado's neck like the ropes attached to the ship's sails. "Come, you will see the gold that your Indian was taking us to for yourself. I sent a scouting party to see what is over this next hill."

"Well Laddie," he thought to himself, "it looks like we had best find the fastest way out of here. The first opportunity that shows its self you skedaddle." To his surprise a horse was brought to him in place of the burro and he mounted, following the Spaniards. The trail led through the sage to the rim overlooking a valley below. A hazy smoke drifted over the bottom, but through it Ian could plainly see an Indian village of neatly set teepees. 2

"There is your gold. When I suspected the slave was lying I had him brought to me." The man interpreting hesitated, for Coronado was speaking so fast and in such fury that the poor fellow couldn't keep up. "He was forced to show where the gold was. He came to this spot and with a little persuasion confessed that there was no gold."

Ian was almost afraid to ask the foremost question in his mind. His voice began to quiver as he asked, "And what has become of Cunga?"

Without bothering to translate to Coronado, the soldier made a gesture across his throat with his index finger. "Cut," he said, "dead."

Ian's heart sank, although he had expected that answer. Nodding his head he followed the riders back down the hill. His emotions ran rampant and he fought to keep the tears from forming. Even though his eyes were closed tightly, moisture still found it's way down his cheeks. The ride back to camp was not nearly long enough. He had to prepare for his escape before the Spaniards vented their revenge on him also. He must leave before he did join Cunga.

1 The supposed cities of gold were actually the Indian pueblos of the modern day Zuni tribe in what is now western New Mexico.

2 The Indian slave had led the party from what is now New Mexico to modern day Kansas.

CHAPTER SEVEN.

Thinking of escape and actually doing it were entirely different matters. With all the soldiers watching him constantly, the difficulty seemed nearly insurmountable. Fortunately for Ian, their numbers had dwindled. Some, believing the gold still existed, had deserted, while sickness had also thinned the ranks. No longer having the luxury of the burro, Ian was relegated to walking again, which gave him much time to ponder his course. Bit by bit the escape plan began to formulate in his brain. At every opportunity he would hide small pieces of essential articles whenever the procession stopped. Piling rocks in the same pattern at every hiding spot, the guards believed that he was simply passing time.

"Muy loco," they would laugh at him. It got to be a joke among the conquistadors as they watched the crazy Englishman dig holes in the earth, only to cover them up again. Whenever he was certain that he was being watched, Ian would do just that. Dig a hole in the earth, and then carefully push the soil back into the empty cavity and pile rocks on top. Powder horns, percussion caps, musket balls and a knife had been buried so far. The larger items presented more of a challenge, so Ian decided to take them just before his escape attempt.

Two weeks into the return trip, Ian had enough supplies buried behind him to start thinking seriously of departing his present company. For once things seemed to be going his way. He was assigned to help with the meals for the men. Which meant that he not only had enough to eat for himself, he was able to sneak some away for later. Taking only what wouldn't spoil his larder grew. Now all he had to do was wait for the perfect opportunity to present it's self, and he didn't have long to wait. A few days later they had stopped for the noon meal and Ian was sent to collect firewood. Carrying an armload of twigs he was also carrying a branch, as big around as his forearm and four foot long, over his shoulder. Nearing the circle of soldiers he spotted a rattlesnake laying across his path. With a blood-curdling scream he swung the branch repeatedly, until the reptile was nothing more than a part of the parched ground. Still he kept hitting it, much to the enjoyment of those watching.

"Hombre es muy loco," one said as he waved his finger in tight circles near his head. The rest laughed and mimicked Ian, swinging imaginary clubs at the ground.

"Laugh, you braying jackasses," Ian thought to himself. "As long as you think I'm crazy, I can do almost anything strange and get away with it." Picking up the pile of twigs and holding the stick before him he walked to the fire, carefully studying the ground before him at every step. Again the mimicking started as one man gingerly walked on his tiptoes and danced around Ian. Ignoring his antics, Ian went in search of more wood, poking the club into every piece of sagebrush as he neared it. For the rest of the day he continued a mock search for snakes, the branch on his shoulder. Nightfall found him sitting with his back against a cedar, legs drawn up until his chin nearly rested on his knees and the branch gripped tightly in his hands. His head continually swept from side to side mumbling incoherently, as if demons that would pounce on him undetected from the underbrush.

"Cover your head with this, fool," the guard that spoke broken English said, throwing the canvas used to cover the food supplies at Ian's feet. "El Diablo will not find you then." The audience grew thinner and still Ian sat in the same position, moving only his head from side to side. In the eyes of the Spaniards the sight of the snake had unhinged the mind of the Englishman. When the rest went to bed Ian was left in that position, much to his delight. He was far enough away from the group to be able to move about unencumbered. This night was perfect for what Ian knew he must do. The half moon threw just enough light to cast broad shadows for him to hide in. The Spaniards had chosen to camp by a fast rushing river, nestled in the narrow valley between two low-lying foothills. The noise of the water rushing over the rocks would cover anything but the loudest sounds. The mournful wail of coyotes, calling to one another from near the camp, caused the horses to become restless. Their whinnies of fear echoed from the walls of the hills.

"It's now or never," Ian said to himself, as he rose from his seat under the tree. He had watched to see where the one to guard the camp was posted, before the rest turned in for the night. He also knew that there was only one guard at camp and one guarding the horses, quite a ways down the draw. Propping the canvas against the tree, he tried to make it resemble a man sitting with it over his head and body. Satisfied that it was as good as it was going to get, he nearly crawled to the base of the large rock that the camp guard leaned against. Putting all of his weight behind the swing, he brought his snake killing stick behind the man's right ear. The only sound he made, was as he slumped down the rock and landed face down in the dirt. Ian was fortunate in that this man was one of only thirteen that carried the matchlock musket. Taking his matchlock, knife, powder and shot, Ian slipped back into the shadows.

The prairie wolves, as the Indians called coyotes, were now in full chorus. Ian caught an occasional glance of one slipping like a ghost through the brush above him. Being a novice to this strange land, he hoped that the beasts were not in the habit of eating humans. Working his way downhill he eventually came to the box canyon where the horses were kept. He knew that a shot would spell disaster for him; he left the rifle and all the gear behind. Holding the club in one hand and the large knife in the other, he crept toward the guard, whose attention was on the animals and attempting to calm them down. The Spaniard was so engrossed with the horses that he neither saw nor felt the blow that rendered him unconscious. Removing the soldiers clothing, Ian rolled them onto a ball and laid the high boots on top of the pile, along with his crossbow, two dozen or so darts and knife.

"If I'm going to steal horses I may as well be hung for a lion as a mouse," Ian thought to himself, eyeing the white stallion belonging to Coronado himself. Selecting a stout Black for a packhorse Ian put on the blanket then the packsaddle. Gathering what gear he had accumulated, which included some of the cooking pots and pans he had been sent to wash earlier, he loaded them onto the rack. The horse stood stoically as Ian finished and threw the canvas cover over the top and tied it securely. The White threw his head as Ian attempted to put the Spanish bit into his mouth. Patting the animal's head Ian soothed him with soft words. "I don't blame you, big one. I wouldn't want such a contraption shoved in my mouth either." The horse settled down and soon he was bridled and saddled.

The clouds were playing games with the moon, sending shadows scurrying back and forth across the valley. Cutting the tether ropes from a half dozen horses, Ian led them out of the canyon and down the trail away from the camp. Many times he did this before all of the animals were released. After retrieving the articles he had taken from the first guard, he returned to where he had left the two horses that he was taking. He mounted the white one and, taking the lead rope attached to the black, he picked his way to where the others of the herd were quietly munching prairie grass. Looking around he made certain that he had gathered everything. Getting a firm hold on the lead rope he dug his heels into the sides of his mount. A sharp slap of the reins and the white reared back on his back legs as he bolted forward, nearly throwing Ian to the ground. Holding the matchlock high in the air Ian screamed as loud as he could and fired. Running straight toward the grazing horses he frightened the poor animals into a panicked stampede. The last Ian saw of them in the moonlight, they were in a head long run over the far hill.

"Now, you Spaniards will know what it is to walk on this miserable ground." With a smile he took one last look toward the camp and set his course on the back-trail. "I've done it now and there's no turning back." Patting his horse's neck he added, "Just get me as far away from this place as you can, old boy. If I get caught I'll get the same thing they gave to Cunga and I'd appreciate being spared that bit of Spanish humor." A tug on the rope running behind him told Ian that the packhorse was having a hard time keeping up. "Sorry old boy," he said softly as he reined the white to a canter. "I don't want to wear you out. There's no way I could carry all that stuff without you." He wondered if perhaps he should have taken an extra horse just in case, but it was too late now. "Seeing as how we three are going to be traveling companions I guess I'd best find names for you two. You'll be Blanco," he said patting his mount, "and you'll be Negre. Pretty clever huh? Spanish for white and black. I admit it isn't fancy but at least I won't have to be calling you, 'Hey horse number one and number two.' I'd likely forget which was which.'"

The trail turned and wound through the flat sage covered prairie as Ian searched the ground for the telltale rock mounds that denoted a hiding place of supplies. He remembered close to where he had buried them, but in the moonlight every bush and rock resembled the next one. He had slowed his pace, as he knew it would be hours before the Spaniards could find enough horses to round up the rest. By that time he would be miles away and even if they came after him, there were enough draws, canyons and mesas to hide in that they would never find him.

The moon was setting before he found the first pile of rocks. Dismounting, he removed the rocks and began to dig in the soft earth. " I wonder what treasure I have buried here?" he said aloud. " Treasure", what a strange word. When this quest began, the treasure was the Seven Cities of Cibola, with their gleaming walls of gold. Even Ian, who would not share in the wealth, had looked forward to seeing them. Now his treasures were simple items that he needed for survival. Not far into the hole he uncovered a spoon and a small bag of salt. "I couldn't buy these in this place with all the Seven Cities of Gold," he thought. "Strange how ones values change with the situation." Satisfied there was nothing else in the hole, he mounted and started again.

Even with frequent stops for rest, Negre was beginning to lag behind and Ian knew the poor animal was getting too tired to continue. At the first site that offered both protection and where he could watch his back-trail, Ian pulled the animals to a halt. The packhorse was the first to get his attention. Removing the canvas cover he slowly removed each article, deciding if it was a complete necessity before placing it in one of two piles. He knew that only the most precious items could be carried. If he overloaded the pack animal, the beast would not make the trek and he would lose almost everything. Keeping one frying pan, two metal pots, two bags of powder and shot, three spoons, two goatskin water bags, an extra tarp and two dozen bolts for the crossbow, Ian discarded the rest. His bedroll was tucked behind his saddle, as was the matchlock musket and the extra clothes from the guards. The crossbow hung from the saddle horn.

"That ought to ease the pressure on your back," he said as he wiped the foamy sweat from the black's sides and back. After taking care of the animals, and hobbling them for the night, Ian looked after his own needs. Afraid to have a fire, for fear that the Spaniards were indeed following after him, he ate a meager meal consisting of a handful of ground cornmeal and dried berries. Happy that he had thoughtfully relieved the soldiers of a bag full of their mornings breakfast, he washed each mouthful down with a sip of water. The gentle breeze wafted through the sage as Ian stared at the starry sky. He wondered if Kale was looking at the same sky and thinking of him also. It had been such a long time since he had heard his friend's voice that he had to strain to remember exactly what it sounded like. It was in this reminiscent state that sleep overtook Ian.

Colleen was awakening him by blowing her warm breath on his neck, as she had done so often. Smiling, Ian turned to kiss her full lips. Opening his eyes he was startled to find Blanco had wandered over to his bedroll and was nuzzling Ian. "You are a poor excuse for a beautiful woman," Ian said as he drew the blanket over his head, but the animal wouldn't give up. Sweeping the covers from over his head Ian sat straight up, "You win," he shouted. Patting the extended nose as he rolled from bed. "You Spaniards sure have a poor sense of timing. I was in the arms of a gorgeous lady and wake up to a face that would give Satan himself a scare."

Once more checking the articles that he was leaving behind, Ian packed the black and saddled Blanco. The sun was barely over the horizon when he pulled up camp. One rolling hill after another greeted him as he continued the trail back to where Cunga had been slain. He really did not wish to go there but he had stashed supplies all along the road, even though he couldn't remember exactly what. The monotonous scenery began to lull him into a sleepy state and he fought to keep his eyes open. Just as he was dozing he spotted another pile of rocks. Climbing from the horse he hurriedly dug beneath them, only to find an empty hole.

"I not only outsmarted the Spanish, I outsmarted myself," he muttered. "I should have marked the empty ones different, now I'll waste time digging for nothing. Oh well, I guess I can't be expected to think of everything." Climbing aboard Blanco he whistled an Irish tune as he led Negre on toward the next hill before them.

The next three holes yielded little that Ian wished to take up space with. He kept a rawhide rope and more dried cornmeal, the rest he threw into the brush. The days ran together and still nothing, except the rolling hills of prairie grass and sage. On the fifth day, since running from the Spaniards camp, Ian topped a high mesa and stopped the horses so violently that Blanco reared back on his hind legs. The entire countryside below him was a mass of moving brown creatures. Ian had seen bison before on the trek up, but never in such numbers. As far as he could see was nothing but animals, slowly grazing and as one disappeared over the hill two more seemed to take its place. The beasts appeared to be rather complacent and sluggish as they moved about.

"It's been a long time since I've had any fresh meat," he said softly as he drew the matchlock from behind the saddle. From his vantage point he could see forever behind him and there was no sign of anyone following him. Loading the musket he carefully filled the pan with powder and, after tying the horses, started down toward the herd. Carefully working his way through the draws and washes he finally succeeded in getting near the outer fringes. Drawing back the hammer he held the heavy weapon braced on his knee, lined up the sight on the shoulder of the nearest bison and pulled the trigger. Expecting the thunderous explosion that usually followed, Ian was puzzled when there was only a metallic click. His target simply raised its head at the noise and went back to grazing.

Checking the musket Ian saw a bit of moisture had gathered in the pan and this prevented the weapon from firing. Hurriedly wiping it dry he poured more powder in the pan and replaced the firing fuse. Lifting the heavy rifle once more he was disappointed to find that the animals had grazed beyond the range of his musket ball. Again he began the stalk until he was within seventy-five yards of the nearest animal. Holding steady on the shoulder he again pulled the trigger. The flash in the pan and resulting noise sent the bison into a headlong stampede. The entire herd turned as one and the thunder of the hooves sent shock waves throughout the valley, as they disappeared from sight, all except one. His fresh meat lay where it had stood but a few moments before. Racing back to the horses Ian gathered the reins and returned to his task ahead.

Surprised by the enormity of the animal, Ian wondered what he had gotten himself into. The largest thing that he had ever butchered was a sheep. "I guess they're all the same inside," he mumbled as he made the first cut. Two hours later he was satisfied with the results of his labors. The skin hung over the sage and the hump and a hindquarter were carved into pieces for cooking. Wrapping the meat into the extra tarp, he rolled the skin into a loose roll. When he attempted to lift the green hide he was surprised to find how heavy it was. "Can't ask you to pack this too, there Negre. This thing weighs as much as everything else on your back." Having no immediate use for the hide he discarded it along with the rest of the carcass. The meat was hung outside of the pack-frame and he resumed his journey once more.

Returning to the trail he soon found the first pile of rocks that he had made. This hole contained a woven reed basket, into which he quickly transferred the meat. The loose weave would allow the air to circulate and somewhat retard the meat souring, at least until he could smoke it.

The sky became dark and threatening as he topped the ridge overlooking the Indian village, where Coronado had taken him. Where the tepees had stood was now deserted and the poles that once held the skins now stood as skeletons dotting the landscape. For as far as the eye could see was horizon, with nothing to break the flatness of the land but an occasional slight bump in the prairie. The vast emptiness made Ian feel more alone and added to his uneasiness. Uncertain as which way to go next, he weighed the options. One thing certain, he couldn't go south or he would take a chance of running into Coronado's men. Many of the deserting soldiers had continued north, so that left east or west.

"Tell you what we'll do fellows," Ian said to the horses. "I'll let you decide which way we'll go. If you turn left at the bottom we'll go west, if it's right we'll head east. First though I need to see if the Indians left anything I can use behind." Mounting again, he headed Blanco downhill and eventually the trail wound into the deserted village. An eerie silence greeted him as he made his way through the abandoned place. The only sound, other than the incessant wind, was the growling deep in his stomach. It reminded him of the fact that he hadn't eaten in a long time and the buffalo meat hanging in the basket. Stopping at a spot, in the center of what once had been the village, Ian dismounted and tied the horses to a log drying rack. Shards of dried meat still clung to the wood. Unpacking the horses he led them to a slow running stream, which ran through the outer edge of where the tepees once stood. A welcome sight Ian soon was shed of the clothes, bloody from cleaning the bison, and was sitting in the cold water. The caked mess was harder to remove than he had imagined and his skin burned from repeated applications of sand. Finally satisfied that the last of it was cleaned from his hair and beard, he climbed from the creek. His teeth chattered as he let the breeze dry his body, while he attempted to wash his clothing.

Once he was dressed in the dry clothes he had taken from one of the soldiers, he decided to try on the thigh length boots. They were about one size too large but, by leaving his moccasins on, they were comfortable enough but the high length bothered him. When he tried to remove them he found that it was nearly impossible. When he bent his leg to pull at the heel the boot bound behind his knee. After many exasperating attempts he started at the top and pulled the boot down his leg, much as a snake sheds its skin. Taking the sharpest of the knives he cut the top away, just below the knee, on each boot. About to discard the top scraps, he remembered something that his father had used at home. Cutting a four-inch wide strip lengthwise, he had a ready-made strop for keeping a keen edge on his blades.

"Not too bad for a novice in this country," he proudly displayed his invention. There were plenty of pieces of wood for his fire and soon bison chunks, impaled on a green stick, hung over a blaze. Cutting the rest into thin strips, he placed them on rocks close enough to the fire that they would dry. The dark clouds had gradually disappeared and the sun was peeking from behind the clouds. Checking on the horses Ian was satisfied that they were, as his father used to put it, "In Irish heaven," Miles of more miles of lush prairie grass for them to graze on. "You two aren't going to want to leave this place," he chuckled.

By the time the meat had lost the pink inside Ian was ravenous. Taking the stick from the fire he cut a bite-size piece and threw it from hand to hand until it cooled. The meat was surprisingly tender, for coming from such a large animal, coarse in texture but very flavorful. Carrying the meat in one hand, he began to search the deserted camp. Bits and pieces of unknown articles were all that were to be found. When he had covered nearly half of the empty shells, that once had been homes to these people, he was about to quit looking further. As he was about to return to the horses, something flapping in the breeze caught his eye. Working his way around the poles he saw a discarded buffalo robe. The hair was worn in most places to the point of being nonexistent. Picking up the skin, Ian was surprised to find the difference in weight between this tanned and the green pelt he had left behind. Further searching led to scraps of tanned skins and a pointed bone awl, poked through the edge of one piece.

By the time he had covered the entire village the sun was nearly ready to disappear. Returning to the horses he passed a mound of rocks. Not a natural formation but one quite similar to the ones he had put by the trail. Carefully removing the flat top cover he peered into the dark space. Much to his delight the entire structure was filled with dried corn and berries.

Hurrying back to the fire he grabbed the reed basket. There would be no need to have the meat inside it now that it was dried. It didn't take him long to fill the container, he then carefully replaced the top lid.

"Sorry about taking your stores, folks," Ian muttered. "I don't know who named you, 'Savages,' but they sure didn't know you." He had never bothered to think much about the ones that had occupied this space. To him they had been faceless nothings that lived beneath skin coverings, over poles stuck into the ground. He had not stopped to consider that they too were living, breathing humans, much like Cunga or even himself. These were not any savages. They were opportunists that took what nature, and the earth, had to offer. Yet, only took what they could use at that particular time. Ian felt guilty for wasting so much of the bison, but he had to live also.

Lost in thought, Ian hadn't noticed that the sun was setting. Before he had completely tended to the animals, darkness fell like a wick of a lantern being turned down, until the flame flickers and dies. Stoking the fire gave him enough light to hobble the horses and prepare his own bedroll. Having lost all faith in the matchlock, he placed the crossbow next to him. Tomorrow he would have to seriously consider even bothering to keep the cumbersome musket any longer, but tonight he was too tired to worry about it. Rolling up in the blanket, he threw the newly found buffalo robe over him. A stomach full of broiled meat and the gentle breeze through the grass lulled him to sleep.

A steady drizzle of rain beating on the buffalo hide awakened Ian. Uncovering his head, he could barely make out a faint glow in the eastern sky. Casting a glance at the horses, he was satisfied that they were safe, so back under the covers he went to attempt a few more minutes of sleep. The next time he opened his eyes, the rain had stopped and the prairie was covered in a misty ground fog. "Great shades of the moors of home," he exclaimed. "Tis like the meadows of the old sod, it tis." It had been so long since he had used the brogue, that it now sounded foreign to him. Shaking the accumulated water from the skin, he rolled it and placed it with the other things to be packed on Negre. The horses were content to munch grass, as Ian loaded them in preparation for the journey.

Once the horses were readied, Ian took one more look around to see if there was anything more that would be of use to him. Satisfied that he had everything, he started to mount Blanco. His foot in the stirrup he saw the butt plate of the musket behind the saddle. Taking his foot from the stirrup, he pulled the matchlock free and examined the weapon. The flash pan was soaking wet and the water had run into the workings of the beastly thing, wetting the powder. In frustration Ian grabbed it by the long barrel and was about to throw it as far into oblivion as possible. A cooler head prevailed and he studied the pros and cons of such a move. The crossbow was more dependable but the musket, when it worked properly, had a greater range and more hitting power. It's twenty pounds plus made it heavy to carry, but the .66 caliber ball would drop anything within one hundred yards. Shaking his head, Ian replaced the musket behind the saddle and, once again, placed his booted foot into the stirrup and swung himself onto Blanco's back.

"Well old boy, the next decision is up to you. Do we go east, or do we go west. I've heard of horse sense and now it's time for you to use yours. The way my luck has run in the past, I'd sure choose the wrong way." With that Ian gave the stallion a nudge in the ribs and looped the reins loosely over the saddle horn. "You lead, I'll follow," he said in a sing-song voice. The horse stayed on a due north course and Ian was about to make the decision for him, when the trail turned abruptly to the left and Blanco followed it's course. "West it is," Ian said patting the horse in the neck, the warm sun casting shadows before them.

The infernal flatlands seemed to go on forever. Day after day of the same sights began to play on Ian's nerves. The only saving grace was the multitude of game animals and birds. Not a day passed that he didn't see roaming herds of bison or deer. Early one morning he jumped a larger animal, resembling the red stags of his homeland. The magnificent beast ran with his antlers nearly touching the light-colored tail patch. There was one near encounter with a she bear and two cubs, but her bluff didn't work and she ambled off leaving a shaken Ian behind.

On the twenty-third day, since leaving the deserted Indian village, the scenery began to change dramatically. The flatlands gave way to rolling hills, which in turn to steeper crags and valleys. The trees became thicker and the game-trails more numerous. He had followed well-worn trails up to this point, so he chose the most used ones as he began climbing. Three days later he stood at the foot of the highest mountain that he could ever imagine existed. The peaks in the distance looked foreboding as he gazed at the rocky surfaces. Surely nothing could climb over such an obstacle, however the distinct game-trails told otherwise.

"I think we've earned a rest before we tackle this one. What say ye lads?" By the time the sun was directly overhead the horses were taken care of and a small fire was boiling water in one of the Spaniard's pots. Adding a handful of the dried corn, a pinch of salt and a double handful of dried meat, Ian soon had a thin soup cooking. The corn was still a bit crunchy, as he savored the meal, but that made little difference. It was tasty and above all nourishing and, when the last of the broth was gone, Ian felt content.

Leaning his back against a large fir he gazed at the task ahead. The peaks seemed to be insurmountable, as one rose just a bit higher than the last. He was even tempted to turn around and go back the way he came, but he was even more uncertain what he would run into if he did. He had come this far, and now it appeared the only way to go was up. A broad game trail wound ahead and then branched into several narrower ones, each heading in a different direction. His challenge would be to choose the one that offered him the safest, and least complicated, route. He was well aware that one false step and there would be no help for him. The loneliness was one thing that he had never considered, before taking off on his own, but then he didn't have much choice in the matter. The one person he trusted enough to take along, now lay dead somewhere near the Indian village. He envisioned Cunga's smiling face and his eagerness to please. His thoughts then turned to Kale. Had he met the same fate as Cunga, or had he managed to escape also?

"Wherever you are, old boy, I hope you're in a better position than I am right now. I'm looking at a mountain that's higher than the entire country of Great Britain if you stood it on end. This must be where God piled everything he had left over when he made this earth." It struck Ian that he had used the word, "God," and credited Him with the creation. Perhaps he wasn't as devout a nonbeliever as he had previously thought. "That's an interesting thought, one that I will have to pursue further." Again looking at the seemingly impossible journey before him, he added, "And I'll have plenty of time to do it in."

It was time for his daily cleaning of the musket. As much as he hated the weapon it was a necessity, and one that had to be taken care of like a newborn baby. If the time ever came that he had to depend on it, he wanted everything to function as it should. The only moving parts were the trigger and the hammer and the constant cleanings had removed most of the lubrication from them.

"I guess it's time to see how good an Indian I'd make," Ian said aloud, then he laughed at talking to himself. "Well, there isn't anyone else around to talk to, so I'll babble to myself." Finding a fallen log, he laid the bison skin over it and lay the musket on top of it. By careful trimming he didn't lose much of the valuable hide. Folding it double length-wise, he used the point of his knife to start a hole then punched the bone awl through both sides. It was a time consuming process, but eventually he had holes down both sides and across the bottom. Next he cut narrow strips from the hide and laced them through the holes. When he was finished he was indeed proud of the crude scabbard he had made. At least the matchlock would be protected from the weather, thus saving the daily cleaning.

Another day was coming to a close as Ian tended to his horses. Making certain there was sufficient forage for them and water to satisfy their thirst, then hobbling them for the night. A bond of affection had grown between him and the animals, and he doted over them like a mother hen. Besides being his only companions they were also his main means of survival, a fact that Ian was more than well aware of. Banking the fire for the night he leaned back on his bedroll. The clean mountain air was sweeter than any he could remember. Little did he dream, when he was in that that cell in debtor's prison or the coalmines of Wales, he would be free in such a beautiful place. All that seemed so long ago and now there was no past for Ian Connor, only the unknown future.

CHAPTER EIGHT.

The trail led through stands of black pines, juniper and scrub-oak so thick that Ian had to dismount and lead the horses through the maze of branches. Deer beds were found in every opening large enough to accommodate the animal. Pinehens and grouse fled before them, as well as rabbits and an occasional wild turkey. Seeing the food was not a problem, hitting it with the bolt from the crossbow was. Ian was still inept at using the weapon, but was improving with practice. A lucky shot would put enough fresh meat in the pot for a day or two at a time.

Ian was aware that the dried corn and berries would last but a short time, so he began to experiment with a few wild greens. Watching what the animals ate he would attempt small portions to see if they made him ill, so far none had. He had been able to find some that he could identify. Twice he had located wild onions and once wild asparagus was growing by a stream. Wild currents were plentiful, as were gooseberries and wild blueberries, if he could get to them before the bears did. These he collected and dried as many as the reed bag would hold. Acorn could be found in the oak thickets and Ian found that, by boiling them and then mashing the nutmeat, they made tasty flour. The only problem was the acorns were also the favorite of the large deer population, so they could be hard to gather.

It was on one of these forages for food that he encountered the strangest creature to date. Early that morning the trail had topped a ridge and below was a bowl-shaped valley. The bottom was covered with lush green grasses, while stands of aspen ran from the far hillside to a stream wandering through the meadow. Ponds formed at several intervals and he could plainly see deer feeding at the water's edge. The beauty and serenity of the place mesmerized Ian as he followed the game trail to the bottom. Finding a shady spot for the horses, with feed and water nearby, was not a difficult task. Everywhere one looked there was ample grass and the small tributaries, flowing from the stream, meandered through the valley.

Once the horses were looked after, Ian took the crossbow and started out to investigate this paradise further. Following the stream, to find it's origin, he worked his way through a grove of aspen. The ground became marshier than before and, as he neared the edge of the trees, he saw the strange brown animal. It was about two feet tall, very stocky and was standing on its back legs, while the front feet grasped a sapling. As Ian watched, the creature was actually chewing through the small tree, the large incisors taking chips with every bite. If not for the flat tail Ian would have suspected it was some giant form of rat, which frequented much of England. Moving around the tree the varmint had chewed a circle through the wood, wide at the top and bottom and narrowing at the center. When there was not sufficient center to hold the weight, the small tree fell. The creature grasped the narrow trunk in his mouth and began to drag it to the edge of a pond, where he manipulated it into the water. Towing the sapling, he swam toward a dam of the same material.

Fascinated by the critter's ability, Ian moved closer for a better observation point. His movement startled the animal and it released its burden and dove beneath the surface of the pond. The last thing to disappear was the flat tail, which slapped the water with a resounding clap that echoed throughout the valley.

"I don't know what they call you, but you are the darndest thing these eyes have ever seen." Ian shouted at the departing rodent. "Seen, seen, seen," his voice came back from the bowls rim. Smiling at the echo, Ian tried it again. It was nice to hear a human voice again, even if it was his own. Following the stream uphill, he saw fish in some of the deep pools, but his attempts to get one failed. He hadn't tasted fresh fish since the coalmines of Wales and his mouth watered for some now. He even tried shooting a bolt from the crossbow into one, but the refracted light gave him a false target and it swam off unscathed, losing the dart in the process. As much as he wanted to be exploring, his belly told him that it was time to put something into it. Like in any Eden, there were bound to be dangers and he had traveled farther from the horses than he had intended.

Hurrying back to where the horses grazed, Ian came to a small tributary that was only a few inches deep. To his surprise there were fish, their backs and sides out of the water, attempting to swim against the flow. Their bright-colored bodies twisting and turning to gain every inch of headway. Using his hands as a scoop, he soon had four fish flopping on the grassy bank. Cutting a willow he hung them together and hurried faster to the horses.

"Fresh fish today," he announced proudly, his appetite growing with every step. Both Blanco and Negre were contentedly browsing and only lifted their heads at his approach, then resumed eating. Ian had to move up the hill, before finding a suitable place to build a fire to cook his meal. The blaze of twigs soon had the skin on all four fish a golden brown. In no time there only remained a pile of bones and crisp tails of his catch. "A full belly, clean air, plenty of game and best of all freedom. What else could a man ask for?" These were the thoughts going through Ian's mind as he lay back and studied the blue sky above the rim of the bowl. "Perhaps I have found the end of my search for a place to settle down." Closing his eyes he formed plans as to where his cabin would be, the corral for the horses and perhaps a smokehouse out back. The combination of a full stomach, the warm clean air and visions of a wonderful future soon lulled Ian to sleep.

The first drops of rain that hit his face awakened him. The sky, that had been so cloudless when he dozed off, was now dark and threatening. Before he could get under the cover of the trees the downpour drenched him. Back home Ian had seen many drizzles and an occasional hard rain, but never anything like this. The mountains echoed with thunder and bolts of lightening shot from peak to peak. Cursing himself for his stupidity, in not bothering to find some kind of shelter before falling asleep, he huddled beneath the green canopy of leaves. The continuous crack of lightening began to agitate the horses, so Ian ran to them and brought them with him under the trees. Between claps of thunder his soothing voice and gentle petting hand settled them as he held their reins.

It was well after dark when the first signs of any letup in the downpour appeared. Gradually tapering off, then renewing itself with a vengeance until Ian was beginning to think it would go on forever. Just when he thought that he would have to spend the rest of the night under the tree, the rain ceased as quickly as it had started. Picking his way ever so slowly toward the hill where he had built the fire, Ian led the horses. Feeling with the toe of his boot before taking a step, he finally made his way to where the terrain began its uphill climb. Shivering from cold it was all he could do to gather dead kindling and pile it for a fire. Pouring a small amount of the precious gunpowder onto a patch of cloth, he carefully placed it on the kindling then added dried shavings over the top. A single swipe of the tinderbox and the powder caught fire to the fine slivers of wood. Soon he was adding heavier sticks to the blaze and holding his numb fingers over the warming fire. Steam rose from his wet clothing, as he slowly turned a different part of his anatomy to the flames. For the rest of the miserable night the rain started on and off again, while Ian fought to keep the fire going.

When daylight finally came, the heavy clouds hung so low in the valley that they obscured the other side. Instead of the beautiful sight that had first greeted him, a gray haze clouded the scene. "Perhaps," Ian thought, "this isn't Paradise after all. Beauty won't feed a body, or keep it warm during winter." He decided that once the sky cleared, and he could see where he was going, he would continue on. His main concern now had to be his animals. The night had been as hard on them as it was on him.

By close to noon the haze lifted and Ian saw miniature waterfalls, dropping from the high points to the bottom of the basin. This added beauty could also mean a more treacherous path out of the valley. The gushes of water had caused great sections of earth to slide, blocking some of the trails. Not wishing to be caught again, he hurriedly divided the load between the two horses and began the exodus from his Eden. Walking ahead of Blanco, he led the animals over mounds of mud and rocks where a well-worn game trail once had been. Fighting for every step, he had barely gone half way to the top when he had to rest. The rarefied air made his lungs feel as though they would burst, and his legs had a hard time holding him erect. Sitting on a large rock, Ian looked over the valley. Rainbows formed in the mist between the waterfalls and the air smelled fresher than ever before. He was seriously tempted to turn around and go back down but, after a short argument with himself, he continued on. By mid-afternoon he reached the crest. Casting a final look at the valley below he followed the rim for a short way, then dropped over the other side.

In the weeks ahead Ian was surprised to discover many valleys as beautiful as the first. By now he had become rather proficient at hitting game with the bolts from the crossbow. The dried corn had long since been eaten and there were fewer berries this time of the year. Meat and an occasional tuber or pinion nuts made up most of his diet. Fortunately the horses were in excellent condition, and Ian patted himself on the back for stealing only the best. With nowhere in particular to go, and no set time to get there, Ian enjoyed his freedom. Frequent stops for rest, and even a few wasted days, bolstered his spirits and rested the horses. This was the way he worked his way to the top of the highest part of his trek. The summit lay just ahead and the anticipation to find what was on the other side grew with each step.

Being well above the timberline, the country was less hospitable and most of the beauty lay below. He felt as though his lungs would never get enough of the thin air, and if he over-exerted his head would spin wildly. He knew that just beyond the crest lay the Utopia that he hoped for. His heart sank in his chest as he gazed over what lay ahead. Nearly a mirror image of what he had just spent the past several weeks leaving. Below were the same black pines that had greeted him on the other side. Numerous hills and valleys descended like giant steps for as far as he could see. This had to be the place Kale had mentioned, for it truly had to be, "Beyond the edge of nowhere." Dejectedly, he sat and looked at the journey ahead and wondered at the wisdom of this whole thing. It was way too late to turn back now.

Ian then remembered a little trick that he had used way back when he was first put in debtor's prison. "Don't dwell on unpleasant thoughts." It had worked then and should work now. Picking up the reins he started off downhill, whistling a jaunty Irish tune as he went. Before long he found that he couldn't both whistle and breathe enough air at the same time, so he was content to simply have the songs run through his mind. Resting often he reached the timberline well before dark. Having learned one hard lesson, he always left enough time to find a suitable place to spend the night. The many caves and crannies, that dotted the hillsides were his choice, but anyplace that offered protection from the elements would do. So far he hadn't had any unpleasant surprises when sleeping in one of the caves. Once he was certain that it wasn't occupied, at that precise moment, he immediately kept a fire going at the mouth. This served a dual purpose. Most caves were cold inside and, more important, the fire deterred any wild critter from ending up in bed with him.

This night he had to settle for a soft bed of fallen pine needles beneath a deadfall tree. The nights were getting cooler and the days noticeably shorter. While he longed for a warm fire, he didn't dare have one in the thick pines, so this evening he had a cold camp. With nothing to pass the time, Ian rolled up in the blanket and pulled the buffalo robe over him. A silent, "Thank you," passed his lips for the faceless Indian that had left it behind. An early start in the morning wouldn't hurt, as he wanted to try to be in the lower hills as soon as possible. Even if he ran the horses all day, there was no way that he could be out of these mountains by the time the first snow fell. He must find a place where he could have shelter, water and food available for both him and the animals.

Either exhaustion from the journey thus far, the darkness in the pines or a combination of the two found Ian still sleeping well after daybreak. It was the whinnies of the horses that finally woke him. The grass was sparse, where he had camped, and he had to find something better. Once the horses were loaded they worked their way through the heavy timber. Often having to backtrack because the deadfalls became so thick that they had to find another way around. Gradually the trees thinned and Ian could see another valley below. The sides and bottom were covered with aspen, their green leaves changed to splotches of reds, oranges, and yellows. At the edge of the pines the grass grew more abundantly, so here Ian let the horses rest and graze as he watched the canyon below.

The mountains did not seem as steep the further down he went; in fact some were nothing more than high rolling hills. Two days, after mounting the summit of the high top, he could see the land in the distance definitely started to flatten out. His calculations put him there in about four more days and not a moment too soon. The winds started to shift from the north, and when the cold rain fell the droplets were thick and on the verge of turning to snow. There was no more time for sightseeing, and Ian pushed himself and the horses to reach the lowlands as soon as possible. If he didn't locate a place, and get it ready before heavy snow fell, neither he nor the animals would make it through the winter.

Ian's calculations were one day off. Instead of four days it took five to reach the rolling hills of the lowlands. Fortunately the weather had held, in fact it was nearly balmy. Finding a high overlook, where the face dropped sharply to the valley below, he scanned the area for a place to call home for this winter. Seeing one or two places that looked promising, he unpacked both horses. Throwing the canvas cover over a juniper tree to mark the spot, he left most of his belongings beneath it. With Negre in tow he rode Blanco down the hill.

The narrow game trail meandered through the cedars, junipers and aspen. In the bottoms an occasional fir grew above the rest. His eyes shifting from side to side, Ian searched for signs of game that may inhabit the area. Dropping onto the valley floor, the trail made an oblique turn to the right then forked. One trail went slightly to the left, while the other followed along the base of the overlook, where Ian had left his belongings. Dense growths of various trees and brush grew tightly against the base of the cliff face and a small stream wound it's way downhill. A narrow trail disappeared into the underbrush, while the most used followed the contour of the hill. The best possible camp spots seemed to be to the left trail, so that was the one that Ian took.

The first place he scouted was too far away from fresh water. He knew that when the freezing winter came, he might be snowbound for a lengthy period of time. Turning in his saddle he looked back to see if the canvas marker was visible. From there he could get his bearings on the next place he had chosen. When he finally reached the bottoms nothing looked as it had from above. The white canvas was quite visible as it flapped in the breeze. The next spot to scout would be slightly west and downhill from where he was now. Just as he was turning in back in the saddle something caught his eye. Nearly hidden in the dense growth covering the face of the cliff, Ian could barely make out a huge dark shadow. Curious as to what it was, he turned the horses back toward the overhang.

Upon reaching the base, again the shadow was invisible. Tying the horses, Ian followed the faint trail upwards. Working his way through the underbrush he climbed the steep hillside. Just when he was convinced the shadow was nothing more than sunlight through the trees, he came upon a cavernous opening in the side of the hill. His heart jumped, for this was possibly the perfect place for him to winter. Further investigation led him to a spring, at the back of the cavern, and evidence of fire-pits and animal bones littered the ground. The back walls and ceiling were black with soot. His excitement mounted as he ran to the horses and hurried to retrieve his valuables from above.

By the time darkness fell Ian had brought all his possessions, loads of firewood and led his animals into their new home. The overhang was about eighteen feet from floor to vaulted ceiling and Ian stepped off twenty-seven paces wide and nineteen paces deep. That was ample room for him to build a comfortable place for them to winter in. His sincere hope was that the spring would still flow during the coldest time of the year. Everything else was perfect for survival, lots of dead wood just outside his front door and abundant game signs. The overhang would protect them from all but the worst driving storms and he had an unobstructed view of anyone, or anything, approaching the cave.

Once the horses were settled for the night, Ian drew out his plans for the interior of the cavern. The soft dirt of the floor made an excellent place to scratch out what he wanted to do. Using a twig he made a crude drawing of the basic shape of the cave floor. After much drawing and erasing, he was finally satisfied with the end result. Tomorrow he would start the building process, but right now it was time for some well-earned sleep.

Ian found the hauling the deadfall logs from the aspen grove, was much more difficult than he had imagined. Without the benefit of an ax, he had to break off the smaller branches and burn off those that were too large. He would set a fire on each side of the ends to form a notch. When he was satisfied the notches were deep enough he would pour water on the flames, so far his idea was working. To get them into the cave he hooked the two horses to the logs, then coaxed them uphill until they were where he wanted to place them. The biggest problem was lifting one log on top of the other. He envisioned three walls of logs for his house and using the cavern wall as the fourth. Try as he might he was not able to lift the heavy logs high enough to get a wall over four feet high. Giving the horses a rest, Ian sat and looked at the squat building in frustration. The uprights held those that he had managed to piece together all right, but he couldn't raise the logs any higher alone. About to give up and think of an alternative plan, Ian threw his drawing stick against the far wall. Sitting with his head in his hands his spirits sank in defeat.

"Nothing's going to be built if you just sit there," he chided himself. "Get off your dead end and figure something else out." The horses pricked their ears at the unexpected sound of his voice. "Maybe I've bit off more than the three of us can chew," he said softly as he approached the animals. Patting each of them affectionately, he studied the task still needing to be

110

finished. Leaving the horses, he saw the stick that he had thrown. It lay at an angle, one end on the ground and the other propped against the cave wall. That was it. That was the solution to his problem. He could build a ramp to the wall and, by using the horses, he could pull the logs up the ramp and into place. He would need lashing to hold the contraption together, which meant that he would have to spend the next while hunting. If he were able to kill even a large deer, he would have meat to smoke and hide to cut for rope.

"Come on fellows. We've rested long enough," his voice carried a sound of renewed hope. Checking the musket, he threw the extra shot bag and powder horn over his shoulder. Leading the horses outside, it seemed the sun was shining a bit brighter than before. His hunt was to be a short one and, for once, the matchlock worked as it should. The largest deer he had been able to find was a heavy doe, but it would furnish both meat and the badly needed hide.

Once the deer was skinned, and the meat hung high over the smoky fire, Ian cut the hide length-ways in strips four inches wide. Laying out the logs for the ramp, he began to lash them together. He had learned the hard way, much earlier, that green hide had a tendency to stretch. Pulling the knots as tightly as possible, he left the frame for a few days to let the hide dry. The rest of the strips he had soaking in the pots filled with water. Satisfied that his efforts were not in vein, he began to lay the logs forming the floor of the ramp. Tying each end to the frame and the middle to the previously laid log, the ramp grew until at last it was functional. Heavy, and cumbersome to move, the ramp never the less worked just as Ian had hoped it would. With one small square opening for a door, and no windows to worry about fitting, the walls went up fast and now only the roof beams remained.

With so much to do before the snow would fall, Ian worked from daylight well into dark. Many nights he worked by firelight, chinking the holes and cracks with mud. Daylight hours were mostly spent gathering cattail roots from the marsh, juniper berries and whatever else he could find to eat this winter. Deer meat hung over the smoke fire, while the pile of firewood grew higher, as did feed for the horses. Growing more confident daily, Ian was proud of what a lad from a farm, clear across the world, had been able to accomplish in this remote land.

The smaller aspen beams were nearly in place, when the first heavy snow came on the heels of a furious north wind. Ian awoke to about seven inches of the fluffy white stuff on the ground and more falling steadily. The aspen had long since dropped the last of their colorful leaves, and Ian knew winter would not be far behind. Anticipating the coming snow, he had hauled the necessary logs inside the cavern. A single two-foot square opening in the top would serve as an escape route for smoke from the cooking fire. The inside measured six paces square and the height a bit over eight feet. The shutter for the doorway was made of saplings, about the diameter of Ian's wrist, which was hung by strap hinges cut from pieces of the buffalo robe. A single log, against the back wall, was his only inside furnishings, while log bins for food supplies were on each side in the corners. A rock fire pit was in the center and extra wood carefully stacked in the front corner. Satisfied that the inside was ready, Ian went back to work on the overhead part. The last beam was finally in place and, when the seams were chinked, he lowered the makeshift ladder through the opening.

The snow fell for most of the day and finally stopped just before sundown. While the overhang protected them from the falling snow, it did little to stay warm inside the cavern. Ian wore one of the blankets, thrown over his shoulders, as he worked putting up a corral for the horses. By making their corral connected to his log structure, the upright walls would serve as a windbreak for the animals. A lean-to would finish the enclosure and, when time permitted, Ian planned to close in the side away from the cavern wall. The progress was much slower now, as he had to stop often to regain feeling in his cold hands. The spring showed no sign of slowing because of the cold weather, but he always kept the two goatskin water bags full in reserve.

It was four days later before the sky turned from dismal gray to bright sunshine again. The light reflecting from the snow was blinding, but the warmth was a welcome relief. The spring did not flow enough to keep it from freezing over in the extended cold, and Ian was fearful of losing his water supply. He had to break away the ice many times a day to keep the spring clear. That was a small price to pay for fresh water, after all what else was there for him to do? While working on the house and horse structures, it seemed there were never enough hours in the day. Now time dragged from one day to the next. Once he had finished the few daily chores, he spent the rest of the day napping or simply looking out over the dismal, snow-covered landscape. Boredom again reared its head and Ian knew that he must either find something to occupy his time, or go mad. He had done, and redone, the horses stable and practiced with the crossbow until he became quite proficient. He had shot the musket once at a wolf that wandered too close to the cave, but the resounding noise inside not only scared the horses nearly to death, it almost deafened Ian. He definitely would never do that again, except in a dire emergency. There had been an occasional visitor which found its way inside the cavern. Magpies and crows were constantly perching on the roof of Ian's home; their incessant chatter a welcome break to the silence. Once a wayward coyote meandered too close to Blanco and received a kick in the side for his inquisitiveness. Packrats and mice made their homes in the woodpile and a horned owl found easy pickings there. Crows and owls are bitter enemies so upon the owl's arrival the fight was on, when the crows were already visiting the roof.

The inside of the shelter was cozy and even the smallest fire kept the inside warm. One or two slight modifications were necessary to make the smoke draw properly. Ian had to remove a bit of the chinking at the back of the room, so the natural draw of air would pull the smoke out of the hole in the roof.

A pile of juniper branches, covered by one of the tarps, served as a bed. This was as comfortable and peaceful as Ian had been since his home with Colleen. He was not nearly the cook that his dear wife had been, and the cattail roots were a poor excuse for Irish potatoes. Of course there wasn't any marketplace at which to shop, so he made do with what was at hand. Even the abundant prickly pear cactus was a good fare. Ian had found that by handling the spiny pieces with two sticks, and then singing the spines off in the fire, he could skin the outer cover. Cutting the cactus into cubes and adding them to a bit of meat and tubers he made a delicious stew. Crushed dried juniper berries made a flavoring for stew or fried meat. Even the stinging nettle tasted a lot like spinach, once the poisonous needles were neutralized by a few minutes in boiling water.

When the weather allowed, he would take the horses out for exercise and allow them to forage for their food. Though it seemed forever, the days gradually grew longer and the winds now blew more from the south. The snows came less frequently and with less ferocity. Just behind the melting snowline the larger game animals, which had congregated in the lowlands, began their migration back to the high country. The howling of the wolves grew more distant as they followed the food to the upper regions of their domain. The winter had been good to Ian. Not too severe and still harsh enough to make him work for his survival. The horses had fared much better than he had hoped for. It definitely appeared that fate was at last smiling on him.

When the ground was no longer a quagmire of mud, Ian saddled Blanco and loaded everything he owned in the pack on Negre's back. It was time to enjoy the outdoors and do some exploring at the same time. Before winter had set in, his searching had been limited to finding food and wood. With the great expanse of country before him, he wanted to see what lay just over the next hill, and then the next, and so on. Strange how he had turned from a soft handed man, who ran an apothecary, to an outdoor adventurer in a land thousands of miles from home.

The sun seemed brighter than usual, as Ian guided the horses through the trees and onto the open flat. He had no plans as to an exact time that he would return and he prayed that no one, or nothing, would claim his home in his absence. Patches of snow covered the ground under the cedars and deep drifts covered the north facing slopes, where the sun seldom reached it. The warmth of the sun at his back, Ian rode toward another high mountain in the far distance. He wondered if he knew exactly what he was searching for? He already had a comfortable home, which he was leaving behind. The game was plentiful and the marsh provided him with cattail roots to eat, reeds to weave and the brown head of seed was a tasty flour substitute. Deep in his heart he knew that he was searching for another human, for any sort of companionship. The eternity since he had heard another's voice, besides his own echo, was weighing heavily on him. Always the one who had enjoyed the light-hearted conversation of others, the solitude was depressing. Even in prison, when the warden had banned anyone from talking to Ian, he was able to gaze upon the face of a guard. As unfriendly as those faces had been, they would be a welcome sight now.

Rivulets of water ran from the slopes, as Ian followed the trail through the bottoms, always headed west. Stands of naked aspen stood against the skyline, while the chatter of jays carried from the trees. Yellow marmots whistled, then disappeared beneath ground, as he interrupted them sunning on the rocks. Thick patches of mansanita made an impenetrable barrier as its auburn, ground hugging branches intertwined into a heavy mass of crooked stems.

On the third day out, the sun was beginning its western downside, when he topped the high point on a bluff. Below ran a wide river that snaked its way through a sage and cedar covered valley. Instead of the blue of the streams that he had previously seen, this one was a curious color of muddy green. From this high vantage point, it reminded Ian of the slime that covered the fringes of the marsh. Giant cottonwoods lined the meandering banks, their leafless branches silhouetted against the slow flowing water. The cliff dropped straight down, from where Ian sat looking at the vista below. There was a strange beauty in the desolate valley and Ian knew that he must investigate it further. Following another trail toward the river, and carefully guiding Blanco through the heavy undergrowth, Ian made his way down the back of the bluff.

The shade of a cottonwood made a perfect place to stop for a leisurely meal and leave some of the equipment from Negre's back. Once the pack was emptied, except for what Ian figured on needing, he led the horses into the valley. The soil was a curious loam-sand mix, providing excellent ground for growing. The prolific plant life seemed to be thriving due to tributaries of the river that watered this desert land. Wild berry bushes, of nearly every description dotted the landscape, while closer to the water nettle and pigweed covered the banks. It was still much to early in the season for any fruit to have formed on the berry bushes, however this was a place to remember for later. The thought of fresh fruit made his mouth water, but for now he must be satisfied with what he had dried last autumn.

The rest of the day was spent investigating what he could of the sage covered flats. The snow had all but disappeared, soaking quickly into the loose soil of the desert. Signs of deserted camps were everywhere and Ian concluded that Indians must travel through here frequently. There were no indications of this valley being permanently inhabited, only areas cleared of brush and remnants of many fires. Scattered shards of broken gray pottery and a scrap of a yucca fiber sandal were found at one sight, but all else seemed to be picked clean. Like Ian, the wanderers had followed the many game trails through the sage. Before the sun began to disappear, Ian turned back toward the river and was surprised to see how far he had traveled from the water. He definitely didn't wish to be caught this far from his supplies, so he pushed the horses back toward the trees.

The sky had turned to colors of purples and yellows that he had never seen in a sky before. If an artist ever painted such a sky it would appear unreal, yet here he was seeing it with his own eyes. The warmth of the sun had faded and the chill of the desert night was taking its place. Birds sang in the branches above him, while the barking of coyotes were heard in the distance. With his back relaxed against the trunk of a tree, Ian gazed out upon the desert where he had explored earlier. The horses were bedded for the night and the sounds of the evening were a soothing end to this day. Before he realized it Ian fell asleep, the empty cup falling from his hand. Sometime during the night the chilled night air awakened him. Shivering, he groped his way to where his blanket and robe were piled with the rest of his belongings. It didn't take long for the bison skin robe to trap the body heat and he was once again comfortable and dozing off.

The floor of the basin was barely seeing the first rays of sunlight when the nicker of one of the horses awakened Ian. Reaching for the crossbow, which was never out of arm length, he slowly shifted his body to look around. About four hundred yards away from where he sat, a band of animals that he could not identify slowly grazed in his direction. They were slender in build, reddish-tan on top and cream-white on the belly and tails. Black horns grew straight from the tops of their foreheads and curled back near the ends. As Ian stood and threw aside the robe, the entire group turned and ran in the opposite direction. Flashes of white rump patches were seen as they disappeared over the hill. Never had Ian seen any animal run so fast and so effortless. What eyesight they must have, to be able to detect so small an object at such a great distance. He decided that he must learn more of this strange creature, as soon as the opportunity presented its self. Besides, he was in need of fresh meat and this was one that he hadn't tried yet.

As Ian was filling the goatskin water bags his reflection in the pool looked back at him. His hair was over his shoulders and the beard nearly to the center of his chest. Using the knife, he began to cut great hunks from the beard, until it was so short that he feared he would cut himself if he continued. His matted hair was next. When Ian was finished, his hair was cropped to just below his ears. The wet shave on the tender face left him wondering if he had partially skinned himself, but a clean-shaven chin now reflected back. He was having too much difficulty shaving under his nose with the large knife, so he decided to leave the moustache there. A quick bath in the cold river and it was time to load the horses and continue the exploration of this fascinating country. Heat waves were already rising by the time Ian rode out of the shade of the cottonwoods. Their shimmering lines distorting the landscape into vague shapes, a sharp contrast to what he had awakened to.

Ian had no real plans, as far as a particular destination was concerned. It seemed that no matter which way his travels took him, there was always something new and captivating to discover. Continuing in the direction that he was heading, the topography showed little change. A slight shift to the south a range of mountains could be seen in the distance, their peaks visible over the bluffs and swales of the desert floor. After spending the winter in the lowlands, the mountains held an intriguing lure so, this was the direction he turned the horses.

Leaning back in the saddle he reminisced of the past. Of time spent with Colleen, and he wondered if perhaps she was looking down on him right now. He was never one to give much thought to the existence of either Heaven or Hell. To a young man there was no need to be concerned over such places, after all he considered himself invincible. The death of his beloved wife gave him cause to wonder about an after-life, but it was nothing that he would dwell upon. Now, with nothing but time, he found himself questioning life and its ramifications more often. At one time his belief was that death was the final chapter in the book of life, that when the cover was closed there was no more. The body was placed in the ground and eventually returned to the earth, and that was all there was. He had little concern about what would happen to his mortal remains, but the thought of Colleen's beautiful body suffering such a fate troubled him greatly. He thought of his mother's rose garden in front of his parent's home. At the end of each fall the bushes, that had held so many gorgeous flowers through the spring and summer, would turn brown and apparently die. With the coming of the next spring, a new growth would show it's self and the same bush would again burst forth with flowers. If there was a Creator and if he would do that for a flower, he would surely do the same for a human. There must be a spot, where the choice of Gods creatures dwelled after their life on this earth ended. Surely his Colleen was in such a place, and eventually they would meet again. These were the thoughts that troubled Ian's mind as he rode through the sage strewn desert, not really noticing the changing landscape.

CHAPTER NINE.

The low desert had given way to plateaus and eventually Ian was climbing towards the high peaks above him. Other than a few scattered spring showers and a flock of sage grouse, that exploded beneath the horses feet sending them into a panicked run before he could get them under control again, the trip had been monotonous. He had seen herds of the strange tan and white animals again, but his endeavors to get close enough for a shot was always thwarted by an alarm within the herd. All he saw were glimpses of them disappearing over the next hill.

So far the assent had been an easy one. Trails led him to the top of the first peak then dropped gradually into a valley, much like the one he had encountered before. There was lush green in the meadow below; the surrounding hillsides were covered with budding aspen. Patches of snow still covered the higher mountaintops, a distinct contrast to the lower desert valley. Following along the ridge, Ian continued to climb. Again he had divided the load between the two horses, so this part of his journey had to be afoot. The soles of the boots had long since worn through, so he had cut pieces from the boot tops, which he had saved, and placed them inside. An occasional rock would find its way through the hole and he would have to stop and tend to his bruised feet. Undaunted, Ian continued the climb, spending the nights beneath any available shelter.

It was on the thirteenth day since he had entered the mountains, when he topped out and the terrain began to drop down to the other side. From the vantage point above the timberline he could see where the mountains gave way to plateaus and mesas, then to rolling hills and gullies for as far as he could see. Directly below him, and well below timberline, was a gradual drop off into a large bowl shaped valley, which was covered with leafy aspens and pines. A high bluff dropped off to a river that wandered through the bottoms. This appeared to be the perfect place for Ian to spend some time relaxing and resting the horses. After all, he was only a tourist who was visiting this land to see the sights. With nowhere in particular to go, this was as good a place as any to investigate.

The progress making the descent was slow, but Ian figured that with the time he was making now, he should be able to gain the bottom in possibly two or three more days. The rests became more frequent, and the duration longer, as the trek continued. The steep terrain was taking its toll on both man and animals. Ian decided that it was not worth pushing to reach the valley, so he stopped for a well-deserved rest in a narrow canyon. Snow fed streams and an abundance of grass gave them everything needed for comfort. With the setting sun deer would meander into the meadow to feed and frolic, giving Ian both much needed meat and entertainment.

When bedding the horses for the night Ian noticed they were acting more skittish than normal. Soothing the animals with soft words and much patting, he returned to his own blankets. The bright moon held his attention as it slowly peered over the crest of the peak, flooding the basin in brilliant shades of pale soft white. A wisp of cloud passed before the orb, barely distorting the moonlight. Ian's mind went back to the dank prison cell and the even darker mines in Wales. In his wildest imagination he would never have dared to dream that someday he would be lying beneath such a sky, breathing the fresh air of freedom. Much too involved in his thoughts to sleep, he threw another branch on the fire and leaned back against the saddle he used for a backrest. The one thing that would have made the night complete would be a glass of Irish whiskey from O'Brien's Pub.

He hadn't thought of the old hangout for years. Why he picked this moment to recall the drinking bouts there was beyond him. He pictured the group of regulars singing, and Murphy's wife scurrying around with a tray full of ale. The many nights when he had to be taken home and poured into bed. He also remembered the terrific hangovers the following mornings. Smiling to himself, he wondered how many times he swore to never drink again?

His reminiscing was interrupted by the howl of a wolf, which was much too close for Ian's liking. Another answered back from directly above him. The horses began to snort at the sounds and Ian could hear them stomp nervously. Taking a flaming brand from the fire, he went to the animals and moved them within the circle of firelight. The howling became more frequent and closer to his camp as more wolves joined the chorus. "It's obvious that there would be little sleep tonight," Ian shouted aloud, hoping his voice would scare off any predators with notions of coming closer. Holding the crossbow in one hand he dropped a large log onto the fire, causing a stream of sparks to rise into the night sky.

The animal noises continued until just before the first faint streaks of light appeared in the east. It was a very tired Ian that packed the animals as he prepared to leave the valley. Not wishing to spend another sleepless night, he led the horses toward the crest of the next hill. Scanning the terrain above, and both sides, for a glimpse of the creatures he had heard throughout the night. Stopping wherever a spot allowed a view of his back-trail, Ian would search the trees behind him, but there was nothing in sight. The behavior of Blanco and Negre indicated that they were not alone however. The constant snorting and the pricked ears, as they looked in one direction or the other, made Ian very nervous and he clung tightly to the crossbow.

Whenever they had to stop for a rest he held the reins tightly, ready to flee at the first sign of danger. His legs were heavy and every step an effort as they descended deeper into the mountain. Finally he could continue no longer without sleep. Taking a chance that the horses would spook and drag him through the rocks, he wrapped the reins around his wrist and dozed off. Without the horses he doubted his chances of survival and dared not tie them, in case there was an attack from the wolves. Last winter he had witnessed a wolf pack pull down a full-grown bison bull, and the picture of the struggling animal haunted him.

Sleep came in snatches, for every movement of the horses would awaken Ian with a start. Giving up any hope of a peaceful sleep, he led the nervous horses toward the river below. The terrain grew steeper as he neared the bluff, making them take a long swing to the south to avoid the drop-off. Long before twilight he had reached the level ground of the bottom, where the rushing sound of water greeted them. Bounded by a thick stand of aspens to the west, a clearing skirted the water's edge. The high bluff offered perfect protection from any marauding wolf and the river would block any attack from the front, leaving only the two sides to watch.

As the horses watered and grazed on the lush grass Ian stood guard. The musket leaned against a convenient tree and the crossbow strung and a bolt placed against the string. "You may make a meal of me," he said in the direction of the thick cover of the trees, "but I'll get at least a bite of you first." Emptying the stale water from the bags, he refilled them in the cold stream, constantly checking his surroundings as he bent over. He was relieved to find that there were no apparent wolf tracks in the soft mud of the bank, only those of deer and a much larger print that he couldn't identify.

A fire was soon started and a pile of wood laid in as the evening camp was set up. The horses seemed more relaxed and their constant snorting and pricked ears were replaced with whinnies, as they nonchalantly grazed. Feeling more at ease Ian removed the dart from the crossbow and laid the weapon on the ground, still close enough to reach in an emergency. Once the horses were satisfied, Ian led them to the shade of the bluff where he tied them, while he settled down for a long, well-deserved sleep. He didn't notice when darkness replaced the dim light of evening. Ian was in one of the deepest slumbers he had been able to have since starting the trek from the other side of the mountain.

The sun sat high in the sky before he threw off the blanket and became aware of his surroundings. Both horses stood grazing, where he had tied them, and the entire scene seemed peaceful and serene. There was a slight breeze moving the leaves on the aspens and the whistle of a meadowlark came from the open area below. A pair of crows frolicked above the trees; their raking calls a direct contrast to the melodious song of the lark. Walking the horses to the stream they appeared to be at ease, but Ian had an uncomfortable feeling that they were being watched. Perhaps it was a sixth sense that he had unconsciously obtained through the time spent in this wilderness. Whatever the reason, he felt that hidden danger lurked somewhere in this peaceful picture. He knew that somewhere unseen eyes were watching his every move.

Ian had no way of knowing just how accurate his feelings were. An Indian lad named Tao had left his village, in search of his vision quest, and fate had brought them to the same spot at this time. Having never heard of an animal like the horse, much less seen one, Tao was frightened by the noises of the beasts. He had heard them in the distance long before they made an appearance at the base of the cliff. Peering over the edge, he watched the movements far below. His vision had failed to manifest itself and he was about to return to his people in failure.

Making his way from the top of the bluff, to a spot close to where he had last seen the strange creatures, Tao hid behind a large rock. Lifting himself cautiously he peered at the spot at the base of the cliff, but it was now deserted. All that remained of the creatures was a burned out campfire and a few scraps of twigs. He wondered if perhaps his eyes were playing tricks on him, but his ears had heard the strange sounds from the beasts.

Having spent two days resting he wanted to investigate the bowl more. Just before daybreak Ian loaded the pack on Negre and riding Blanco went farther upstream to explore. Finding only oak brush thickets and heavier aspen growths, he rested the horses in a grove then turned back toward the bluff.

Following the tracks made by the horses on the initial trip Ian picked the way across a sage strewn flat. Ahead lay another aspen grove and beyond that the meadow where he had first made camp. The trees had thinned considerably and upon entering the edge of the growth; he could barely make out a buck and doe deer. They were feeding on the grass by the river, occasionally lifting their heads to look about, then returned to their grazing. They seemed to be working their way back toward the tree line and he could do with some fresh meat. Tying the horses he pulled the matchlock from the bison skin scabbard and carefully made certain that it was ready to fire. Picking his way through the undergrowth, he slowly made his way closer. The deer seemed unconcerned, as they were now at the far edge of the trees and gradually getting closer to Ian. Resting the heavy musket on a fallen log, Ian waited for the quarry to move closer for a clean shot. He watched as they raised their heads in unison and wandered into the thicket, where they both seemed to be sniffing the air. This was as good a time as ever. As Ian pulled back the hammer on the musket, both animals took off running at the sound of the metallic click. In headlong flight, they ran back into the meadow just as he pulled the trigger. The recoil and thunderous noise told Ian that the rifle had functioned, as it should. Through the smoke from the burned powder, he watched the doe crumple in a heap in the grass. Returning to where he had tied the horses he again wrapped the bison skin around him. He had previously learned that it was the only way to keep from getting scratched up going through trees.

From the hiding place behind the rock, Tao had also been watching the deer. He also wanted fresh meat, but the distance was too great for his arrow to find its mark. He was about to return to the top of the bluff when the deer exploded from the aspens, where only a moment before they had peacefully meandered. The sound of musket fire was new to him and when the deer fell dead at the very sound, it both amazed and frightened him. What he saw next was even more amazing. It appeared that a creature half buffalo and half beast entered the clearing. Following that creature was a smaller one of similar build, except that it had a large hump on its back. What Tao saw next made him rub his eyes and wonder if he was dreaming. The lead beast broke in half, the top part completely separating from the bottom, whereupon both the bottom part and the beast behind began to nibble grass as the deer had done earlier. This must indeed be the answer to his vision quest, for surely no such animals could really exist.

A combination of fear and curiosity held Tao's eyes riveted to the beasts. As the top half of the first creature approached the fallen doe it threw off its outer skin, and Tao saw that it wasn't a bison creature at all. It walked like a man, but none that he had ever seen before. The skin was a pale white, while the hair was the color of over ripe corn silk. What he had believed to be a skin, was actually the hide of a bison that now lay in a pile behind the creature. In one hand the man creature carried a long stick that reflected the sunlight. As the man beast bent over the deer, he drew a long object from his side and before long the skinned carcass was hanging from the lower branch of an aspen.

The uncomfortable feeling of being watched bothered Ian again. Lifting his head he searched the surrounding area, but there seemed to be nothing out of the ordinary. After starting a fire, he cut a piece of the back-strap from the doe and went to unload Negre. As he untied the rope holding the canvas, he felt that there was definitely something behind him. Spinning around, he pulled the knife to defend himself, but there was nothing except a magpie pulling at the deer hide.

"Guess I'm getting too jumpy," he said as he finished unpacking the horse. Taking the frying pan, he returned to the fire and soon the odor of frying venison permeated the air. The thought of the meat cooking may tend to attract wolves, was never far from his mind. Constantly scanning for any sign of something out of the ordinary, Ian chewed the tender meat. "I remember once when Cunga told me of places where spirits lived," he said aloud. "This must be one of them, for I sure have an uncomfortable feeling here." Blanco raised his head at the sound of Ian's voice and then returned to the tender grass.

The smell of frying meat was nearly more than Tao could endure. His only recent food had been a handful of grubs that he had found beneath a rotting log. His belly was gnawing at the odor, but there were more important plans to be made. If he could take one of the four-legged beasts back to his village, the elders would have to believe this vision. At first he thought of attacking the man beast, but the stick that bellowed thunder frightened him more than the tribe elders did. He decided that he would return to his place of hiding and, when night fell, he would sneak in and steal one of the animals. Backing slowly away, so as not to be detected, Tao crawled back to the safety of the fallen log where he had spent the night. Well away from the strangers, he began to formulate plans as to how he could manage to get one of the beasts, without getting himself killed in the process. This would be a long and busy night, so Tao wrapped himself in his robes and drifted off to sleep, dreaming of the grand entrance he would make into the village.

Never one to believe in spirits or ghosts, Ian was ready to make an exception in this case. He was bothered by the unseen danger that he felt. He had heard no cry of the wolf, or for that matter seen anything that would cause him harm. Still he could not shed the uneasiness that was nibbling at him. When the last bite of venison was gone, he reloaded the pack and silently left the valley to whatever it was that was haunting it.

Finding a trail that led slightly south, and one not so steep, Ian rode out of the basin. Constantly looking behind him, but seeing only the swaying of the aspens in the breeze, he rode on. Topping the summit and dropping over to the other side, the uneasy feeling seemed to leave, much like one drawing a drape closed over a window. Following the rim he cut more canyons. It was near dusk when he felt that he had put enough space between whatever was behind him. Dropping down into the ridge below, he found an overhang where he could spend the night. The feeling that had been so prevalent earlier had become only a dim memory as he prepared for the night. There was no water close so he watered the horses from the goatskin bags and hauled wood for the fire. Ian cursed himself for not cutting more of the meat that he had hung in the tree. A thick cut of venison would far surpass the dried berries that he was eating now. Tomorrow he could take better care of his needs, but for now he wanted sleep. The flow of adrenaline had ceased and now he was drained of any energy what so ever.

The midday sun beat down on him before the stirring of the horses awakened him. Impatient to be fed and watered, they were snorting and pulling at the hobbles. Wanting another twelve hours of sleep, Ian forced himself to get out of the blanket and tend to his stock. Using the last drop in one water bag he temporarily satisfied the thirst of both him and the animals. He hated to use more in case he couldn't find any potable water in this area. Dividing the load, he again led the way toward the trail above.

His boots kicked up puffs of dust, as he trudged over the path used for eons by various animals. Upon reaching the rim, he noticed that the trail narrowed to a point that he feared taking the loaded horses on it. One slip and it was too far to the bottom for anything to survive the fall. The sun was in his face when he led the animals down a less used trail skirting the aspen groves. Ian knew that if he continued west, somewhere beyond was the great ocean, however he had no idea exactly how far. He did know that Cunga had led them on a north by east course and his had been fairly well to the west and a bit south.

Daydreaming, Ian was startled when a young buck mule deer exploded from the trees in front of him. The nubbin antlers, barely visible between the large floppy ears, covered in the soft velvet. Before he could react the deer disappeared into the aspens. All Ian could do was simply gawked at the spot where it had vanished so quickly. Not wishing to be surprised again, he held the crossbow at the ready, while his eyes watched carefully for any foreign movement. Just as he thought that it would be dried berries for supper again tonight, he heard a strange cackle just ahead. Leaving the horses, he softly made his way to the edge of a small clump of oak brush. He had seen tame birds like these on his father's farm, but never had he laid eyes on a wild turkey before. Raising the crossbow to his shoulder, he carefully aimed and pulled the release mechanism. There would be fresh meat tonight. The hen gave a few feeble flaps of its wings and lay still as the bolt found its mark.

A whoop of delight escaped Ian's lips, as he held the bird high, examining the prize. The sound of his voice sounded so good that he did it again. After cleaning and feathering the bird his next chore was to find a suitable spot to camp, preferably one with water close by this time. His hands were sticky from the bird's entrails but he dared not use more from the goatskin bag, so wiping them on his trousers, he returned to the horses. He had found in the past, that there was usually water in the bottoms, so that was his destination. The aspens were so thick that he was forced to stay on the trail, sometimes holding wayward limbs aside for the horses to pass. Long before he had left the heavy cover he heard the sound of rushing water. As they exited the trees, onto a small meadow, Ian thought he saw a shadow disappear into the trees to his right. Hoping it was only another deer; he led the horses to the stream where he unpacked them.

Tonight's fire would be a special one. Not only giving the comfort of the flames, but the air was filled with the smell of turkey roasting. Parts and pieces were skewered on green sticks, and hung near the glowing coals that Ian had pulled from the blaze. More wood meant more hot coals and the fire blazed high as he added logs. Pulling more coals into the trough, he turned the meat to another side. Seeing the horses were grazing contently, he picked up the crossbow and wandered upstream to do a bit of exploring.

Patches of snow were visible on the south facing slopes, where the trees sheltered the ground from sunlight. Reaching a spot where the stream emerged from the trees, Ian stopped cold. That hadn't been a shadow after all. In the soft mud of the bank were the unmistakable paw prints of a large wolf. Hurrying back to check the safety of his animals, Ian shouted. "Why is it that every time I find a perfect place to rest, it's either occupied by wolves or ghosts? Is there no quiet sanctuary in this place, where a man can simply find peace?" His only answer was his echo bouncing from the cliff behind him.

The horses seemed quite undisturbed as he entered the campsite. Quickly Ian moved his animals to a spot beneath a high rock and gathered what wood as was close at hand. Filling the water bags, he then gathered the sticks full of turkey meat and carried them all to the new place. The final move was to be all his equipment from the pack. Bringing coals from the fire, he started a new blaze in the semicircle of wood that he had laid out. With him and the horses inside of the fiery barrier, he hoped that no wolf would cross the flames. It also came to Ian that this would be another sleepless night. He barely noticed the fragrance of the turkey roasting. His complete attention was on the fringes of the aspens and the edge of the meadow. By now he knew the horses well enough to know that they would sense danger long before he would. All he had to do was watch for the nervous prance, pricked ears and the snorts as they tested the air. Tonight he wouldn't hobble them, for if a wolf should get through the fire and past the crossbow he wanted the horses to have a chance at escape.

Ian was anxious for the sun to set and get this night over with. As soon as it appears safe to leave, he would put miles between them and this valley. It was not long before he got his wish and the sun disappeared behind the western hills. It seemed that it was a signal for the wolves to begin their howls, which sent shivers down Ian's spine. The echoes made it impossible to tell where they were, or just how far away. Laying the bolts in a line on the ground between his legs, he prepared for a long night of waiting. The firelight made it hard for him to see beyond the circle of light, but once or twice he caught the brief reflection of eyes in the darkness beyond. The horses no longer pricked their ears; they were now laid back against their heads. Their eyes wide open and rolling in fear, the poor animals fought to get loose and run. Ian dared not take his attention from outside the light, so he could only speak to them in soothing tones. Grabbing a bite here and there of the turkey, he kept the vigil through the night. Sometime just before dawn the horses eased a little, and Ian knew that the predators had withdrawn, at least for now.

As soon as the sun was over the horizon, Ian loaded the pack on Negre, saddled Blanco and made fast tracks for the next ridge. Trying to travel in fairly open country, he wove his way around the stands of trees and through sage covered flats. At least that way he wouldn't be taken by total surprise if the wolves should attack. The only part of the turkey, which he had grabbed before leaving, was the large breast. To his displeasure only the outer part was cooked, while the main piece was still raw. He was tired, hungry and plain disgusted with this frontier. Even the mines were beginning to look attractive to him right now. Even though he was treated worse than he treated his horses, he still had three meals a day, a place to sleep, usually in relative peace, and someone to talk to.

Constantly checking behind and to the sides, they made their way to the crest of the next ridge. Pulling up the horses, Ian scanned the open valley. It also appeared to be a mirror image of the one where he had spent the night. Snow on the slopes, across from him, peered through the waving aspen branches. A sage covered bottom worked its way up and into the thickets on the side hills. Looking for a place to rest the horses and cook a slice or two of the turkey breast, Ian followed the trail to a small clearing just below the ridge. He didn't want to go too far down, as he was planning to leave the area as soon as he finished eating.

As he dismounted from Blanco the saddle slipped with his weight shift. In his hurry to leave the other canyon behind, he had neglected to tighten the cinch sufficiently. Tying Negre to a sapling, he led the white to the bare spot below and removed the saddle and bedroll. Returning to the packhorse, he untied the rope and, because he planned on only being there such a short time, simply threw the canvas back. Carrying the frying pan, Ian sauntered the short distance down to where Blanco waited. In a short time the fire was going and strips of turkey sizzled in the pan. The constant slapping of the crossbow against his back, and the weight of the bolts at his hip, was becoming a nuisance.

"As soon as I finish with you, I'm going to shed these things and get comf...." Ian's words were cut short by a series of growls from the vicinity of where he had tied Negre, followed by a sound of stark terror from the black horse. Spinning in his tracks, Ian saw a pack of wolves descending on the tied horse. In his panic Negre reared and his feet slipped from beneath him. As he fell the lead rope snapped, freeing the terrified animal. Everything seemed to be happening in slow motion. Ian watched as the frightened black ran headlong back toward the top of the hill, with two of the pack in pursuit. Four others were circling toward Blanco, their bellies barely off the ground. Running to the horse, which had now dropped his head and was lashing out with his hind feet at the closest wolf, Ian grabbed the reins and vaulted onto the bare back. Before he was set, the horse ran down the hill with the wolves on his heels.

Ian had no time to wonder as to why the horses had not sensed the wolf pack before they had gotten so close? His only thought now was to hang on to the heaving back of Blanco. Flat on his back, in the midst of a bunch of snarling wolves, was the last place that he wanted to be. Digging his heels into the horse's sides was an unnecessary gesture, as the animal was already running through anything in its path. As they reached the bottoms and started up the far side, Ian glanced behind them. The wolves had fallen back and reverted to the loping pace, which they could carry on for miles, eventually wearing the prey down from exhaustion. Scenes of the bull bison flashed in his mind, and he wondered if Negre was suffering the same fate.

A rocky out-crop near the top offered a place to take a stand, it was there that Ian loosely tied Blanco. From this point he could plainly see the wolves move ever closer. They had split into two pairs. One pair headed directly at the rocks, while the other circled to come from behind. The musket lay back by his saddle and the only defenses he had were the crossbow, nine bolts and the large knife. Gathering a pile of rocks, that averaged in size that of his head, Ian glanced from side to side checking to see which pair was closest. The ones coming from the front would be nearest first, so Ian concentrated mainly on those two. Blanco was stomping the ground and whinnying in terror, as the first of the front two burst from hiding behind the large sage. Ian raised the stock to his shoulder and let fly with the bolt then, without even looking to see the result, hurriedly cocked the bow and placed another bolt in the slot. Looking for a target he found none. The lead wolf lay where the bolt had hit him, his breathing barely visible as his sides heaved, then were still.

Ian was so intent watching for the lone wolf in front, that he neglected those coming from behind. Blanco nearly knocked him to the ground in an attempt to run from the pair, which was a scant twenty yards away. His feeble attempts to push the horse away were as futile as trying to change the course of a river with a sieve. Dodging the flailing head, Ian made his way around to get a better shot at the running predators. Holding on the base of the throat of the leader, he released the trigger. He failed to lead the animal, and the bolt buried its self in front of the hindquarters of the one directly behind. The cries of pain from its mate failed to even slow the large male, and he charged directly at Blanco. It was a mere ten feet away when Ian loaded the next bolt. There was no time for aiming, so he pointed the weapon from his hip and released the string. At that close range he surely had to hit the beast somewhere, vital spot or not it would at least slow the charge. The wolf was dead even before the front legs crumpled, the momentum carrying the carcass into the front legs of the panicked horse.

With a mighty heave Blanco pulled the reins free from the bush he was tied to. As he started by Ian grabbed the loose hanging reins. The Spanish bit, which he had cursed so often for tearing up a horse's mouth, was the lone thing that kept Blanco from getting away. As the bit wrenched against his tongue and the side of his mouth, the horse turned sharply to avoid further pain and fell on his side in the process. Approaching from behind, Ian kneeled on the thrashing animal's neck, attempting to get him under control and prevent him from injuring himself. Holding next to the bit, he talked softly and the frightened animal finally calmed enough that Ian dared to let him to his feet. A fast examination showed nothing more serious than cuts and abrasions from the rocks. Running his hands down the horse's legs, he walked him around; fortunately there was no sign of a limp or a favored leg.

Once the horse was tied, well away from any wolf carcasses, Ian went to retrieve the spent bolts. Two of the short arrows were still imbedded in the dead wolves, but the third he never found. Unless he could locate the other bag, he had only eight of the darts left. His first thought now was to find Negre. Besides his concern for the animal, nearly everything he owned was in the pack and the last he saw it was bouncing up the trail away from the attacking wolves.

Ian was aware there was no way he could make it back to where his belongings were before nightfall. Besides being cut and bruised, Blanco was near exhaustion from the run for their lives and he needed attention. His own condition was a known factor, however Negre's was not. Ian couldn't take a chance of losing both animals, and he couldn't sacrifice Blanco for the remote possibility that the packhorse had gotten away. It was a heavy-hearted Ian that led the surviving horse away from the three dead wolves.

Taking inventory of his current possessions, he found that other than the crossbow and darts, he had the knife, a tinderbox and a six-inch wick for the matchlock. These few items, and the clothes on his back, were all he had to insure his survival in this seemingly hostile country. Picking the way around rocks and brush, which the horse had either gone over or through in his flight, Ian made it to the bottoms. The gradually melting snow formed small pools of water in every indent and depression in the mud. It was to one of these puddles that Ian led Blanco. While the animal was satisfying its thirst, Ian removed his shirt and, after soaking it in the icy water, began to clean some of the wounds on the horse. Lather mixed with dirt had caked into clumps of dried mud, matting the mane and hide. Most of the wounds were superficial scrapes and cuts, but one gash on the shoulder worried Ian. Carefully scrubbing the horse clean he led it to a patch of grass, far away from the cover of the aspens where an ambush could occur again.

"Tomorrow we will start back to gather some of our gear and attempt to find your partner," Ian spoke softly to Blanco. As if he understood the words, the horse nuzzled the man's shoulder. After securely tying the animal to a sapling, Ian returned to a pool to satisfy his own thirst and gather wood for his nightly fire. There was still one wolf unaccounted for, so he wanted plenty of fire to keep it at bay.

Once the sun set the evening air turned cool. A shirtless Ian sat as close to the flames as he dared. He found that the portion of his body facing the fire became too hot, while the opposite side was a mass of goose pimples. This is how the morning light found him, shifting from one place to another to keep warm. Kicking dirt on the remnants of the fire, a very tired Ian led Blanco back up the side hill towards where he had last seen Negre. His still damp shirt, thrown over the horse's back, flapped in the morning breeze as they entered the first stand of trees.

Progress was slow, as they trudged through tangled undergrowth and thick trees. They hadn't even reached halfway up the first hill when Ian knew that he must sleep. His head was pounding with every beat of his heart, and his legs were having a hard time holding him erect. Ahead stood a large clearing, and it was here that he would rest beneath the shade of a single clump of aspen. Buttoning his soiled shirt he tied the horse close to him, lay against the tree and was instantly asleep, the crossbow clutched tightly in his hands.

The call of a jay, in the tree directly above him, awakened Ian. Judging from the position of the sun he had slept for only two hours or so, but it was enough to rejuvenate his tired bones a little. His empty belly was more of a problem right now. Without some nourishment he would never make it back to where his belongings were scattered. He recalled seeing Cunga catch and eat an assortment of insects on the journey north, but the thought revolted Ian. The Indian had assured him that the bugs were a source of protein and were really quite tasty. He had found a handful of acorns but without a pot to boil them in, the bitter nutmeat was not palatable. The worst part was the lack of drinking water. He had to travel close to the slope, where patches of snow still lay under the sheltering trees.

His big concern was that some varmint would tear apart the goatskin bags before he could get to them. These were the thoughts that occupied Ian's mind as he placed one foot in front of the other; constantly looking to see in the crest was getting closer.

By late afternoon he found a spot, on the summit of the hill, where he could make a fairly decent camp. A hapless hare had made the mistake of stopping just ahead of them and a shot from the bow would mean meat for tonight. The snow was sparser on top, but Ian found a few puddles from which he could water the horse and himself. Once the rabbit was reduced to a pile of bones, it was time for an exhausted Ian to catch up on some well-deserved sleep. As he dozed off, his final thoughts were of the safety of the black horse that had served him for so long and so well.

CHAPTER TEN.

When Tao returned to the meadow he was surprised to find there were no sign of the beasts that had been there earlier. His hopes of taking one of the four-legged creatures back to his village faded. It was with a heavy heart that he began his journey over the mountains to meet his people. As he was about to enter a thicket of scrub oak, he heard a rustling in the heavy brush. Drawing the arrow to where the point nearly touched the bow, he waited. A spot of black was seen through the tangled branches. Then directly before Tao emerged the very beast he had watched in the meadow many hills past. At the sight of the Indian boy the creature stopped in its tracks, the pink nostrils sniffing the air. Easing the arrow Tao laid the bow on the ground and slowly approached the black one. Uncertain as to what the large beast would do, he talked to it in soft tones as he reached out his hand. At first the creature shied away from the offering, then reached out his muzzle and sniffed Tao's palm.

"I will not harm you large one. All I ask is that you extend the same courtesy to this person." When each was convinced that the other meant no harm, Tao examined the beast. Mostly cuts from tree branches were visible on the front and sides, however there were severe wounds on the rear flanks. Making a poultice the Indian lad bandaged the injuries. Investigating the strange boards on the animal's back he found two pots, of a material that was seemingly indestructible. A white covering strung out behind the contraption, which was of a material unknown to Tao.

Backtracking, his travels eventually led him to the spot where the wolf attack had occurred. Leaving the animal, which he now called, "Mine," on the other side of the hill, Tao investigated the abandoned campsite. There was no way he could have known that across the valley, and one peak away, the man who's belongings he was now going through, was also moving in that direction. Investigating farther he found the saddle. What this heavy object was he had no idea, so after examining it closely he left it and turned his attention to the frying pan. Scraping the burned scraps from the round, flat pot he carried it with him. It would make a fine gift for his mother. The thunder stick, that made the deer fall dead at the very sound it made, leaned against a log. Carefully examining the strange object, Tao could see the front part seemed to be made of the same shinny material as the pots. No matter how he shook it, or what he did, the stick would not repeat the noise that he had heard it make back in the meadow. Seeing that it was a heavy and useless piece of nothing, Tao grabbed it by the shinny part and threw it into the trees in disgust. Returning to the main part of the campsite he hoped to find the object that had skinned the deer so quickly, but the search was of no avail. Nothing else seemed of interest, or use, to him so Tao followed the trail to where he had tied Mine.

As Tao was cresting one hill, Ian was nearing the top of the one directly across the valley. The boots had worn huge blisters on both feet, making every step agonizing torture. What he should have been able to walk in one day, now took the better part of two. A swelling developed on the front hock of the horse, so he dared not ride him and chance crippling his only companion. Ian was uncertain as to exactly where his camp had been. For all he knew he had passed it and was wandering in some other canyon. Too tired and sore to really care any more he dropped to the ground and, for the first time in recent memory, Ian uttered a prayer for deliverance.

His answer came about an hour later in the form of a drenching downpour. Huddled beneath the limbs of an aspen didn't offer much protection from the driving rain. Not wishing to spend the night in the open he staggered to his feet and continued the climb to the top. The leeward side of a large boulder offered some protection from the weather and, drawing Blanco in close as possible, Ian huddled tight against the windbreak. Around twilight the rain turned to drizzle, then stopped all together, leaving a clean smell to the mountains but a very wet and uncomfortable Ian.

With barely enough time before dark he gathered what dry wood he could find. Before long steam rose from his soaked clothing as he stood over the flames. He had taken for granted the usefulness of the cooking pots. He had used them for so many various reasons, that it seemed nearly everything he did involved them in one way or another. Nothing to haul water in, or make stew or even mix ingredients in. Food like nettles, acorns and some tubers that needed boiling before they could be eaten, were now beyond his reach for nourishment. If he had only bothered to unpack the horse, he would still have these things. But hindsight being one thing and foresight another, it was too late to change anything now. At least he would have the frying pan, once he reached his old camp. The reflected heat had dried his clothes, now he must try to find a place that wasn't mud in which to spend the night. Carrying large rocks to the fire, Ian laid them out to form a rough bed. It wasn't comfortable but it was dry. Removing the wet boots he tended to the broken blisters on both heels. If he had been in his apothecary in England, he would have had no problem treating them with balm. In this wilderness he had no clue as what to put on them. Facing his feet to the fire, he catnapped off and on throughout the night.

The dismal weather disappeared with the warmth of the sun, as did some of Ian's doubts of survival. Tearing a sleeve from his shirt, he bound the sore heels, slipped on the boots and resumed his trek in search of his possessions. Traveling downhill pushed his feet deeper into the toes of the boots, thus taking some of the chafing away from the back of his feet. He just topped a small knoll, in the center of the side hill, when directly across from where he now stood he recognized the spot where the wolves had jumped him. A shout of joy escaped his lips as he nearly dragged Blanco down hill and up the other side, his sore feet forgotten in the excitement.

His joy was short lived though for the camp had been ransacked. The frying pan was gone, the musket lay thrown into the trees, and what hadn't been taken was covered in mud. His saddle lay on its side and the blankets scattered down the hillside. The rain had washed away any signs of the culprit that had ravished his possessions, but what animal would take a heavy pan? The only apparent damage to the matchlock was a chip out of the end of the stock, where the butt-plate connected. The powder horn and extra clothes lay undisturbed, rolled up in the bison skin robe. There was no time to lament his misfortune; there was too much cleaning to do. Washing off the saddle was first, followed by the muddy blankets and lastly the clothes he had on. The recent rain had turned his camp into mire, but also had filled many troughs in the rocks with water.

After hanging the wet blankets and clothes on tree limbs to dry, he led Blanco up the trail where he had seen Negre disappear. The downpour had erased any signs of either the horse or the wolves. Only broken branches and trampled brush testified that something had come this way.

136

Going deeper into the aspen forest, Ian held the reins tightly in one hand and the loaded crossbow in the other. Suddenly Blanco started to pull back on the reins, his familiar snorts warned Ian of danger. Searching the trees and ground ahead, he saw the outline of a wolf hiding in the grass just off the trail. Raising the bow he let the bolt go. Even though he made a direct hit on the beast, there was neither sound nor movement from it. Working ever closer and ready for another shot, Ian threw a rock towards the gray head. There was still no movement so he walked closer, until he stood over the carcass. There had been no need for his bolt, as the wolf's jaw as well as his neck, was broken. It appeared that Negre had taken at least one of the two with a kick under the muzzle. Retrieving his spent bolt, Ian led Blanco back toward what was left of his camp. It would soon be dusk, and he had no desire to be caught in this thicket at night. Tomorrow he would continue his search for his lost horse. As remote as his chances were, and fearful of what he may find, he never the less couldn't give up hope of finding him alive.

It was to be three days before Ian could resume his search. His feet became so swollen that he could not fit them into the boots. Lying around camp and tending to himself and the horse time passed slowly. Blanco's cuts seemed to be healing nicely, while the swelling in his hock had reduced and there seemed to be no fever in the leg. Wrapping his feet in the two blankets, Ian made clumsy footwear that allowed him some protection as he did only those things that were absolutely necessary. Again water, or the lack of, was the biggest problem. Ian had tied knots in the legs of the trousers and stuffed snow into them. Emptying the snow into the deepest depression, he waited for the sun to heat the rock enough to melt it. A flock of pine hens had settled in the trees and Ian had been able to kill two before the rest flew off.

Finally he was able to fit his feet into the well-worn boots and, by the time the morning sun arrived, he was ready to travel. A flock of magpies rose from the carcass of the dead wolf as he rounded a curve in the trail. Carefully searching for any sign of Negre, he would check every broken twig or anything that appeared out of the ordinary, but to no avail. The aspens closed in on the path, then opened up again as they thinned, then stopped altogether just short of the top. The trail widened as Ian looked down into the valley below. There had been no sign of the horse, or of his missing gear. As he looked over the landscape a motion caught his attention.

Just below and to his right, at the edge of a thicket of oak brush, something was moving in the gentle breeze. Leading the horse to that spot Ian's hopes returned, for clinging to the branches was a piece of the canvas cover for the pack. At least he knew that Negre had come this far, but where from here? Following the trail would have been a natural route, but the terrified animal could have gone in a dozen different directions.

Looking for any signs of the large horse breaking through the brush, Ian followed the winding game trail. At the point where the oak thinned a bit then thickened again, he saw what appeared to be freshly broken branches. The trail was definitely wide enough for Negre to have made it. Rocks had been turned over and the ground churned up, and Ian was certain that this was the way that his horse had come. Tying Blanco at this point, Ian entered the tangled brush. Ducking low hanging branches, he wondered how the horse had gotten through here? Following the torn up ground he emerged from the oak into a clearing that overlooked a ledge, and below that the valley opened up. This was where the signs ended. The rain had sent miniature mudslides down the hill, obliterating anything that would indicate the animal had passed this way. Dejectedly, Ian returned to where Blanco patiently waited. His heart was heavy, for he now knew that he would never see Negre again. Bitter tears rolled from the corners of his eyes and ran down both cheeks.

"Is this the way You answer my prayer to deliver us from this wilderness?" Ian shouted at the sky as he sobbed and wiped the tears away. "Come on Blanco. I guess if we are going to survive, it's going to be up to the two of us." Leading the remaining animal he back trailed to collect his gear, and plan just how they would get out of here alive. He scarcely noticed the deer that stopped and watched as they approached, his mind was elsewhere. The sound of the hoofs against the rocks brought him back to reality, as the doe scrambled for the oak brush. "Don't worry mama," he said softly, "right now I have deeper things on my mind than having you for dinner."

Ian was not sure whether he was so sad because he had lost the packhorse, or because the metal pots were gone. He could pack what few possessions he had left on Blanco, but the soft eyes of the black horse would definitely be missed. Sentiment was one thing, but no way to even boil water was quite another. The pots were invaluable to him and, while Negre had been a great comfort to Ian, the kettles could not be replaced. Rummaging through the campsite, Ian was delighted to find the other bag of short arrows for the crossbow. They lay with the two water bags behind a rotted log. Evidently the one that ransacked the camp had set them there, and then forgotten these prizes. Pulling the stopper from one of the goatskins, he drank deeply then filled a shallow rock depression for the horse to water from.

His movements came as much from repetition, as from thought. Gathering wood, building a fire, rolling out the bedroll, tending the horse, eating and sleeping, had become such a daily habit that he knew automatically what to do next. Elated that he had found the water bags and bolts, his spirits rose and he began to feel the gnawing in the pit of his belly. There had been no sight or sounds of the wolves since that first incident, so he felt safe leaving Blanco while he hunted in the nearby aspens. Much to his disappointment the only living thing that stirred was the black and white magpie. He was definitely not ready to eat one of those disgusting birds, so he returned empty handed. Perhaps a fine deer or partridge would grace his fire tomorrow, but for tonight it would be what scraps of meat he could forage from the bones of the fool hens.

The rising sun brought with it an urge to move on. Carefully examining every inch of Blanco, Ian determined that he was fit to ride. With little left in the way of belongings, he rolled most things in the bedroll. The water bags hung from each side of the saddle horn, as did the spare bolts, the powder horn and shot. The musket was tied behind the cantle on top of the bedding. With the crossbow slung over one shoulder, Ian departed for parts unknown. The range to the north of where he had briefly tracked Negre looked somewhat promising, so north it would be.

The mountains gradually gave way to the familiar shrub covered hills and flatlands. If God had truly created this country He hadn't used much imagination. This side was like the myriad of others that he had seen since leaving the cavern. The basic lay of the land would change, adding a stream or peak here and there, but the scenery was basically the same monotonous thing. These were but a few of the scattered thoughts going through his mind, as Ian sat on the high knoll overlooking more rolling hills covered with the usual sage and stunted junipers. Shadows and light were playing across the area as he stood to return to where Blanco was tied.

Taking one last look, he noticed a faint movement below. It had been only one quick glance, but there definitely had been something move just over the side of the knoll. Running as crouched as he could, Ian pulled the musket from the scabbard, primed the pan, cocked the crossbow and slithered back to where the movement had caught his eye. If the wolves had returned he would be ready for them this time.

Carefully rising, to see over the sage that was hiding him, Ian caught his breath. The ridge no longer hid the animals. The side of the knoll was covered with the strange tan and white critters that he had seen before. Most were contentedly grazing, but it seemed that some always had their heads up, as if watching over the others while they fed. He had already witnessed the tremendous eyesight that these creatures possessed, so Ian made no movement. As the herd meandered closer, he selected a medium sized one on the outskirts of the rest. He could not tell if it was buck or doe, for all but the youngsters had horns. When the animal was within fifty yards, Ian slowly raised the musket, took careful aim and fired. At the report from the muzzle the herd disappeared in an instant. The sixty-caliber ball had done its job and there would be fresh meat once more. The critter smelled like one of the goats on his father's farm, as Ian skinned the carcass. He had eaten goat before and, while it wasn't one of his favorite meats, it was still palatable and certainly better than the reptile he had tried to eat last night. A shudder passed over him as Ian remembered the snake with the pointed snout and a head shaped like the end of the shafts for the bow. Try as he might he wasn't able to force himself to eat the thing once it was cooked.

Once Ian had removed the hide, he was surprised to find how small the creature actually was. Throwing it over his shoulder was no chore at all. With his dinner on his back he walked to where Blanco met him with a nicker. This was as good of a place as any for tonight's camp, but tomorrow he must find water. One bag was totally empty and the other half full. As much as Ian hated to ruin the bison skin robe, he had to sacrifice a portion of it. Cutting a two-foot square from one end, he draped it over a circle of rocks, forming a pool for Blanco to drink from. Hanging the meat as far from the ground as possible, Ian cut out the choice tenderloins for this night's meal. Inch thick slices hung over the fire, on pointed sticks, as he cut away strips for smoking. Cutting forked branches from the junipers he layered the strips on one, then placed another branch over the other side of the strips. The tops of the forks were tied together with strips of bark and, hopefully, it would serve to hold the meat away from the flames and cook it slowly.

Blanco was showing no signs of any injury; in fact he appeared to thoroughly enjoy being able to run along the game trails. He would toss his head and attempt to take the bit in his teeth, giving him and not Ian control. A sharp jerk on the reins would change his mind, as the Spanish bit pulled at the corners of his mouth and rasped against his tongue. For the first few nights, after Negre had disappeared, he whinnied and carried on as if he was wondering where his companion had gone. Now it was only an occasional call that would suddenly erupt from his throat, then his ears pricked as if listening for a return. Ian was also getting used to the absence of the second horse and, while he missed Negre, he realized that he had been more of a convenience than a necessity. As Ian looked at the once majestic Blanco, he noticed how the tail had been worn ragged by snagging brush. The once sleek coat was now mud splattered and pink scars, from the episode with the wolves, stood out on the heavy neck. The matted main showed signs of neglect, but there was nothing to curry Blanco's coat with. There was little Ian could do to maintain the outside, but he relished in the fact that looks were indeed deceiving, and the animal was in good physical health. Running his hands over his own hair and beard, he wondered if he looked as ragged as Blanco did?

The roasted meat was surprisingly tasty, as Ian munched on pieces of the overcooked antelope. The sunset was unusually picturesque, as he leaned against the robe that he had draped over the saddle. High overhead a ferrous hawk circled, as he searched for a meal that had wandered too far from its hole. The evening was peaceful and, with a full belly, Ian felt at ease. The red of the setting sun, set the scene before him aglow, like embers before the fire finally gives up flickers and dies. He had a definite feeling of guilt, for being so outraged when he thought his prayers hadn't been answered. They were indeed answered, just not in the manner that he had expected them to be. He felt a bit foolish, as he looked heavenward and offered another brief prayer. This time it was one of apology and, nearly as an after thought, thankfulness for divine protection this long journey. Checking the welfare of Blanco he returned to his bed, and found even more comfort in his dreams.

He was sitting beside Colleen as the buggy bounced along the country back roads. The musty odor of the peat bogs hung heavy on the night air. These had served as fuel for Great Britain eons before the discovery of coal. Nestling closer to Ian, Colleen held his hand tightly in hers, her perfume drowning out the smell of the bog. The call of wild geese drifted back to them from the river, and an occasional flock passed in front of the full moon. A peaceful night, his Colleen sitting next to him and not a care in the world, what more could any man ask? Pulling up before the white fence that surrounded their home, they sat in a long embrace while the mockingbird whistled his song. So went the entire night. When one dream ended, another one about Colleen replaced the previous one. There were a great many memories that were stored in the brief years they were together. It had been such a long time since he had lost her, but the love for her had not diminished, in fact it had grown stronger.

He awakened slowly, trying to hold onto the last vestige of the dream before he had to face the reality of the world that waited for him. A sense of melancholy always haunted him whenever he spent nights like the one past. He would finally convince himself that he had no time for this kind of foolishness and faced whatever lay ahead. This day would be no different than the many times preceding it, and the dreams shelved in the back of his mind. He must find water and something to eat besides meat. He knew that his body needed greens and he had no taste for sagebrush. Chewing on a cold piece of meat, he decided that it definitely tasted better hot. The flavor was too strong for him and he spit out the mouthful of half chewed food.

Blanco stood quietly as Ian threw the saddle over his back, and only protested a little as Ian attempted to put the bit in his mouth. Making certain that the cinch was tight this time; he loaded the gear and led the horse to the top of the knoll. As he gazed over the broad expanse before him, he debated on which way to explore next. In the far distance, to the north, he saw the tip of tall trees and that usually indicated water. Mounting the horse he guided him in that direction.

It had been months since he had waited for the snow to melt enough for him to leave the protection of the cave. The mornings were definitely getting cooler, and Ian knew that fall was just around the corner. If he was going to spend the coming winter in these parts, he must start looking for a place that offered him protection. The cavern had been a one in a thousand find and, he was well aware, that his chances of finding another were slim. Steep ravines hindered his progress as he dropped from the rolling hills onto the flats. The line of trees was much closer now, but the detours around the drop-offs added hours to the trip. Using the last of the stored water, Ian drank deeply and gave the rest to Blanco. The smoked meat was too strong to eat so he threw the rest away, knowing that there will always be game to replace it.

It was well past midday when he stood on a high overlook and peered into the river below. Over the centuries the rushing water had eroded a deep gorge through the rocky bed. From this vantage point he could see islands in the wide stream, and flocks of geese dotted the banks. The land slowly flattened out upstream and this was where the trees were lined on either side. Picking his way around giant anthills that abounded on the rim, he slowly followed the trail toward the lower river. Sounds of rushing waterfalls came up from the gorge below and Ian would often stop to gaze down on the sight. Mist from the falls rose into the air so thick that, at times, it would obliterate the view of the water. It seemed that, even-though the time and distance he traveled stretched on, the trees grew no closer. The open space had been deceptive and Ian realized that they had been much farther away than he had thought. With the last of his water gone he knew he must reach the lower river before he could rest. There was no snow here to melt, as he had before.

Spurring Blanco on with a new sense of urgency, he searched for trails leading down to the water. Finding a few, that were way too steep to take the horse down, Ian wondered what kind of animal could possibly negotiate such terrain? The first piece of the sun was disappearing behind the horizon when he finally dropped down to the banks of the wide river. Massive old trees lined the banks and it was beneath one of these that Ian chose to spend the night. The muffled sounds of the waterfalls, far downstream, were heard but here the river ran slowly. Where the water had under-cut the bank large tree roots protruded over the eddies, as they cut deeper still into the soft earth.

After he had made Blanco comfortable for the night Ian turned to his own needs. He wondered at the wisdom of throwing away the smoked meat. Even-though it had been nearly unpalatable, it would have at least filled the void he was now feeling in his belly. In his haste to reach water he had given no thought to replenishing his food supply. The dried berries had long since been eaten, leaving him nothing to take the edge off his hunger. This was not the first time that he had suffered hunger pangs, and he knew that it wouldn't be the last. Sitting close to the fire he pulled the robe over his shoulders and tried to ignore the gnawing that was growing stronger. He could hear Blanco moving about, as he fed on the grass, and was glad that at least one of them would have a full belly tonight. Tomorrow he would find something to fill his stomach also, but for tonight he would have to suffer.

A strong wind blew down the river and the night sounds carried along. The hoot of an owl directly above him and the yap of coyotes in the distance broke the silence. Ian was just dozing off when he was suddenly awakened by a sound that he had not heard forever. It was faint, but he swore that he had heard the sound of voices, human voices carried on the wind. With mixed emotions he listened for the sound to repeat its self, but it never did. Had he been dreaming? If there had been voices, did they belong to the Spaniards that he had run from? Had he traveled all this way only to meet the ones that had killed Cunga, and probably had the same plans for him? He realized that the death of Cunga would have been swift and merciful, compared to what he would suffer for stealing Conornado's own horse. Quickly dousing the fire, as to not give himself away, Ian sat in the dark. The sounds of the night grew more ominous without the comfort of the firelight. Holding tightly to the crossbow he waited for dawn. At least he had something to think about besides his empty stomach, but it wasn't any more comforting.

A thousand thoughts ran through his mind as Ian sat in the darkness. He tried to formulate a plan of escape, and if that was not possible, one of defense but was unable to come up with either. His thoughts jumbled together as the night wore on. He didn't want to be caught by winter trying to return to the cave, and perhaps it wasn't the Spaniards whose voices he had heard after all. The words were muffled and inaudible, but definitely human. Perhaps he would sneak for a closer look at who made those sounds. If he was careful, he could be undetected as he spied on those with the voices. If they posed a danger, he would attempt to escape into the many arroyos and gullies that abounded in this country. If the deep crevasses could hide so many herds of game, they could surely hide a single man and horse.

A sliver of light, appearing in the east, alerted Ian to the coming morning. Using the toe of his boot he scattered the blackened coals that had once been a comforting fire. As soon as the light trickled through the branches of the trees, he saddled Blanco and led him slowly up river. Keeping to the heaviest cover available, Ian scanned ahead for the first sign of possible danger, but everything appeared serene. Deer wandered down to the riverbank to water and jays scolded him from above. He watched as a weasel stalked a meadow mouse, made a swift attack and had his morning breakfast. The faint odor of burning wood would occasionally waft his way on the breeze. Stopping often to listen, he picked his way around deadfall and hid behind large boulders as he searched ahead. The wind had quit earlier and the air was still, as he was about to round a broad swing in the river. The smell of smoke grew ever stronger and was now visible, as it hung close to the ground.

Tying Blanco deep in the trees Ian made his way to the curve. The definite sound of voices was heard above the rush of the water, as it slapped against the near bank and made its way over the rocks and sandbar. Crawling on his belly Ian drew close enough to see around the bend in the river. Parting the top twigs of the sagebrush he was using for cover, he was astonished to see a large group of Indian tepees set not four hundred yards from him. Women carried water from the stream to the village, while children ran about involved in their games. The entire area was set in a meadow flanked on two sides by high bluffs and a place where the river seemed shallow enough to ford. The place reminded Ian of the ant beds that he had left at the top of the overlook. People were scurrying here and there, involved in their various activities.

Ian lay in one position, watching the activities, until his cramped muscles made him slowly draw back to where he had left the horse. The Indians seemed peaceful as they went about their business, but how would they react to a stranger? The few that he had encountered in the past, were friendly towards the whites simply because they had seen neither one with white skin, nor a horse before. What many had considered as savages, had knowledge of survival that Ian lacked. He needed their expertise on tanning hides and wilderness lore if he would continue to live in this wild country.

He realized that so far he had blundered through the hardships of the past, but would his luck continue to hold? The bison robe was getting thin and he had only fourteen balls left for the musket. The powder horn felt nearly empty and he had no idea how many loads were left in it. He had marveled at Cunga's ability to live off the land, but had never paid much attention as to how he did it.

Ian was still debating with himself as to what his course of action should be, when his mind was made up for him. He had just put his foot in the stirrup and swung into the saddle when an Indian boy of about thirteen suddenly appeared from the thicket. Freezing in his tracks the lad dropped the two fish that he was carrying and stared momentarily at the strange creature before him. The only sound he made was a sharp intake of breath before he turned and ran back into the trees.

"The fat's in the fire now," Ian said to himself. "Whatever you decide to do, you'd better do it fast 'cause soon you're going to be neck deep in Indians." Following Kale's advice of not bucking a pat hand, he slowly walked the horse directly into the center of the tepees. The cocked and loaded musket held ready for any emergency. Ian figured that the noise of the matchlock would be almost as an effective weapon as the musket-ball its self. The hair raised on the back of his neck as he waited for an arrow, from some unseen bow, to pierce his skin. Women had hurriedly pushed children into the lodges and eyes could be seen peering from the darkened tepees. Walking unmolested through the camp, Ian wondered exactly what he should do next? Pulling Blanco to a halt in front of the largest lodge, which was set in the center of the rest, Ian looked around him. From his high vantage point he could plainly see men holding bows, hiding in the grass and bushes. Doing as Cunga had shown him; he raised his arm with the palm of his hand facing out.

"Friend," he said in the least threatening tone of voice that he could muster, "I come as a friend." Slowly lowering his arm, he again put his finger on the trigger of the musket. "I may be friendly but I'm certainly not an idiot," he said softly, as he looked around with a strained smile on his face, showing as many teeth as he could muster. One by one the men came out from their hiding places, arrows notched and ready should Ian become a threat. Spotting the lad he had encountered in the trees peering from behind a rather stocky man, who was coming toward him, Ian held the fish to him. "I believe these belong to you," he grinned. Hesitantly the boy took the fish and quickly disappeared again behind the man holding the bow.

It seemed an eternity that he sat atop Blanco waiting for the next move. It happened in the form of an elderly man that calmly walked from the opening of the lodge. His braided hair hung down to his waist, and the wrinkled face reminded Ian of the dried plums back home. Again Ian smiled broadly and, holding out his palm again, said, "I come as a friend." The elder Indian mimicked the hand gesture and mumbled something that Ian hoped meant he too wanted to be friendly.

Taking this one to be the leader of these people, he wished there were something that he could give him that would make an impression. Reaching into his belt he took the smaller of the two knives and handed it, hilt first, to the old man. With no apparent hesitation, or reservation, the gift was accepted. Carefully examining the knife from every angle, the elder ran his thumb along the blade's edge. Before Ian could stop him the sharp blade had done its damage. Dropping the knife the chief stared at the gash dripping blood on the ground.

Jumping from Blanco's back, he quickly grasped the hand and applied pressure to the wound. The next thing he knew, rough hands had yanked the matchlock from his hands and he was thrown to the ground. As he focused his eyes, he was looking at the business end of a dozen arrows. A sharp word from the old man and he was helped to his feet and the musket returned to him. Tearing the bottom from his shirt Ian applied a bandage to the cut, then picked the knife from the ground and returned it to the old man. A long exchange of words followed, between the leader and others, before Ian was motioned to follow the elder inside. Concerned over leaving Blanco alone he hesitated, but the chieftain pulled at his arm, insisting that he follow him. Appearing to be safe, at least for the time being, Ian did as he was bid.

The interior of the tepee was much more spacious than the outside indicated. A small rock fire ring was in the center and buffalo robes lay against the interior walls. A young woman scurried to hide beneath one of the robes as Ian entered. Ignoring her the chief motioned for Ian to sit. Neither said a word but studied each other intently, the old man from curiosity and Ian because he was trying to read the expressionless face. Just as he was feeling a bit more relaxed the man across from him shouted something, and instantly another man entered the lodge. Words and exaggerated hand motions passed between the two. The other man turned and left, only to return shortly with a large bowl of food. The smell of roasted meat made Ian remember how hungry he really was. So much had happened that he had completely forgotten the hunger pangs that haunted him before.

Taking the bowl the elder man tore a hunk of meat from the bone and chewed at it, never offering any to Ian. Another piece followed the first and, when he was finished, he wiped his hands on his bare chest and only then was Ian given something. This was to be his first lesson in tribal manners. No one ate until the chieftain was full and he was given the choice cuts. Grateful for any morsel, Ian devoured what was left. When the bowl was taken away, the old man pointed to the musket and jabbered something that Ian had no idea what was said. Shrugging his shoulders, he looked quizzically at the wrinkled face. Again he pointed at the musket and repeated himself. It finally dawned on Ian that he was curious about the weapon. Anxious to impress these people, he stood up and motioned for the man to follow him outside.

Lifting the flap he was surrounded by men, women and children of all ages, sizes and description. Motioning everyone aside, the elder indicated for Ian to lead on. Looking for a likely target, Ian spotted a drying rack of heavy logs nearly twenty yards away. Making certain that everyone was well behind him; he raised the musket and fired. Large chips flew from the rack at the impact of the sixty-caliber ball hitting the dried wood. Turning to receive his praise for such a wonderful feat, Ian was surprised to find he was standing alone. Those that hadn't ran and hid, at the thunderous explosion, were lying prone upon the ground. Whether he had impressed the Indians or not was a mute point. One thing certain he had gotten their attention. Gradually they came from the various hiding places and those on the ground stood up. Many of the men had sheepish looks on their faces. As defenders of the tribe, they were among the first to disappear.

Walking to the rack, Ian drew his remaining knife and began digging at the splintered wood. Prying out the flattened musket ball, he walked to the chief and dropped it into the old man's hand. Turning it over and over, it was thoroughly examined by the ancient eyes. A group had gathered at the rack and was chattering among themselves, as they poked fingers into the hole made by the ball. "That's my first lesson to you," Ian smiled. "You may not understand my language, but you certainly must understand this. Now for my next magic trick."

Blanco had drawn a crowd of curious, but very apprehensive, tribal members. Standing well away they talked among themselves. Some even lay down to study the underbelly of this strange beast. A very small boy, who was too young to understand the danger this demon may possess, calmly walked up and touched the horse's leg. When Blanco dropped his muzzle to investigate the lad, a gasp of terror escaped the lips of the boy's mother. Snatching her child away, before the beast could eat him, she held him tightly to her breast while the boy struggled to free himself.

Calmly walking up to the horse, Ian patted the head that was extended to him and spoke in soft tones. "Okay old boy, it's now your turn to show off for the folks." With the best showmanship that he could muster, with an exaggerated flourish, he slid into the saddle. A gentle touch of his heels and Blanco was off at a dead run, through the village, to the base of the cliffs and back. Having never seen such an animal before most stood with mouths agape, as Ian reined the white to a halt before the large lodge. Dismounting, he walked to the woman that was still holding the wiggling boy in her arms. Smiling, to show his friendly intent, Ian took the lad from her arms and gently placed him on the horse. Frightened for the child his mother protested loudly, but was restrained by fear of her own safety. Her son was already on the back of the great beast and there was little she could do to save him now.

Placing the boy's hands on the saddle-horn, Ian led Blanco in a circle around the crowd. Fortunately the horse was on his best behavior and the lad squealed with delight, while his mother hid her eyes in fright. Once around the circle and Ian carried the child back to his mother, then turned to the head of the tribe. Extending his hand he offered to help him onto the seat vacated by the child, but received a shake of the head. A few gathered enough courage to mount the creature and ride once around the center of the village. When the rest saw that there appeared to be no danger of being eaten by this beast, they lined up for their turn. Even the chief eventually gave in and was given an extra long ride. By days end most of the village could identify Blanco as, "Horse," and him as, "Ian," even though they pronounced his name as, "Yawn." He also learned that these were a tribe of the Shoshoni Indians.

149

It was a very tired and lathered Blanco that was settled for the night, and a very elated Ian. His musket and strange animal had earned him a place of high honor this day. He was led to a lodge of his own, and offered a Bannock woman captive as a companion. The former he accepted, however the latter he graciously rejected. Leading her back to the tepee of the chieftain three times before she didn't return again. That was to be his second lesson on tribal edict, never refuse a gift offered in friendship. The woman was a chattel, and as such held no more value than one of the many curs that darted in and out of the village.

Almost as tired as Blanco, Ian reclined on the pile of buffalo robes. The activities of the day rushed back and forth in his mind. With the rising of the sun he had wondered if he would survive the encounter with this tribe of people, and here he was a celebrity of sorts.

Just as he was dozing off, a loud commotion brought him to his feet. Lifting the flap Ian stepped from the opening and looked in the direction of the noise. The Bannock Indian woman, that he had returned, was being driven before a group of women and young girls wielding stout willows. Blows fell on the defenseless back as the Bannock tried to run from her tormentors. Ian had no idea what the young woman had done to deserve such treatment, but he did know that he couldn't stand by and let her receive such abuse. Placing himself between the girl and her pursuers Ian yelled for them to stop. They did not recognize the words, but his intentions were clear and the group fell back.

"Come with me," Ian said to the terrified woman as he led her into his lodge. "No one will beat on you as long as I'm here. I wouldn't treat a horse that way." At the mention of the horse, she cocked her head and looked at him quizzically. That was the only word she had understood and couldn't understand why this strange person was comparing her to such a giant beast. Was he going to make her carry him around on her back? Ian motioned for her to sit beside him, as he studied the close-cropped hair and soft facial features.

Using his shirt as a pad, he soaked it in the water bowl and patted the cool liquid on the welts left by the willows. Exposing her back Ian could plainly see that this was not the first time that she had been beaten, but as long as he was here it would definitely be the last. She flinched at the touch of the cloth on her bruised back but silently endured the pain. Soaking the shirt again, he gently laid the cloth over her entire back.

The flap was pushed aside from the outside and the large man, that had brought food to the chieftain's lodge, peered inside. A knowing grin spread over the aquilline face, then the flap was lowered and they were alone again. "There may be Hell to pay for this, but maybe I can bluff my way through it again." As long as he had the magic stick that spewed fire, he felt completely safe. But what would happen when the powder ran out? "I guess I'll take care of that problem when it arises," he said softly. The girl raised her head to see if he was speaking to her, then laid her cheek back against the robes. Whoever, or whatever, this man with skin the color of snow is, he seems to pose no threat to her.

CHAPTER ELEVEN.

It was with more than a bit of apprehension that Ian stepped from his lodge the next morning. The uncertainty of how the tribe would look upon him, for saving the Bannock woman, dug at his mind. Before stepping through the flap he checked the musket one last time, then with a deep breath he stepped forward to face whatever lay ahead. Ready for any antagonistic move he gripped the matchlock tightly, but those he met greeted him with smiles and knowing glances. A rather large group was already gathered, at a respectable distance, and was watching Blanco as he grazed. Receiving pats on the back and broad smiles, as he worked his way through the crowd, gave Ian the impression that there was little to fear.

"Horse," said the man who had entered the tepee as Ian was wiping the woman's back, pointing to Blanco. "Shoshoni," he smiled pointing to himself. "Yawn," he added proudly, indicating Ian with a nod of his head. The rest of what was said he could not even guess, however it drew laughs from the crowd.

Ian sauntered toward the horse, in a manner intended to impress those watching. Throwing the blanket, then the saddle on the animal's back, he hoped that Blanco behaved himself when it came to the bridle. For once he didn't fight the bit as it was placed between his teeth, and Ian gave those watching a broad smile as he swung into the saddle.

"Now I'm going to give you all a lesson on what a gentleman Ian Connor is." Picking his way through those assembled, and the even more that were coming, Ian worked his way to his tepee. Dismounting, he went inside only to return holding the Bannock woman by the wrist. Her eyes were down cast and, like any good slave, she was the picture of subservience. Pointing to the woman he had in tow Ian said in a voice that all could hear. "Yawns woman." Having once been the equivalent of a slave himself, he would save everyone he could from that fate. Lifting the girl into the saddle, Ian swung up behind her and slowly walked around the

152

whole village. When he was certain that all had seen that she was indeed his woman, and no longer a slave, he set the heels to Blanco. The white stallion sprung into a full gallop, nearly unseating both the woman and Ian. Only the grace of God allowed him to hold her tightly and, at the same time, keep himself on the bouncing back of the running horse. He would have had a terrible time trying to explain why he couldn't control the beast that he so bravely rode.

Reining the anxious horse to a stop at the base of the cliffs, Ian made certain they were still in sight of the village. The group of spectators grew by the minute and all eyes were on Ian and the woman. Sliding from his spot behind the saddle he helped the Bannock woman dismount.

"I can't be calling you, 'Woman,' all the time. I need to know your name.'" Pointing his finger at the dumbfounded girl, he asked, "Name?" From the quizzical look he received in return he knew she didn't know what he wanted. Patting her on the shoulder he again asked, "Name?" A smile crossed her face and a twinkle appeared in the dark eyes.

Patting herself on the chest with an open palm, she replied, "Name." Patting Ian on the chest she said, "Yawn." "Name,…. Yawn," she repeated as she gestured toward her then Ian. The smile of success broadened as she kept repeating until Ian threw up his arms in defeat.

"It's original, I'll say that for your new name," Ian muttered as he wondered how to make her understand. No sooner were the words out of his mouth than she parroted, "Name," as she patted herself once again. "Okay, 'Name' it is, but remember it was you that chose it, not me. I've always been partial to the name, 'Gloria,' myself, but if you want to be called something stupid like …."' Ian didn't finish the word, as he didn't want to get her started again with the patting and "Yawn and Name." Motioning for her to follow he held her hand as they strolled back to the village, leading Blanco and giving everyone plenty of time to watch Yawn and his woman.

The succeeding days were both learning, and a teaching experience for Ian. He figured that if he was to mingle with these people, the first thing he must do is to learn their language. Picking up a few words here and there he attempted to mimic them, as Cunga had the English words. A few of the customs he just couldn't get used to, one was the habit of community swimming. The swimming part didn't bother him, but the fact that no one wore any clothing while they swam did. While the rest were cooling off in the river, Ian would sneak off to a more secluded place and have his private dip in a pool of the river. One day, thinking that he was all alone, he stripped to the skin and waded into the cold water. Just as he was up to the waist, and beyond the point of no return, he heard laughing behind him. Turning his head he saw a dozen of the tribe standing on the bank gawking at him. The sun had tanned the exposed skin, while the parts in between were stark white in contrast. Embarrassed, Ian dove beneath the surface of the water. Holding his breath as long as possible he prayed that they would all be gone when he surfaced. No such luck, in fact they were taking off their clothing to join him.

"Wapiti," one of the men said pointing at Ian, "Wapiti," he repeated and everyone laughed. From that time on he was seldom called by his name, and was known simply as, "Wapiti." When he asked Name what Wapiti meant, she placed both hands, with her fingers spread, against each side of her head. Stretching out her neck, she made a whistling sound. Whatever he was being compared to must be strange indeed.

It was on one of the many hunting trips, that he was allowed to accompany the hunters on, that he found what a Wapiti was. The party had just entered a thicket of pines when a whistle, followed by a series of grunts, came from just ahead. The man closest to Ian laid a hand on his arm and made a motion for silence. "Wapiti," he whispered, pointing to his right. Ian was surprised when the hunter answered the call, which was to Ian's ears nearly a perfect imitation. The whistle came again and so did the answering call and grunts from the hunter. The animal that burst from the heavy timber was one that Ian had seen before in his trek. The largest deer he had ever seen came directly toward them.

One shot from the musket and the huge animal fell. Clapping Ian on the back the hunters congratulated him for such a fine shot. One of the men carved two incisor teeth from the dead animal and presented them to Ian. "Wapiti," he said as he pointed at the antlered animal that Ian was still marveling at.

At their base the antlers were as big around as his wrist and Ian could nearly stand erect between the tines of the spread. It was indeed a privilege to be named after such a regal creature. "Wapiti," he said proudly, pounding his own chest. A quizzical look came over his face as the entire group began to laugh.

The man who had given him the elk's teeth took Ian by the arm and led him to the rear of the carcass. Lifting the tail he pointed to the cream-colored patch surrounding the tail and extending down inside the hind legs. "Wapiti," he said patting the rump of the elk, then to his surprise the Indian patted Ian's backside also. "Wapiti," he repeated with a broad grin.

Then Ian understood. They weren't comparing him with this animal because of any magnificent feature. They had given him the name when he was swimming nude and was seen by some of the tribe. His bare flanks were what they had seen as he dove under the water. A somewhat embarrassed Ian simply shook his head in resignation. "I guess I'm fortunate that they didn't call me, 'Skunk,' or something less glorious than this animal,'" he mumbled to himself. 3

The carcass was quartered and carried in triumph into the village. Shouts, and much pointing at Ian, punctuated the parade through the tepees. Men yelled, as each wanted to be the first to tell the rest of Ian's weapon that fell this beast where it stood. Raising imaginary muskets to their shoulders, they attempted to mimic the explosion and how the elk had fallen dead. To Ian it was all rather comical, however the musket was not anything magical to him, as it was to them. It was then that he thought that he had better try to impress them with the crossbow. How many more shots were left in the powder horn, he could only guess.

Name was waiting outside of their lodge and Ian left the rest and went to her. Bowing her head in a sign of obedience, she lifted the flap for him to enter. "How can I make you understand that you are no longer a slave? You are equal to any woman in this village now." Taking her gently by the arm, he urged her through the opening ahead of him. They had barely sat when a succession of handclaps came just outside the tepee. Lifting the flap Name held a brief conversation with one of the hunters. Dropping the skin door she pulled at Ian's arm for him to follow her. The rolled green hide of the elk was deposited just outside the entrance. The woman tried to pull the large hide around to the back of the lodge, but it took both her and Ian to move it. Once it was unrolled, flesh side up, Name staked it to the ground. With a sharpened bone she began scraping the hide vigorously, removing all the meat and tissue. Much to her surprise four other women soon joined her, each carrying their own scraper. The five jabbered as they went about the task at hand, and by nightfall the hide was cleaned to her satisfaction.

155

The fire-pit had been filled as soon as they had returned with the meat. Large chunks of glowing coals filled one end of the trough, as fresh logs were added to the other end. Long before sundown the air was filled with the fragrance of the elk slowly roasting on a green spit. This night there would be feasting, dancing and stories of the hunt, but for now Ian just wanted to close his eyes and sleep.

It seemed that he had barely dozed off when the thumping of the drums, and chants of the dancers, brought him back to the real world. Name sat silently beside him and, as he rolled over on the robes, she gently stroked his head. Pushing himself to a sitting position Ian studied the face before him. The high cheekbones, so prominent in most Indians, were less pronounced, while the nose was narrower and smaller. The lips were not full as those of the Europeans, more of a delicate line placed between the base of the nose and the cleft chin. Her deep-set eyes were so dark they were nearly black in color. Ian tried to picture what this face would look like once the raven hair was allowed to grow. The woman had a natural attractiveness, not what he had previously considered beautiful, but still an unknown magnetism drew him to her. Without the use of the paints and powders, used by the Europeans, a glow seemed to radiate from the dark skin.

Pulling the boots on he helped Name to her feet and led her outside. Two fires were burning in the center of the village. One blazed brightly, while the other was more of a bed of coals that was roasting the elk meat. Finding a place on the fringes of the dancers, Ian watched as the many hunts were reenacted to the beat of the drums. The chief, who Ian had learned was called, "Gona," sat in the place of honor. Even at his advanced age, there was still a look of majesty in the way he carried the frail body. His arms crossed over his chest and the eagle-feathered headdress, cascading down his back, he was the picture of authority. Once the meat was pronounced cooked, he proudly produced the knife that Ian had given him. Cutting away the portion he wanted for himself, he then handed the knife to one of the men, who began to carve the meat for the rest. The Shaman was served next, then the hunters, then the village elders and finally the rest. There was no shoving or pushing, that Ian had expected to see, everyone stood waiting for their serving. He had observed the same actions in a wolf pack, where there seemed to be a certain feeding order. The dominant male and female had the first feeding and so on down to the last getting the scraps. The difference was that here everyone was given equal portions, once Gona had his large serving. The snarling and fighting of the wolves was totally absent among these people.

Ian sat with his arm about Name's shoulder, as he watched in fascination, as the tribe was fed. When the hunter's turn came, he was pulled to his feet and ushered to the head of the line. It was evident that he was being honored for bringing this meat to the village. Pats on the back and broad smiles, as he walked past the others, made Ian a bit uncomfortable. He wondered if they truly were honoring him, or if it was through fear of the musket he was receiving so much attention? Either way he hoped that it would continue for as long as he chose to stay.

The dancing lasted until a slight tinge of light appeared in the east. Ian wondered at the endurance of the ones involved in the shuffling and prancing. With barely a moment break in between, they had gone on all night from one dance to another. Some dances were slow and almost sensuous, while others were fast and furious. The one that intrigued Ian was the dance where the young girls, of marrying age, formed a circle, facing out. Slowly side-stepping to the beat of the drum, they would show their best side to the young men. One by one they would leave, as the man of their choice selected them, and the couple would depart to their new lodge. "An interesting way of courtship," Ian thought to himself, as he pulled Name to her feet and they went to their own tepee. A long day and short night, along with a full belly and Ian was asleep shortly after lying down.

The daily hunts continued as the tribe readied for the coming snows. The drying racks sagged beneath the weight of the bison, deer, elk, bear and antelope. Woven ropes held split fish halves, which would swing in the breeze like some macabre banners. The rock enclosures were filling fast with pinion nuts, dried berries of all descriptions, cattail roots and vegetables, grown in the rich soil by the tribe. Skins from the various animals were staked out to dry. Once the meat and hair was scraped clean, a mixture of fat and ash was rubbed into both sides and left to tan. The stiff hides were then soaked in the river and, when flexible again, the job of chewing the hide began. To Ian this was disgusting, but to the women it was natural. They knew no other way to break down the hide and soften it enough to work it into garments. Name had made a pair of moccasins from the elk hide, to replace Ian's well-worn boots. Remembering the laughs he had drawn when the tribe saw him nude, he refused to wear the breechcloth worn by the other men. Name worked from sunup to well after dark, making him elk skin trousers and a deerskin shirt. All of his clothing, and that he had stolen from the Spaniards, were now nearly shreds of cloth. When Name presented him with her creations, it was none too soon. The supple hides molded to his form, but the heaviness of the garments took some getting used to. His long hair was the next thing to have her attention. Sitting him by the warming fire, Name would spend the evenings pulling her fingers through his mane to remove the mass of snarls. A bunch of dried prairie grass was tied into a bundle and served as a crude comb. The braids hung just below his shoulders when she finished. She wanted to braid his beard next but Ian thought that was a bit too much, so he shaved it instead.

Waterfowl constantly flew overhead in their migration south, purporting the winter was nearly upon them. Huge piles of dried wood were stockpiled against the time when they would be snowbound. The edges of the water started to have thin ice build up in the mornings. The people had built a shelter for Blanco, which was equal to some homes he had seen in London. It was constructed close to Ian's tepee; at times he wondered which they revered more, him or the horse? Fodder and all kinds of silage were stored in one end of the enclosure. The walls were covered so not a sign of the cold wind would find its way inside. Watching the ease with which they constructed the shelter, Ian remembered his own trying experience building the one inside the cavern.

The first snow came on the heels of a cold north wind, blanketing the landscape in a mantle of fluffy white. The drying racks had long since been emptied and now stood useless until next season. Flat rocks covered the openings to the rock silos, which held the provisions for the winter. Hopefully, all was ready for the season of cold and depravation. Most of the time the deep snows would hinder the gathering of fresh game and the ice would have to be broken to fetch water. Clay vessels of every description served as cooking pots, plates and bowls. Learning from generations past, the village was prepared for the onslaught of winter. The food would be rationed to each tepee, by one of the elders, and whatever game was harvested was shared equally. Name would heat water in the clay jar by taking hot rocks from the fire, and lower them into the liquid. Ian marveled at the ingenuity of these supposedly savage people. Compared to them the civilized world was not so intelligent after all. How long could they survive if they suddenly had no markets where to buy their food, or shops for their clothing? Ian watched Name use the bone awl to make holes in a hide. She would then thread strips of lacing through them to form a legging to protect his legs from the branches and thorns. Savages, indeed.

Other than for daily trips to the river and an occasional hunt, when the weather allowed, the majority of time was spent inside the tepees. With nothing to keep him occupied Ian began to grow restless. After tending to Blanco, and a few other chores to take care of every day, he searched for something to do. He grew tired of the language lessons, but was proud of the progress that Name was making speaking English. His own grasp of the Shoshoni dialect was not doing quite as well. While he could somewhat communicate with the others, he would become frustrated when the words wouldn't come to him. Name would gently prompt him with the word he was looking for and he tried to remember it for the next time.

A mild thaw came that lasted for over a week. Everyone took this opportunity to renew friendships and fill the somewhat depleted food coffers. Ian would take Blanco on long rides, usually with Name in the saddle before him. She had attained a status, nearly equal to that of him and Blanco, among the tribal members. No longer was she looked upon as a slave, or even a former slave, but the woman of Wapiti. Even Name had changed. No longer did she cast her eyes to the ground when addressing Ian, or act in a subservient manner. The respect and manners were still there, but those of a wife not of a servant.

Returning from one of the runs, they found some of the men engaged in a shooting contest. A deerskin stuffed with cornstalks was suspended from between two poles. One by one the men would step up and shoot an arrow at a white patch in the hair. Perhaps this was the chance Ian had waited for to introduce them to the crossbow. After watching for a while he was handed a bow and arrow by one of the hunters, who indicated for Ian to try it. Placing the arrow to the fiber string, he pulled back and released the arrow. The missile flew wildly missing the target by twenty feet or more. The group laughed then Ian was handed another arrow, which he declined. Leaving the gathering he returned shortly with the crossbow. Loading a bolt he stood ten yards farther from the target than the others and released the trigger. His practice paid off in a hit through the white patch, then completely out the other side. Everyone wanted to examine the new weapon at once. Shouts brought more to the gathering and before long, the eight or ten original contestants grew to encompass nearly the entire village. Ian was urged to show the capabilities of his strange bow and squat arrows over and over again. Fearing that he would either lose or break the precious bolts, he called a halt to the demonstration after a half dozen shots.

Leaving the rest, Ian went to check on Blanco one more time, then returned to the tepee where Name had his supper ready. As usual, the exchange of language lessons continued through the meal and into the night. Unable to clear his mind, a restless Ian tossed and turned in his robes. The strange words and phrases were a perpetual blur as he attempted to file them in his memory.

It was the howl of a wolf and the snorts from Blanco that brought him to his feet. The beast sounded like it was too near for comfort. The previous encounter, that he had with the pack, made him doubly uncomfortable. Name was also awakened by the noise and stood by Ian's side, as he pulled the trousers on and slipped into the moccasins. Loading the crossbow, he took a burning brand from the fire, opened the flap and stepped into the moonlight. The reflection on the snow multiplied the moon's brightness many times over. First checking in the direction of the horse's shelter, Ian waited for another sound from the wolf, but none came. Walking to the fence, encompassing where the horse was kept, he looked for the tell tale footprints in the snow. He could hear the horse stomp nervously inside. Other men carrying spears and bows joined him. A call from the far side of the village sent everyone rushing to that spot. A pair of prints indicated that two wolves had indeed entered the perimeter of the village. Satisfied that the threat was over everyone returned to their lodges, all but Ian. Stopping only long enough to grab his robes, he returned to Blanco's shelter. Opening the buffalo skin door Ian spoke softly to the anxious animal. Spreading his robes just inside he pulled them over him. If anything were going to go for his horse, it would have to get past him first. The musty odor of manure and sweat permeated the interior and Ian thought of how comfortable his own lodge was.

The adrenaline rush made sleep impossible, so he lay in the darkness just thinking. Visions of past times with Colleen played in his mind's eye. Four short years together and a lifetime of memories. Before long he found himself comparing Colleen and Name. "That's like comparing butter and eggs," he said softly. Completely different backgrounds, nationalities and cultures separated the two women in his life. Each had qualities the other lacked but both, at one time or another, were devoted to Ian. He wondered again, "What would they be doing now if only Colleen had lived?" The large home that he had shared with Colleen seemed ostentatious when compared to the one he now shared with Name. In England, his position in the community had demanded that he have a home denoting his station. In this wilderness it was necessary to be simple, comfortable and functional. In their own element each woman would stand head and shoulders above most. How would Colleen have survived in the undeveloped frontier? Conversely, could Name exist in the phony life of the big city? In London survival had meant being seen at the posh theaters, and dining at the best restaurants. Here it meant eating snake, when necessary, to keep from starving and scrounging enough dried wood with which to build a fire.

Ian felt a tinge of remorse as he reminisced how his life had changed. Meeting and marrying Colleen, the apothecary and the wealth he and his partner amassed, and the fine house he purchased to surprise his wife. It seemed when things started to go bad for him, it all happened at once. Colleen's illness and death, his own bout with the fever and his partner selling the business and running off with the money, leaving Ian destitute. His yearning for revenge softened over the years, but there was still a glow inside that refused to die. Deep down he hoped never to meet the thief that had caused him to be sent to debtor's prison, for he was unsure how he would handle the meeting. Besides the physical change in Ian, there had been a drastic mental change also since his incarceration. Refusing to give up, both changes were necessary to survive.

A gentle snowfall greeted Ian as he pulled back the buffalo hide and stepped into the world in which he now lived. If only the boys at O'Brien's Pub could see him now. His braids and animal skin clothing were a far cry from what they were used to seeing him wear. The game of darts had been replaced with the musket and crossbow for survival, while the hardest drink he had downed in years was muddy swamp water. Yes, his priorities had definitely changed.

There was still one thing bothering him. Even in his youth Ian had never been what anyone would call religious. As a young man he had been involved in a few harmless flings with the fairer sex. When he married Colleen, that all ended and he walked the straight and narrow path of morality. Now he was sharing the same lodge with a woman, that was not his wife, and that bothered his conscience. He had witnessed many marriages since arriving at the village. None were what any Christian would consider a true marriage, but a ceremony none-the-less. The chief officiated and a small cut was made on the wrists of both the man and woman. The wounds were bound together with a piece of buckskin, allowing the blood to mingle, and they were married in the eyes of the Shoshoni people. He joined Name in this ceremony that very afternoon. To him it was something to clear his nagging conscience, to his new wife it meant much more. Since being taken in a raid on the Bannock village, and as a slave, she had been a non-person. Her new masters dictated her actions and habits. She was told when to eat, when to sleep, what to do when, even that her head must be shaved as a sign of her slavery. Now, she had become the wife of the only man that even the Shoshoni Shaman feared. His stick that spoke thunder, and the strange bow that shot arrows twice as far as those of the hunters, made him the most powerful man in the village. Her days of slavery would be put behind her forever.

The winter was short and rather mild and by early April the ice cracked and began to leave the river. Fish traps were set and fresh meat was again abundant. As soon as the ground thawed the rows of corn, squash and beans were readied. A digging stick turned over the soft ground and the fish entrails buried with each seed. Needed repairs were made to the various tepees and more rock silos were constructed. Name had finished Ian's new leggings, along with a pair of elk skin footwear that tied just below the knees. After telling him three times what they were called, and Ian still couldn't pronounce the name, he gave up trying. "To heck with it," he muttered, "they'll be Indian boots as far as I'm concerned."

Short hunts went out nearly every day and Ian accompanied the hunters on most of them. Once in a while he grew tired of the group hunting, so he would saddle Blanco and go alone. It was on one of these trips that he nearly lost his horse and his own life. Crossing a shrub dotted meadow, he stopped to water the horse at a small stream. With no warning, Blanco shied to the side and threw Ian to the ground then ran headlong through the scrub. The crossbow was slung over his shoulder and when he landed, the weapon was beneath him. His head spun, as the last of the air was pushed from his lungs and try as he might, he couldn't get his breath back. Rolling onto his stomach, he watched as the horse disappeared over the next hill, the reins dragging the ground.

Pushing himself to a kneeling position, to relieve the pain in his stomach, Ian stared into the face of a huge bear, which was studying him from not thirty yards away. The black nose sniffed the air and the click of the beast's teeth was as plain as if they were next to Ian's ear. He had been told that bears had poor eyesight, however their hearing and sense of smell more than made up for it. Moving ever so slowly Ian pulled the crossbow from his back. Holding the butt against the ground he locked the string into place, then loaded a bolt into the groove. The beast swung it's head from side to side and the teeth clicking grew louder, then it came directly at Ian. The bolt must have hit something, for it suddenly veered and snapped at the spot where the throat and chest join. Ian didn't wait to see what it would do next, he was too busy trying to reload the bow. When he looked up again the beast was in full charge and not ten feet from where Ian knelt. Instinct took over and he fired the second bolt then rolled to the side. His momentum landed him on the edge of the shallow stream and, before he could move again, the bear was upon him. Blood dripped from the open mouth into Ian's face and the foul breath was filling his lungs. In his wildest dreams Ian had never believed that this was the way he would die. Freezing, starving or caught in a slide maybe, but chewed up by this behemoth, never. Protecting his face with one arm, he attempted to reach the knife at his side. He could feel the teeth tearing at his arm, then the crushing weight that knocked his breath out again. Waiting for the animal to finish the job, Ian plunged the knife deep into the bear's side. With a shudder the beast rolled to one side, it's hind legs jerked violently, then he was still. There was no movement, and the only sound was that which Ian made as he gasped for air. Using his good arm, he pulled himself free from the front leg that draped over his chest and, for a moment, lay beside the silver tipped mound.

Strangely the arm was void of the excruciating pain that he had expected, as he studied the limb. The deerskin sleeve was shredded and his arm was torn from elbow to wrist. "Okay doctor, see what you can do for yourself," he said as he submerged the arm in the water. The sudden pain came like a thousand hot knives being driven into his arm. His head began to spin and Ian could feel himself start to lose conciseness. Lowering his face into the cold water helped to restore his senses and he continued to administer to his wounds. Using his teeth, he held one end of his sleeve, while cutting the garment away from his arm. The wounds were bleeding freely and Ian knew that he must bind them. Tying a strip of sleeve above the wounds he slowed the flow, then staggered off to find Blanco. There was no way he could walk back to the village, without the horse he knew that he was a dead man.

Calling the horse's name as he walked, Ian followed the trail left by the bolting animal. Topping the hill, where he had last seen the horse, there Blanco was. The dragging reins had caught in a large sage. Ian thanked the Spaniards for showing him how to tie a knot in the free end of the reins. They did it to free both hands in warfare and still have the reins available, as they were needed. The horse stood as if nothing had happened a short time ago. The usually effortless task of mounting into the saddle became an ordeal, which sent jolts of pain through Ian's body. His head spun as he turned Blanco back toward the village. In his haste to find help he left the crossbow and darts beside the dead grizzly.

How and when he returned to his tepee Ian was to never know. Whether the horse found it through instinct, or he steered Blanco, was a blur. He awoke to Name bathing his forehead and the Shaman applying a foul smelling poultice to his wounds. Chants and grunts accompanied the old man's ministrations, as he wound strips of hide around Ian's arm. Holding a gourd cup to Ian's lips, Name urged him to drink a strong liquid that seemed to burn all the way to his belly. When the last was consumed Ian lay back on the robes and a merciful unconsciousness over took him. In and out of awareness, he spent the next six days in oblivion. The Shaman administered to him daily, while Name never left his side, except to bring water with which to cool his fevered brow.

As much as she fought the weariness, Name could not keep sleep away any longer. Unaware that she was giving in to fatigue, her head slumped to her breast. The vignettes of dreams were anything but comforting and seemed to run one after another, with no connection or separation. She pictured Blanco running free across the vast prairie, sans the bridle and saddle, and the white tail flowing behind as he disappeared from view. Immediately her visions turned to when she had been captured and taken to the village as a slave. Kneeling by the stream, she had been watching a few small fish at play in the pools. She had no inkling of the four warriors watching her from the willows. One blow to the back of her head rendered her unconscious and she was slung over the shoulder of one of the Shoshoni hunters. One minute a carefree thirteen-year-old Bannock maiden, and then whisked from her home the next. As she had done many times, she imagined her father and mother wailing for their lost child. The worst part of the whole thing was not the hardship of slavery, but not knowing the welfare of her parents. Were they even still alive, or had their spirits joined those of her ancestors?

A groan escaped Ian's lips as he turned in a twilight sleep. The sharp pain brought him to reality and he opened his eyes, to find Name opening her eyes and looking into his. A smile drew at the corners of her lips as she soothed his brow. The touch of her hand was as soft as a spring shower as it fell gently on the prairie flowers. Attempting to raise to a sitting position, Ian fell back, too weak to hold himself up. Name placed an arm behind his shoulder and, between the two, managed to prop his upper torso against the pile of robes.

The throbbing in his wounds was gradually lessening, and there was a hollow spot in his belly that demanded to be filled. A gourd cup of thin broth was held to his lips and Ian drank deeply, before Name took it away and shook her head. He knew better than take too much too soon, so next time he took only a few small sips before Name took the gourd away. Resting his head against her arm he drifted asleep once more.

Waking only to take nourishment, and the drink the Shaman gave him daily, Ian was in and out of his senses for the next three days. When he finally opened his eyes, the sparkle had replaced the dullness caused by the fever, and the pain in his arm was now but an occasional ache. A day after that he was taking short walks through the village. He was concerned about his horse but the worries were found to be groundless. Under Gona's direction the animal had been walked around the camp, while the children fought to see who was going to be first to wipe him down after the exercise. The hunters had followed his trail to the great bear and returned with the hide and the crossbow. Stretched, scrapped and treated with the mixture of ashes and fat, the skin would grace their lodge.

The Shaman visited one night to remove the wrappings from Ian's arm. Nodding his head in satisfaction, he proudly inspected the souvenirs the bear had left Ian. A pair of parallel scars appeared as wide welts from the elbow to the wrist, while a number of healed cuts were inside and outside his entire arm. Motioning for Ian to flex the limb, the Shaman pushed the arm until it was bent double at the elbow. Jolts of pain accompanied each motion, but the limb responded to Ian's commands. He considered himself very fortunate. An injured arm and a lot of anguish were a small price to pay, for the outcome could have been much worse. An involuntary shudder passed through his body as he relived the attack. The smell of the putrid breath in his face and the sight of the teeth near his throat were all to plain in his memory. He was to go on many hunts after that, but never again did he go alone.

3 The American elk is called, " Wapiti," which in the Shoshoni language means, " White Rump," for the light patch at the tail.

CHAPTER TWELVE.

Summer had followed spring three times since Ian had found the Shoshoni village. Two years ago Name had given birth to a baby girl who Ian named Kaleen, after his friend Kale and his wife Colleen. She was now heavy with another child and the heat made every day miserable for her. Sitting with her feet dangling in the cold water of the river, she watched the sunlight play through the leaves of the canopy above her. Kaleen sat by her side throwing pebbles into the water, giggling with delight as the spray splashed on her mother. As with any Indian child, she was loved, protected and well taken care of. If it meant that the adults went without food or other necessities, the children always came first. Preparations for the new baby were made well in advance and, having been through this before, Name was busy as her time grew nearer.

The prairie grass was turning from the green of early summer, to yellow-tan from the burning rays of the sun as autumn approached. The crops flourished as the tenders watered the rows daily, one stand at a time. Fine silk topped the ears of corn, while the squash, gourds and beans grew in abundance. It was a season of plenty for the tribe, with the drying racks full and all the fresh meat and wild fruit everyone could eat. The store cashes were ready for the winter supplies to be placed inside and more were being built, to accommodate the growing members of the village. New babies joined them daily and, though there were also deaths, the tribe grew in number. The old chief joined his ancestors during the last winter and his position passed to his eldest son. The knife that Ian had given him was his prized possession and was buried with him.

As with most newborns this one decided to enter the world in the middle of the night. Chased from his lodge by two portly women, who had come to aid Name with the birth, Ian paced as he heard the cries from his wife just inside the hide covering of the tepee. When his daughter was being born Ian had retired to the stable for solitude. He was in no mood for the babbling of the women and friendly joshing of the men. So it was this time. Sitting on a pile of silage he softly talked to Blanco and waited to be summoned by the midwife. The night dragged into early morning before he was called back to the lodge. An exhausted Name smiled weakly as he entered. "You have a son," she whispered as he bent over her and kissed her cheek. A mixture of pride, joy and the same apprehension he had felt at the birth of Kaleen. The mortality rate among babies was high and he prayed that theirs would not be one that was taken from them.

Ian watched, with tears forming, as Name laid the new baby in the lap of his big sister. Kaleen played with him as she would with one of the cornhusk dolls. When she tired of the baby she pushed him toward her mother and ran to Ian. Tugging at his trouser leg to be lifted up, she made squealing sounds until he bent down and took her into his arms. Raising his eyes heavenward he uttered a silent prayer.

"Please Lord. Watch over these infants and their mother. Protect them from harm and the sicknesses that claim so many of our young. They are innocent of any wrongdoing and, if you must extract vengeance, do so with me. As we are with Mother Earth we are only stewards of these children, a gift from You that we may enjoy only as long as You see fit. If I have offended You, in any way, punish me but not my innocent family." His daughter, wrapping both arms around his neck and squeezing him in a hug, cut his message short. The tears flowed unashamed while he returned her embrace. Sitting by his wife's side, Ian looked about the lodge. Everything that he owned, except for Blanco, was inside this small enclosure. The musket stood against one wall, now a useless relic for the powder had long since been used up. The crossbow, with a rawhide strip replacing the broken string, and half dozen darts in a quiver. One bearskin rug from his encounter with the grizzly, one well used knife and the clothes on his back. His most prized possessions cuddled next to him and, for the first time since his much younger days, Ian felt wealthy. The material things that he had previously worshiped were now unimportant. The trials and hardships he had endured, made him appreciate the many everyday things that he had taken for granted. He recalled the time that he had gotten impatient with God for not delivering him from the hardship before him. He now realized that like a fine blade, in order to keep a keen edge, a life must be tempered also. Too little and the blade is soft, too much and it becomes brittle and breaks under the slightest stress.

"Are you happy my husband?" Name asked as she took his hand. "There are tears in your eyes. This is not a time for sorrow, but one of great joy. You now have a son to teach the ways of your people to. I only ask that you remind him of his other heritage also."

"You are my wife and the Shoshoni are my people," Ian replied. "I will tell him of the people in the other world and the marvelous things beyond the ocean. I will also tell him of the cruelty and of the quest for riches that never ends. I hope to instill in him the wisdom that has been given me in the past many years. I once wanted gold more than anything on earth. Now it is no more valuable than any rock by the river. A whole lodge full of gold would not buy me one scrap of buffalo hide. I am now rich beyond my wildest dreams." Kissing Name's brow he laid Kaleen by her mother's side and stepped outside into the noonday sunlight.

While he cinched the saddle tightly on Blanco, Ian was still deep in thought. He wondered if perhaps somewhere Colleen was looking down on him and remembering also. He smiled, remembering the fine restaurants where they had dined on squab and seasoned vegetables at outlandish prices. The theater they had attended, or the time wasted at the ballet, at least as far as Ian was concerned it was a waste. Leading the horse from the paddock, Ian swung into the saddle and urged him into a trot. Tomorrow he would take Kaleen for her ride, but today he needed to be by himself for a while.

The winding trail took Ian to the top of the cliff overlooking the village. The view was spectacular, as he reined the horse to a halt and dismounted. Sitting on a rocky overhang, he watched as a dust devil swirled across the plains below, eventually blowing its self out the wind settled again. Looking at the far horizon Ian wondered what lay just beyond the scope of his vision? "Forget it old boy. The days of you wandering off are gone forever. There is nothing out there that will equal what you have directly below you." His thoughts turned to Negre and he felt guilty for not spending more time looking for the black one. What had happened to him he had no way of knowing but with all his heart he hoped the horse had somehow survived.

In this wilderness he had finally found a religion that he could believe in. Not the dictatorial teachings of the Church of England, that for so many years had turned his homeland into a theocracy rather than a

169

monarchy. Nor was it close to that of Spain, which in the name of religion, had tortured and burned innocent people for so called heresy. This primitive religion taught that the Great Spirit had given man Mother Earth to use but never abuse. That there was an inborn spirit in every living creature and, if that life was taken, an offering and apology was to be made to the spirit. It had seemed strange to Ian, the first time he watched, as the hunters pet a deer they had just minutes before killed. The words were as fresh in his mind as if it was yesterday. "I thank you for the meat that you have provided for my family and the warm hide that will cover my child. I am deeply sorry that your spirit must leave such a beautiful body in order for us to survive." Sprinkling a pinch of salt onto the head of the animal as an offering of apology, the ceremony ended. He had snickered inwardly the first time he had witnessed this scene, however the longer he lived among these people the more he believed as they did. There was no wanton waste, nor was there the selfishness he had so often witnessed among the whites. Other than a few allowed personal possessions, everything used was for the betterment of the entire village.

In the far distance a herd of buffalo grazed lazily. Clouds of dust rose as some rolled in the loose dirt of a prairie dog colony. It was Ian's turn to be thankful that God had put so many of the shaggy beasts in this place, to feed and clothe his children, and his children's children. Surely there never could be an end to the giant herds that roamed freely for as far as the eye could see.

The evening shade crept across the eternal prairie as Ian mounted Blanco. Above him a golden eagle called as he rode contentedly toward the valley where his loved ones waited for his return. There was no doubt that there must be a Supreme Being to create such a beautiful and peaceful spot, and for this Ian was grateful. This was not beyond the edge of nowhere; this had to be the beginning of creation.

After putting Blanco away for the night Ian strode to his home. The smell of impending rain filled the air, while dark clouds were building in the north. Kaleen was playing in front of the lodge and as Ian approached she ran to him. Holding her doll, as she had seen Name do with the baby, she cuddled it to her tiny chest. Presenting the cornhusk effigy to her father, she proudly announced that this was her baby. Swinging his daughter into his arms Ian held her close, until she wiggled to be put down.

170

Running ahead she waited impatiently for her father to open the flap to the lodge.

Name was shucking ears of corn while the new infant slept in the cradleboard. The novelty of the baby had worn off for Kaleen and she couldn't understand what good it was. Every time she tried to pull it out of the board to play, she was scolded. Once she tried to feed him some of her supper, and again she was told not to bother the baby. If he couldn't play with her and all it did was sleep, then it didn't have much value as far as she was concerned. Ignoring the sleeping infant she sat beside her mother and pulled at her sleeve. Bits of sibling jealousy was evident and, try as they might, there was no way her parents could make her understand. She had been the center of attention since her birth, now it seemed this newcomer was replacing her. When there was no reaction from Name, the girl slipped under her mother's arms into her lap. There was no way she could be ignored now, as she draped herself across both of Name's legs and stared into her face.

Lifting the child from her mother's lap, Ian tossed her on his shoulders and dashed through the doorway into the twilight. Running about, and imitating the sounds made by Blanco, Ian threw in an occasional jump, which always drew a squeal from Kaleen. Holding tightly, with both hands full of Ian's hair, she giggled as her father pranced around the camp bowing to those he met. Her small braids bounced with every step and she clamped her legs tighter around his neck. This is as life should be, not one of strife and bondage but of freedom and love. War was not new to the Indians; in fact it was almost a way of life. Raids on other tribes gained food, slaves and prestige among the warriors. Though Ian was always invited to accompany the rest on such raids, he would politely decline. He had seen enough misery, suffering and slavery in his life. Perhaps by instilling in his children the evils of such raids, he could play a small part in eventually ending these practices.

It was a nightly tradition that, after the evening meal was over, Kaleen would spend time with Blanco. The routine was always the same and, after petting the animal, she would wave goodnight as Ian led her back to her bed. This night Ian let her linger a bit longer, before carrying her away and putting her in her robes. Name was feeding the baby, whom they had decided would be called Kelly after Ian's father. The contented noises coming from the small figure as he ate drew a laugh from his father.

Seeing the cradleboard was no longer in use, Kaleen quickly leaped from her bed and placed her doll inside the laces. Ian opened his mouth to protest, then thought better of it. She would soon be asleep and then Kelly could have his bed back, meantime she was having her way. Laying the board next to her, as she had seen her mother do, the little girl went to sleep with a smile of contentment on her face.

While Name was absorbed in the feeding of the infant, Ian stared into the flames of the small fire. He had spent many hours doing just that same thing. The nights he had to have a cold camp were the longest of his trek. There seemed to be comfort, as well as heat and light, from the flickering flames. Somewhere along the way the tinderbox had been lost, and he was glad that it hadn't happened while he was someplace on the trail. The Shoshone had shown him how to start a blaze by striking stones together, something that he could have used many times before. A pitch knot popped, sending a shower of sparks into the air, where they glowed brightly then died. Thinking of when the wolves had attacked and he had lost Negre, Ian wasn't aware of his surroundings, until the noise of the fire brought him back to reality. Kaleen stirred, then drifted back asleep at the sound. Gently lifting the cradleboard Ian handed it to Name, who placed the sleeping baby inside and laced the front.

With the children asleep, it was the time that Ian and Name set aside for themselves. Silently they stole form the lodge and sat just outside the entrance. Name never tired of hearing of the large cities that Ian had lived in. Every night she urged him to retell about the carriages that were pulled by teams of horses, or the dresses the women wore. Being used to things that were either practical, functional or both, she couldn't imagine a woman wearing the things as Ian had described them. When he told of the men's tight-fitting trousers, shirts with flared cuffs and coats with tails she burst out laughing. Somehow that kind of dress just didn't fit her Ian. His description of the restaurants, where food was served on silver platters, or wine in glasses that one could look through, were her favorite stories. It was hard for her to imagine lamps that did not burn wood for light and especially the thing Ian called a, "Stove." To cook on something that was made of the same substance as the barrel of his musket, was too hard for her to comprehend. She did not want to hear of the prisons he had been in. To her way of thinking it was much worse than her kidnapping by the Shoshoni. At least she could still see the sky and listen to the song of the meadowlark. To take away someone's freedom was a death sentence to someone like her. She expressed, more than once, how grateful she was that the Indian Nations would never be confined in such a manner.

"That is something that you will never have to worry about my dear. There will never be enough people in the whole world to fill the broad expanse of this wilderness. There is nothing but mile upon mile of land, that nothing occupies, and the only humans I've seen are a few hundred Indians." Patting her arm, Ian put her fears to rest. "Besides," he added, "there isn't room for people with all those bison roaming all over the countryside."

An autumn chill filled the air, as they finished their chat and went inside. It would soon be time to wear the heavy robe over the buckskin shirt, to keep in all the body heat possible. Ian used to hate the winter, with its snow and extreme cold temperatures. He realized that it was a necessary evil, for without that discomfort there would be no water during the hot summer.

Name climbed beneath the covers and beckoned for Ian to follow. He simply nodded as he pulled the robe up to her chin. "I'll be there shortly," he whispered. Mentally he was going over the many things left to do before snow falls. His attention was again drawn to the flames, as though he would find the answers in the flickering light. How long he sat there Ian could only guess. Name's heavy breathing indicated that she was fast asleep and his own lids were getting heavy. His gaze shifted to his left, where a kangaroo rat was busy eating the dinner scraps dropped by Kaleen. As he watched the little rodent, he reflected on how small and insignificant he himself would appear in this vast country. He would live maybe another thirty or forty years at the most, then there wouldn't even be a footprint in the sands of time to mark that he had ever been here. His posterity would be the only evidence that Ian Connor had ever existed. Pulling the robes over his head he joined the rest of his family in a welcomed sleep.

Epilogue.

Ian Connor could not have been more wrong about not leaving a footprint in the sands of time. Centuries later the legend of the one with skin the color of snow, riding on a beast larger than a bull bison, still are told around the fires. If anything, his powers have grown through the years as the stories are passed down from generation to generation, but Yawn was never forgotten.

Both Name and Ian lived to see their grandchildren grow to the age when they too married. In his later years, Ian would sit and watch as Blanco grazed on the foliage provided for him daily by the children. His arthritic hands prevented him from even cinching the saddle strap. For the past few years Blanco's brief daily exercise had been limited to taking his grandchildren around the compound bareback.

When the magnificent horse lay down, never to rise again, Ian was by his side. When the last breath was taken, a pinch of salt was sprinkled on the head that had served Ian so loyally for so long. A prayer, more sincere than any that Ian had ever offered, was sent heavenward on behalf of the spirit of his loyal companion. The drums sounded, as they had for the departed spirits of other members of the tribe, and the burial would have rivaled that of royalty. Atop the pile of rocks the saddle and bridle were placed as a monument. Through the eons of time the leather and wooden saddle have rotted away. The hated Spanish bit still lies beneath a mound of earth and sage, waiting to be found by some modern day traveler.

It was a few seasons later that the funeral drums sounded for Ian and, shortly thereafter, for Name. They were also buried in the fenced enclosure that had been Blanco's corral. The musket, knife and crossbow were placed in the grave with Ian; then the last vestige of European culture was covered with earth and rocks.

Fortunately, Ian never lived to see the vast herds of bison decimated to near extinction, or the prairie carved up into cities, that gradually drove the wildlife onto smaller and smaller domains. Roads that brought more settlers west turned his beloved grasslands into wastelands. The free flowing river was dammed to provide water for the new immigrants, at the expense of the migrating salmon. No longer was this the edge of nowhere, but only the beginning of the pillage of Mother Earth.

On January 29, 1863, just short of three hundred years after Ian settled in his valley, the last of his progeny was to disappear from the face of the earth. In a winter campaign some U.S. soldiers surprised a group of Shoshoni and Bannock Indians in their camp on the banks of the Bear River. Believing they were responsible for raids plaguing the Overland Trail, the soldiers attacked the village. In a four-hour fight two hundred and twenty-four Indians lost their lives. Perhaps the most ironic part of the whole massacre was the name of the colonel who led the soldiers, which eliminated Ian's seed forever. The man in charge was Colonel Patrick Edward Connor, a last name he shared with Ian.